Assassin
Next Door

Bad Boy Inc. 1

Eve Langlais

New York Times Bestselling Author

Copyright © December 2016, Eve Langlais
Published July 2017
Cover Art Razz Dazz Design © September 2016
Edited by: Devin Govaere, Literally Addicted to
Detail, Amanda Pederick, Brieanna Robertson

Produced in Canada

Published by Eve Langlais ~
www.EveLanglais.com

1606 Main Street, PO Box 151
Stittsville, ON, Canada, K2S1A3

ISBN: 978 1988 328 53 9

Prologue

Tick tock. Time passed, sluggishly slow, probably because he remained all too aware of it. Calvin hated waiting. However, some things just couldn't be rushed. Who'd coined the phrase, kill it once, kill it right?

Didn't matter. It still remained the motto he lived by. It wouldn't be much longer now. He knew the habits of his target. Every night, Theodore Robinson paid a visit to his office before going to bed. Mr. Robinson enjoyed smoking a fat stogie while browsing porn. The information came courtesy of the maid Calvin had bribed. A peek around the office confirmed it. The lingering smoky scent and the history on the laptop gave Mr. Robinson's vice away.

Tonight, Calvin's target hosted a small party, just a few guests sharing conversation along with food and wine. So much wine. When Calvin arrived—slipping in through the back garden, the stone wall easy to scale and the guards dogs repelled by the aerosol-sprayed scent of a bear— the staff had begun to dim the lights in the house, bathing it in shadows.

I like shadows.

Some music still played in the main entertaining area, soft and slow strains, the kind meant to lull people. The kind to put a man to sleep. Calvin remained awake by eating from a tray he'd filched from the kitchen when backs were turned. The canapés being served were superb, some sort of crab cake with cheese. The wine, though, was a rather cheap offering. Not that it mattered. Calvin never drank on the job.

While he chewed, Calvin catalogued the rather boring space in which he chose to wait. Mr. Robinson had old-style views on what an office should look like. Decorated in dark wood paneling, the room held bookcases full of pretentious leather-bound titles. A carpet of dark colors and thick weave hid the gleaming wood floor. Stuffy and overbearing, the room seemed a pompous attempt to appear wealthy. Personally, Calvin preferred a light and airy space for when he worked at home.

At a creak outside the door, Calvin straightened from his slouch and readied himself. The door opened, and a rather corpulent man crossed the threshold. The long-awaited target flicked the light switch before shutting the door, sealing his fate.

"About time you got here," Calvin muttered even as he struck. The sharp blow to the man's temple dropped him. The large man didn't rise, which meant Calvin had to wait again.

While the fellow napped, Calvin set the stage, propping his target in a chair. "Would it have killed you to hit the gym a little more?" he grumbled as he handled the largesse of the man.

Body propped in a chair, Calvin placed the gun he'd found in the desk drawer just out of reach. He would note he wore gloves, special gloves that wouldn't leave behind trace evidence of his presence.

When the fellow stirred, Calvin was ready. He tapped his target on the cheek. "Rise and shine, you tubby-assed buttercup."

"What the f-f-fuck," the guy slurred. "Who the hell are you?"

One of these days, for shits and giggles, Calvin would totally reply and call himself Death. But this was business, not playtime. "I see someone doesn't wake in a pleasant mood. No wonder you're being divorced again." Four wives now and counting. The guy really didn't learn. Most men would have stopped getting married by now. The alimony alone would have killed them. Except, funny thing, Theodore Robinson's exes always seemed to suffer fatal accidents a few months after the final papers had been signed. Foul play was suspected but never proven.

Someone's rich daddy didn't care about proof. His little girl was dead, and he wanted vengeance.

I am that vengeance. Calvin almost smiled.

He slapped the cheeks of the guy whose eyes drooped again. "No more sleeping for you. We have things to discuss."

The fellow stirred and batted feebly at Calvin's hands. "Fuck you. I'm not talking to you. You'll regret this."

Misplaced bravado. Why did guys always attempt it even when the odds were stacked against them?

"Now that's where you're wrong, Mr. Robinson. Or should I call you Teddy? You don't look very cuddly to me."

Lifting his head, Teddy glared at him. "If you're here to rob me, then take the money in my desk and go."

"Rob?" Calvin chuckled. "I'm not a simple thief. You wish I was here to steal. Alas, dear Teddy, I am here on other matters. You've been a bad boy. Killing people to save a few dollars."

"I don't know what you're talking about."

"Don't you? Do the names Chloe, Marina, Jennifer, and Henrietta ring a bell? They should because you were once married to them—and later killed them."

"I didn—"

In a flash of motion, Calvin held the gun in front of Teddy's face. "Wrong answer. I guess I should have warned you I really hate lying. And for the sake of full disclosure, I should mention that, while I am being paid to kill you, I probably would have done it for free because I don't think I like you, Teddy." Calvin followed only a few rules in life. One of them was he didn't kill women or children. Not because he was a hero, but because, oftentimes, those people were innocents. It was the person hiring the hit who often needed to go.

"Someone paid you to kill me?" Teddy

sounded much too surprised.

"Really, Teddy, think about it. I don't work just for the hell of it." Pro bono was for those without home renovations and retirement funds that needed padding.

The fat man licked his lips. "Whatever he's paying, I'll pay you more."

"That's not how it works." Calvin clicked on the lamp on the desk, finally lighting the office. The gooseneck of the standing light bent so that it shone on the face of the man sitting in the large and quite expensive leather chair.

Teddy didn't look too good. His florid face, with its thick jowls, shone with a sheen of perspiration. His eyes, bloodshot and small, blinked rapidly. His mouth didn't have much to say, probably on account of the gun currently residing between his lips.

"Oops, how did that get there?" Calvin smiled, and then placed a pen in Teddy's hand. "You need to start writing. I, Teddy the asswipe. No wait, forget the asswipe part. Asswipes never reveal their assholish power. So let's go with I, Teddy, do declare myself responsible for the deaths of my—"

"Mgsgfsgd." The pen rolled from Teddy's fingers.

"That doesn't sound like you writing, Teddy." Calvin shook his head. "You really should be cooperating. The faster you do, the faster I am out of here. I know I'd rather be back at my hotel right now, enjoying a late-night glass of whiskey, perhaps reading the latest assassin thriller." For laughs because authors did so embellish reality.

"Nmgggdsgew."

"I thought you might see things my way." Calvin once again placed the pen in the man's stubby fingers. The tip of it scratched across the surface of the pad. "Good boy, Teddy. Now, one more thing. My poor client, I don't think he deserves to bear the entire cost of this endeavor. I mean, if you weren't such an a-hole, I wouldn't even be here. You need to pay your fair share. Give me the number of that account you've got offshore. Be sure to add a tip for making me wait." He wiggled the gun.

Scratch, scratch.

Fuck you.

Calvin read it and cocked his head. "Really, Teddy? Is that appropriate language? One way or another, you're going to die. Whether you die with dignity or in absolute shame is up to you."

Teddy glared. Stupid man, he didn't think Calvin would shoot.

"Are you sure you don't want to even try and bribe me into not splattering your brains?" No missing the stench of urine when Calvin shoved the barrel farther.

Scratch. Scratch. The writing was hesitant but clearly numbers. Enough numbers for Calvin to use a specialty app to verify. One-handed, Calvin took a picture with his phone and let the app check it out. It took but seconds for Calvin—an eternity for Teddy—to get a reply.

Money transferred, via so many layers it could not be traced. Calvin loved technology.

He tucked the phone away. "That's a good boy. I knew you could do it, Teddy. Now you might want to close your eyes for the next bit."

Rather than listen to Calvin's advice, his target's eyes widened, bulging so much from the sockets they looked as if they might fall out. Teddy's breath expulsed in one last huge exhale, and he slumped, the weight of his head pushing on the gun. Calvin pulled the gun free, and Teddy's face smashed against the desk.

With gloved fingertips, he felt for a pulse.

None.

Dammit. This was supposed to be a suicide. Guilt over what he'd done. Yadda. Yadda.

The gun in his gloved hand looked so disappointed. The matte black metal of it begging for use. Beautiful weapon. But he couldn't exactly shoot a dead man.

Forensics being what they were, they'd know Teddy had been shot after dying. Being a thorough fellow, though, Calvin placed the man's gun in his hand, closing still flexible fingers around the grip before sitting it on the desk.

Not what he'd planned, but the improvisation would work. Later this night, or in the morning, Teddy would be found, dead of a heart attack, the thought of suicide sending him over the edge. A man whose conscience had finally caught up with him.

Or so the newspapers would claim.

Calvin didn't care one way or another. The client had paid to have the truth come out and the culprit killed.

As always, Calvin delivered.

Job done. Time to go home.

Being a cocky fellow, Calvin left via the front door, snaring a sweet dessert on the way. He borrowed a lovely red sports car. Very expensive, he'd wager, and worth every penny. He ditched it at the train station. A few blocks away, the car he'd rented got him to the airport for his flight home. Adjusting his tie, Calvin boarded a plane for home. In suburbia.

An assassin for hire, living in the 'burbs.

Someone should write a book about it.

Chapter One

Time to start a new chapter in their lives. A good one with a happily-ever-after—that didn't involve a witness protection program or mommy wearing an orange jumpsuit.

Justifiable homicide was much harder to prove these days, according to her lawyer. Lily dared anyone to walk a mile in her shoes and not have murderous impulses.

"Are we there yet?" The lisp of her child drew her from the dark thoughts.

"As a matter of fact, we are. Welcome to our new home," Lily sang as she pulled into the driveway of the house she'd rented, a cute place in suburbia away from the city and the lack of parks. Situated in a great school district and far from a certain ex-husband's influence, or so she hoped. She'd wanted to go farther from the city, but her lawyer had vetoed the idea as soon as she broached it.

"Your ex will never allow it," said Lisa Cummings, Lily's legal counsel in the divorce and child custody case.

No kidding, Brock would never let Lily go too far. It didn't stop the urge to flee, as far and fast as she could. Away from here. Away from all the baggage and memories. Away from the violent thoughts she kept having that said death was the only way out.

"It's pretty." The piping voice from the back seat belonged to the reason Lily couldn't just take off. Much as she hated her ex, he was still Zoe's daddy, and Zoe deserved to have two parents—even if one was a total douchebag. If Lily could turn back time, she'd never go on that first date with him.

But if that happened, she wouldn't have her greatest treasure.

"I'm glad you like it," Lily said as she turned a bright smile on her daughter.

The house was actually very quaint with its yellow siding and white picket fence. The lawn could use some help, the grass struggling against the weeds, and the shrubs lining the house in need of a good pruning. The work would be nice, though. Lily had spent so much time in court fighting that she needed something to relax her. She couldn't wait to get her hands dirty. She was finally going to get her life together. She was even going back to work. *I have a job.*

It was Lisa who'd helped her find it, working for her law firm as a legal secretary since theirs had left on maternity. While only a temporary position, it would give Lily the experience she needed to get on her feet.

Having a job also gave her a sense of purpose. With Zoe starting preschool in a week, Lily needed to do something, and that something shouldn't be plotting ways to get Brock out of her life for good.

"Come on. I want to show it to you." Opening her car door, Lily stepped out and inhaled the fresh air, not tainted by the fumes of passing cars or the smell of fried foods. Just grass and flowers.

As for noise? The faint, distant hum of a lawnmower as opposed to engines and honking.

Welcome to a better life. *I hope.*

Not hoped. It would happen. She'd make it happen.

Time to bitch slap Lady Bad Luck to the side and take back control of my happiness. The driver's side door clicked as she shut it. Lily peeked at Zoe through the passenger window. Her daughter's tongue stuck out, and she made a monster face. Such a ham, her perfect girl. *She deserves a good life.*

Lily opened the passenger door, the child lock making sure her curious child remained safe. Her daughter, who'd already unbuckled herself—*because I'm a big girl now*—hopped out. When had she gotten old enough to do so many things without help?

Zoe skipped past Lily straight to the front door. No fear of the world. Not yet.

Not ever if Lily had a say.

At four, Zoe no longer felt a need to hold her mother's hand all the time. Actually, since the summer and the knowledge that she'd be going to school soon, her daughter didn't cling at all. She took to independence too well.

Doesn't she realize how close I came to losing her?

Of course, Zoe didn't. Lily had kept her out of the courts. She wouldn't use her as a pawn, and for all his faults, at least Brock didn't either.

Mommy and Daddy might have split up, but their child had bounced back without any ill effect. Lucky girl. It was Lily who was left with the nightmares.

I have a bogeyman. But now that they didn't share a bed and closet, would she finally be free?

Somehow, she doubted it. Brock was nuts.

She didn't care if three doctors claimed he was fine, and that Lily was the one who might possibly be suffering mentally. *I know he's the crazy one.*

So crazy, he insisted they share parenting instead of completely taking Zoe away. People thought it was nice they could share despite the divorce. They didn't understand it was part of his plan to win Lily back.

Devious, really. And how would he react when it didn't work? How long before he tired of waiting?

The smart thing to do? Grab Zoe and run. Run before Brock achieved his full potential as a nutjob. But, apparently, leaving the state with her kid permanently was considered kidnapping, or so her best friend, Jenny, had explained over a few glasses of wine. Jenny also reiterated Lisa's claim that murder wasn't a solution.

A pity I don't know any hitmen. Then again, what would she pay one with?

Zoe skipped across the concrete patio stones. The generic squares that led from the driveway to the concrete stoop. No cedar deck here. Not for this price. Lily could see where they'd patched it, the newer stuff discolored and not evenly blended in, but it was a porch. Her porch, and wide enough for a chair. Lily could sit out here and watch Zoe do cartwheels, or at least her version of them, on the lawn.

Up close, the white front door showed signs of peeling paint and the aluminum screen door needed the mesh mended. A little shabbiness never hurt anyone. The upkeep would give Lily things to do when the hours stretched. Insomnia sucked.

Entering the house with Lily leading the way, sunlight chased them, lighting the dust motes that hung in the air.

"Look, Mommy, dust fairies." Zoe laughed happily and danced forward, jumping as she tried to catch them. What a nice change that, for once, Lily didn't have to shush her or curb the enthusiasm. They were in a house now. Not an apartment in the city with cranky neighbors who didn't remember what it was like to be young and full of energy.

The clomping of Zoe's feet and her giggles bounced around the inside of the house. The place was currently empty, even of furniture. It would remain fairly empty even once Lily moved their things. She'd chosen to leave most of her furniture behind when she left Brock. Most of the house-sized stuff wouldn't have fit in her tiny apartment. She also wanted a fresh start, one without the memories.

"This is going to be our living room," she told her daughter, who stepped into the empty space, her running shoes squeaking on the worn parquet floors. A perfect-sized room for the two of them. Lily even had a couch for it, courtesy of Lisa, who was using Lily's new place as an excuse to clear out some stuff in her basement. Lily would have refused the charity except Lisa's husband had begged.

"You have to take it. It's the only way she'll get rid of it." What Gary didn't mention was that he had hopes of turning the basement into a man cave. She didn't have the heart to tell him Lisa was angling for a craft room.

What must it be like to have such mundane problems in a marriage?

"Where's my room?" Zoe asked. A reply was apparently not needed, given her daughter dashed off. Let her explore. The place had only one floor with the basics. Living room, kitchen, bathroom, and two bedrooms. Zoe wouldn't have a problem picking hers out, given the smaller one already boasted light pink walls. A moment later, she heard the squeal as Zoe found it and declared it, "So pretty!"

It would be even prettier once Lily was done with it. She'd cover over the marks on the wall with posters of her daughter's favorite characters. She would be shopping the garage sales and second-hand shops for furniture. She had her fingers crossed she'd find a table and chair set sized for a child so that they could have tea parties together again like they used to. The previous table they'd had didn't survive a temperamental fist.

Don't think about it.

Stay out of the dark place. She'd escaped. She would never go back. And Zoe would never have to deal with it because if he ever laid a hand on their daughter…

The theme song for *Psycho* rang from her back pocket.

A chill went through her.

She didn't need to pull out her phone to know *he* called. The high-pitched squeal of the music score gave it away.

Ignore it. Don't answer. She really, really didn't want to, but she knew ignoring it would only make things worse. With a sigh, she pulled the phone from her pocket and answered. "What do you want?"

"I want my wife and daughter back where they belong." The low words emerged silky-smooth. Then again, everything about Brock was smooth and slick. It was how he hid the monster inside.

But I see it now.

"I'm not starting this argument again, Brock. You know why I left, and that hasn't changed." He would never change.

"Zoe belongs with her father."

"The courts gave us split custody. She's mine during the week. Yours on the weekends."

"And only weekends," he growled. "You made sure of that when you moved out to suburbia."

"The schools out here are good." It was also far enough from Brock that he couldn't easily claim he'd driven by her place for the fifth time that night because he was running errands.

"You're playing hard to get."

He seemed so convinced. He was so wrong. "I did what was best for her." *And me.*

"What's best for her is a mother and father together. Zoe should be here, in her house, in her room! And you should be with her."

"I don't belong there."

"You'll always belong. You're mine."

Those words about summed it up. Brock's world was all about *his* needs. His things.

"Since you didn't call for any good reason, I'm going to hang up. See you on Friday when you come to get her." It just about killed Lily each time he showed up. She worried about his state of mind.

Brock played the visits perfectly, though. He never did anything Lily could use against him. It didn't stop her overanxious mind from imagining the worst.

"This isn't over, Lily."

"Oh, yes it is." Lily hung up and stared at her phone for a minute, expecting it to ring again. To shrilly demand she obey.

Once upon a time, Lily used to do what she was told. She apologized even when she wasn't at fault. Brock worked hard. He was under a lot of stress. Then, she saw Brock snap at their daughter one day over something stupid, and Lily wondered how long before he hit her, too.

What would it take for Lily to stop accepting his behavior? She couldn't even say she put up with it because she loved him. That excuse had stopped being a reason a long time ago.

So why couldn't she leave Brock? She never really understood how she'd let herself become his punching bag, but when he threatened her baby, when he got that look in his eye with their daughter…

What Lily wouldn't do for herself, she would for her precious girl. She'd left, and she wouldn't go back. There was nothing Brock could say or do that would sway her.

He'd fought her leaving every step of the way, but subtly. On the surface, he always seemed so bloody perfect. The loving and doting father who couldn't understand why his wife was acting like this. He fought Lily in court, painted her as unfit. To the point that Lily feared she'd lose Zoe.

Then Brock relented. He gave Lily a bone. He told the judge that because of his work schedule, he would like shared custody. She could have cried, except even then, she saw it as a ploy. He gave her something because then it gave him something he could threaten to take away.

Jerk.

Lily tucked the phone back into her pocket and stood for a moment with her eyes closed. She took a few deep breaths. She couldn't let the taint of the past affect the future. This was a new start.

The beginning of a new life.

He won't let you live here.

He wouldn't have a choice.

You'll never be free.

Then she'd better learn to look good in orange and eat ice cream while she could.

"Hey, Zoe, want to walk with me to the corner store?" There was one a few blocks away. It would do her daughter some good to exercise. Living in the city meant no yard to really play in and a confined space that didn't do much to expend the energy of a growing child.

"Zoe?" Lily wandered from the living room into the hall and the doorways that branched off it. A peek into the first bedroom showed it empty. She'd thought the pink walls an omen when she'd first seen the place for rent.

Next, Lily checked the master bedroom, not exactly master-sized, but it was a space of her own. A room she could put a real bed in and close the door at night so no one would hear her cry. Much better than the sofa she'd been sleeping on so Zoe could have the only room in the apartment.

Jenny teased that now Lily had her own place she could start dating again and have sex.

Date and risk being wrong again about a

guy? No, thank you. Lily had sworn off men. As for sex? She thought it rather overrated. She had more fun by herself.

With no sign of Zoe in the bedrooms, she checked the kitchen next. It didn't take long as the Formica counters were bare and the white-painted cupboards shut. The kitchen was empty of a child with her brown hair in pigtails wearing light-up runners.

"Zoe?" The word emerged tremulously as she looked around, wondering where her daughter could have gone. The place wasn't big enough to hide. She noticed then the sliding glass door slightly ajar, the stick that kept it jammed shut, sitting on the floor.

She flew across the kitchen and wrenched open the door, spilling out into the backyard. A fence surrounded it, big enough to keep a child and small dog in, but nothing that would keep a determined predator out.

The grass thrust up from the hard ground in patches, scraggly and poorly kept. A massive oak tree at the back loomed and blocked most of the sunshine.

Still no sign of a precocious four-year-old. Where the hell could Zoe have gone? She'd lost track of her for only a few minutes.

Panic fluttered in her breast.

"Zoe!" She shouted her daughter's name as she ran back into the house, once again passing through all the rooms, looking and hoping she'd somehow missed her. She poked her head in the bathroom.

Nothing.

Her breathing came fast as the same panic that had crashed over before threatened again. Zoe was fine. Just hiding. Children did that; the book on parenting she'd read mentioned the games they liked to play. The book forgot to mention the game of hide-and-seek from mommy wasn't any fun.

At all.

She headed for the front door and flung it open, only to scream at the man looming in it. There was nothing truly menacing about him, and yet his appearance sent a shiver through her. He stood tall and fairly broad, but that was the only truly intimidating part of him. His brown hair was neatly trimmed, his beard, as well. He was dressed quite fancy, too, in a trench coat that gaped over a suit. A businessman by all appearances, wearing a string necktie and cowboy boots, odd for the area, but it suited him. He also wore a fearsome scowl.

"Can I help you?" she stuttered.

"Does this belong to you?"

She peered down from the stern gaze to note the little person he angled in front of him.

With a gap-toothed grin, Zoe said, "Hi, Mommy."

Lily burst into tears.

Chapter Two

Mommy?

The woman in front of Calvin appeared much too young and fragile to be a mother. In her hip-hugging jeans, faded T-shirt, and hair scraped into a ponytail, she looked not far into her twenties, surely too young to be the mother of a child that old.

She was also much too attractive. Being a guy, he, of course, noted—and admired—her feminine attributes. How long since he'd been with a woman? Work had kept him busy of late.

It's been too long.

But he wouldn't break his streak with the neighbor next door. Cute or not, the hottie came with baggage. Calvin had two rules in life—don't poach too close to home, and no single mothers. The life of a family man didn't appeal at all. Not even if the mother was hot.

This one was hot and sobbing. Not loudly or noisily. Just big fat tears escaping blinking eyes and rolling down her ashen cheeks.

How could he properly chastise her about her parenting if she cried?

I can't. He stiffened. *So that's her devious plan.* She wouldn't trick him so easily. What did she have to cry about? Calvin was the one who'd almost run over the damned child while pulling into his driveway. He'd had to abruptly brake because the little girl stood in the middle of it. He'd exited his vehicle with a frown on his face. "Who are you, and what are you doing here?" The child had looked unabashed.

"Hi." The little girl smiled and waved.

"Are you lost?" Should he call the pound for children?

Pigtails bounced as she shook her head. "Not lost." She giggled and jabbed a finger in the direction of the house next door.

Just freaking great. A new neighbor was moving in. Pity. Calvin had quite enjoyed the peace since the last tenant moved out.

What a shame the landlord wouldn't sell because now the game started over. Calvin would have his work cut out for him, convincing the new tenant of the merits of living elsewhere. He should also provide instruction on watching her kid. Some people just didn't know how to parent.

You have to be firm with them. "Go back to your place." He'd shooed the little girl. It seemed the most understandable gesture, and yet she blinked at him. "You can't stand there." He'd pointed at her house. "Go find your parents and insist they watch you more closely."

The little tyke then smiled. A gap-toothed brilliant thing that could have blinded a weaker man. She blinked long lashes and lisped, "Will you take me to my mommy?"

"Uh…"

She dipped her chin, and her eyelids fluttered. Little freckles across her nose crinkled. "Please."

Good God. The child was possessed by a dark force. Surely, she possessed some kind of insidious evil because Calvin had held out his hand and didn't flinch when her sticky palm slid into his. Still under her dark spell, Calvin had said, "Come with me. I'll take you home."

Call a fucking priest!

And that was how he'd ended up on a concrete porch, looming over a tiny woman as she cried. It looked bad. Other neighbors might be watching and judging. Perhaps even calling the cops.

This shit is why I don't get involved.

He took a step back, and still, the woman hiccupped. He clenched his hands lest they reach out to offer comfort. Why would he comfort her?

He needed to leave. "Bye."

She sniffled and lifted her head. "I'm sorry for wailing like a wuss. I got scared when I couldn't find her. Thanks for bringing her back. I swear I don't know what got into her. She's never wandered before." Her teary-eyed stare then dropped to the child Calvin had returned. The woman wagged a finger and took on an expression Calvin recognized, the one that said, *You are in so much shit.* "Zoe Eleanor Fitzpatrick, you get your butt in here right now. You had me scared half to death."

She should have been scared. Letting a

little girl like that wander at will. Despite the mother's frazzled appearance, it didn't mean Calvin gave her any quarter. "You should keep a better eye on your kid." The rebuke served to blanch her features.

It didn't last long. Her shoulders went back, and her chin tilted. "I do keep an eye on her. But we're new here, and she obviously forgot the rules about exploring without a parent." She cast a stern gaze to the child, who chose to smile adorably instead of appearing chastised.

"I wanted to go see the colors. The man has flowers in front of his house."

Not planted by him. He preferred just plain grass that needed only a little bit of mowing.

"You should have asked."

"Sorry, Mommy. Can we go see outside? The man has a pretty car. I want to touch it."

The thought of grubby fingers patting his pristine paint almost brought a shiver. Especially since, how could he prevent it? One did not shoot children in suburbia for touching cars. But a man could and should demand respect from his neighbors. "No touching the car." He presented his best stern face.

The little girl batted incredibly thick, dark lashes, and her gaze siphoned part of his soul. "No touching." Said with a lisp and smile.

Calvin got the feeling he'd be seeing little fingerprints soon.

Apparently, the mother recognized the truth, too. "No touching, Zoe. You are not to go over onto his property at all. As a matter of fact, you are not to leave this house or the yard without permission, little missy." She rebuked the little girl, whose eyes began to well with tears. Her lower lip trembled.

It seemed rather harsh. The poor thing hadn't really done anything wrong.

He should say something.

Say what?

Calvin frowned. He should applaud his new neighbor for reining in her obviously errant child. Instead, he wanted to say "don't worry about it" and ask the mother out to dinner. Or they could skip right to dessert in his bed.

No point in denying that Calvin was attracted to his new neighbor. As a man, with ample testosterone, he noted her petite stature and curvy hips. Her full lips moved, and she gestured as she spoke. Her dark eyes flashed, and given her also darkly colored hair, he wondered if she had some fiery Italian in her.

She was not a great beauty, but there was a vivaciousness to her that rendered her quite fascinating.

The lips kept moving, and yet it took him a moment to realize that she spoke.

"…new." The woman offered him an apologetic smile. "Sorry she bothered you. I will make sure it doesn't happen again."

And with that, she stepped into the house, child in tow, and shut the door.

Click.

Had she seriously just locked it?

Finally, she'd done something smart, so why did he feel so insulted?

He left her front step and returned to his home. He did his best to ignore the window overlooking the neighbor's place. He cleaned his guns. He checked his email. He went to bed and got friendly with his hand.

The next morning, he spent a few minutes checking the paint on his car, buffing imaginary smudges while taking peeks next door. The old, plastic blinds didn't twitch. A little girl didn't come flying over to ask questions, nor did the hottie emerge in skimpy attire, looking for a newspaper. Perhaps that only happened in certain erotic movies?

Calvin stood there longer than needed, but never caught a glimpse of the mother or the child. The lollygagging meant he was late for his meeting.

It didn't go unnoticed.

Sherry, manning the reception desk, her hair perfectly piled atop her head, her glasses perched on the tip of her nose, raised her head long enough to say, "They're already in the boardroom." Then she went back to micromanaging the office affairs. She and her long, red-lacquered nails did the job quite well, almost as well as she micromanaged Harry, her husband and the general manager of this place.

Given his tardiness, Calvin didn't bother hitting his office first. He strode right into the meeting room. Everyone within abruptly stopped talking the moment he opened the glass door. From the outside, he couldn't have said what was going on; the room was soundproofed.

He offered a wry grin. "Sorry I'm late. I was unavoidably detained."

"Don't let it happen again, or you're fired." Jerome wagged a finger at him before laughing. The man was always smiling, even though a football injury had left him with a bum leg. It didn't stop the man from tossing barbs. Or playing pranks. Bad habits the academy they'd all attended never managed to completely eradicate.

Calvin preferred to toss knives and play Russian roulette. He'd aced his class in the first and had won every time in the second.

"What have I missed?" He took his seat and relaxed, knowing that, other than his house, this was probably the safest place to be. In this room, he could talk freely about his last job where the client had keeled over before he could kill him properly. The admission would never leave this room because, despite the fact that the sign said *Bad Boy Inc.: Specialists in international realty*, the truth was, they were much more than property dealers.

After graduating from Secundus Academy—an institute that taught more than just language and math—Calvin had faced two choices. The first involved hiring out as an independent contractor, which, in turn, meant working alone most of the time. It could be done;

however, true success came with a proper team. Big jobs with big payoffs needed backup. Which was why he worked for Bad Boy Inc.— international problem solvers.

"Now that we're all here, let's focus on the important stuff. Right now, there're slim pickings on the board," Harry announced.

"Does this mean we're getting time off for a few weeks?" Mason perked up. "I've been eyeing this golf course they just built out on the East Coast."

"If you're going to take vacation, then might as well do it now while there's not much available."

"What's 'not much?'" Calvin asked. He'd been eyeing a hot tub for the backyard.

Harry held up a tiny remote and clicked it. The image on the screen flicked to show an aerial view of an arid ranch property. Brown landscape dotted with a few darker blobs of bush and rock. "This is Ranchero Del Diablo. A non-original name just like the owner, who thinks he's living some kind of seventies power trip. Parties, drugs, alcohol, and orgies, he's the mafia lord for his region and a few others that he's taken over."

"So someone wants to put a bullet in him?"

Harry shook his head. "Not at this time. The job is to go undercover and ferret out information. It's believed he's got links to other organizations that aren't so flashy about their business."

Infiltration jobs paid well, but they were hard and dangerous work. Calvin didn't need the funds that badly. "If it changes to termination, let me know, but I'm not going deep." He'd planned to be done with the tiling in the master bath by next weekend if work didn't get in the way.

"Sex, drugs, and rock and roll. It might not be a bad gig. How much is he paying?" Declan questioned.

Mason shook his head as he tapped a finger on the table. "Does it matter how much? Those guys down south are trigger-happy. You'd have to cough up some serious bucks to take this job on."

"A quick and easy way to get a man to talk is to lead him by his dick." Jerome winked at Kacy.

In reply, Kacy held up her middle finger. The petite Latina wasn't one to waste words.

"We are not whoring out our only female operative." Pretending to be loose with morals for a night or two was one thing, but Harry ran a tight ship. Which meant that he didn't bargain his employees' lives or their bodies for money.

"How out of place would a white or black dude look working for this guy?" Calvin asked, turning the question into a more serious one. "Other than Kacy, all of us would stand out like a sore thumb if we went down there."

"If we tried to blend, we would stick out, but what if the person was on an ocean-side vacation?" Declan interjected. "A tourist angle could work. I might do it in that case."

"How about we see if it can be done before we accept the offer." Harry clicked the remote button again, and the screen on the wall changed from an image of the arid walled compound to that of a beach, the white sand stretching along the edge of clear blue.

"I'll do it." Mason wagged his hand.

Harry turned to look at him. "I haven't even said what it entails."

"It's in paradise. Who cares?"

"If you insist. I'll submit a bid for you."

"Sweet. Can't wait. Light packing for me. Bathing suit. A few Hawaiian shirts. Sounds like a dream job. What's it entail? Rich dude wanting to see if his wife is cheating? Hidden money on the island? Drug ring?"

"Shark fins."

Mason's happy smile froze. "Say what?"

"You'll need to infiltrate the underground fish market for delicacies. Someone is flooding the market with shark fins, and you need to find out who. We'll set you up as a fishmonger."

"What's that?" asked Calvin, doing his best to look innocent.

A scowl covered Mason's face. "The guy who is covered in fish guts every day."

Calvin hid a grin behind his hand. That would serve Mason right for not listening to all the facts. Even at the academy, he'd been prone to hotheaded tendencies in his choices.

More of the assignments being offered on

the Dark Web—that sub-layer of Internet only available to those who knew how and where to look—were perused. Many were dismissed out of hand. Harry didn't believe in needlessly wasting their time or endangering the lives of his operatives on impossible gigs.

What did surprise Calvin was the last thing Harry pulled up on the board. A newspaper headline.

Young Socialite Overdoses

The article went on to talk about the young lady in her third year of college being the fourth rich kid in as many months to die from an overdose.

"Is there a point to this article?" Calvin asked.

"It's related to a job."

"A job in our city?" Declan shook his head. "We don't do those."

"I have to agree with Declan. If this is about busting drug dealers, then let the local cops handle it," Jerome said.

"The cops aren't doing anything." Harry shut off the screen and took a seat. "No one is."

"If they're not acting, there's a reason." This, from Benedict. He dated a lot of cops. He liked the fact that they weren't wigged out when he asked them to use the handcuffs.

"Ben's right." Mason leaned forward with a frown. "If the cops aren't doing anything, then that tells me we shouldn't get involved."

"Sergeant Kringle always did preach,

'don't shit in your bed.'" Jerome loved quoting the more colorful phrases.

Ah, yes, the good old sergeant. He'd retired to a quiet farm in Omaha. Calvin visited from time to time to drink and hear some of the stories.

"I know we usually steer clear of things close to home. But I am still going to insist we take this job."

"I don't like it. This kind of thing, so close to home...it feels like a trap." Kacy finally chimed in with her usual suspicion.

Harry shook his head. "I can assure you, it's not. I know the person offering the job."

"A friend?" More than a few brows rose. "Since when do we cater favors?"

"We don't. This friend is going to pay us big bucks to discreetly look into this."

"Have you gotten Mason to vet him?" Mason being their current information retrieval specialist.

He took care of their tech needs. A geek at heart, Mason loved anything to do with computers. Just don't call him a geek or nerd to his face. At six-foot-eight, the guy could crush a skull with his bare hands. Calvin had seen it firsthand on a mission. The memory kind of stuck with a man.

"No need, and besides, Mason's going to the island to investigate shark fins."

"I'll dump the fish job to do it." Mason waved his hand.

Harry didn't quite manage to hide a smirk. "Very well. Mason will be looking into the digital aspects of the crime. We'll want autopsy results, police reports. I want to know what exactly killed them and what the cops found."

"I know someone over at the precinct working for the drug squad. I'll see what he's got to say," Ben offered.

"Sounds good. Declan, you check out the clubs the kids hang at. I want to know who their local connection is. Who their friends are. Calvin, I want you to hit the clubs the kids' daddies belong to. See if perhaps there's a link there."

"And, let me guess, the Latina girl should talk to her *hombres* to see what they have to say about the rich kids and their designer drugs." Kacy rolled her eyes.

"Actually, I need you to go shopping for girly stuff because you're going to be assigned to a special security detail starting next week."

Her brows drew into a point. "I'm not a babysitter."

"Are you sure about that? It pays more than your last two jobs combined." Harry's smile stretched with devious delight.

The struggle didn't last long, and the acceptance, "Fine, I'll do it," emerged begrudgingly.

The protests followed right after. "How come she gets a gravy security detail job?" Declan interjected.

"Would you like to shave and dress as a

hot chick so you can pretend to be this guy's girlfriend while protecting him?"

Declan shrugged. "Depends on if I've got to put out."

"The right question," Ben said with a grin, "is the client hot? I'm in between boyfriends right now so I'd do it, but I might have a hard time passing as a girl." Ben was not only a big man, he sprouted more hair on his body than any human should.

"The client is heterosexual and already has a male bodyguard, so Kacy will be the secret one hidden in plain sight." Harry opened a folder and slid a black credit card across the table's surface to Kacy. "Go out and buy whatever you need. High-end stuff. Our man moves in important circles, so you need to look the part."

Lucky girl. Harry tended to be tight with the expenses.

The room emptied, but Calvin remained behind, as did Ben and Harry. They spoke idly of mundane items as the door opened to let the others out. Only when it sealed shut did Harry nod.

"Go ahead and ask."

"Who is this friend, and why is he asking you to do this? What does he know about us?" In other words, had their cover been compromised? Calvin knew they had a good thing going here, but it would take only one misstep for the whole thing to crumble. If it happened, he, and the others in this group, would scatter and never look back. The academy had taught them to always have a backup plan.

"You don't have to worry."

"Famous last words, right up there with hold my beer." Ben shook his head. "I don't like this playing-at-home shit. Our cover depends on us staying out of the local cops' way. Getting involved in a possible murder scheme isn't staying out of the way."

"You're only ferreting information for now."

"As soon as we start poking, someone will notice," Calvin argued.

"If they do, then we'll handle it." By handle, Harry meant eliminate the problem. "But first, let's see if there's anything to find."

"What are we doing with any information we find? Feeding it to the cops?" Ben asked.

"No cops. Because if the client is right, then the precinct is dirty. As in drugs are going missing from their lockup dirty. Rumor is they're resurfacing on the street and might be the stuff that's killing the kids."

Calvin shook his head. "You mean this case might be about dirty cops? All the more reason to stay out of it."

"Kids are dying."

"Drug addicts are croaking." Calvin spread his hands and gave a shrug. "Still don't get it. Why are we risking ourselves for rich druggies with Mommy and Daddy issues?"

"Because we think whoever is doing this

used to be with the academy."

"That seems to be a pretty big leap, so you might want to explain." Dealing in drugs wasn't something the specialty school taught or condoned. The use of poisons wasn't usually recommended, as they left a trace.

"The reason I know they're related is because the drugs found on the kids all had this emblem on their packaging."

Harry held up a hand and flashed his ring. It bore the symbol of the academy, the jewelry a sign they'd graduated from a school built around the concept of second chances. Harry understood, as did Calvin, that it was possible to copy the emblem. The academy was a renowned private teaching establishment on the surface. Renowned enough that if someone copied the emblem, they knew it would be linked back to the school.

Not on my watch. Calvin had made some of his best memories and friends there.

"All right, let's nail this thing." After all, the ten-year reunion fast approached, and Calvin would like to rub it in a certain school rival's face.

And the added bonus of getting paid while remaining close enough to home to still work on his renovations kind of appealed.

Perhaps working from home wouldn't be so bad. It would give him more time to keep an eye on his new next-door neighbor.

Chapter Three

The clock ticked, mocking Lily from its spot above the kitchen fridge. The tail, dangling from the bottom, swished and the eyeballs at the top twitched. The novelty cat, made into a clock, had some nervous tics—and possibly escaped the wall at night to murder people—but she'd paid fifty cents for it at the thrift shop. The deal was almost as good as the coffee pot she'd gotten for three dollars. A little bit of electrical tape from the Dollar Store fixed the cord.

Sitting at the kitchen table Lily had scored from someone's curb—the wooden surface scratched but clean—Zoe hummed as she colored, her head bent over the page. At least she was occupied and couldn't see the coiled tension in her mother. Never noticed the way Lily jumped at the slightest noise.

Fridays got harder to handle each week. Most people had a Thank-God-it's-Friday mentality. She wished Friday would never come.

When the knock came, she almost jumped out of her skin. She didn't immediately rise. A part of her thought she shouldn't answer. Maybe he'd go away.

Zoe didn't lift her head. She wore her little Miss Kitty ear buds and listened to some silly songs on her iPod. The buds had been Lily's idea, as she didn't want Zoe hearing anything that might be said by Brock. Her daughter didn't need to hear the ugliness. Or was Lily just fooling herself?

Zoe has to have heard the fights. And who knew what Brock said when Lily wasn't around.

He wouldn't talk much if he was six feet under. Knowing Brock, though, he'd come back as a zombie just to torment her.

The second knock sounded just as Lily left the kitchen. Why did it fill her with such toe-dragging dread? Why couldn't she have great big brass balls?

Because he broke them.

He had not broken her. Bruised, yes, maybe cracked a little, but Lily was getting better.

Stronger. *I can do this. He can't hurt me anymore.*

Tell that to her trembling fingers. They shook as she clicked the bolt open and grasped the knob. Inside her chest, her heart beat a rapid flutter much like a bird panicking, trying to break free of its cage.

I did fly free. He couldn't do anything now.

Knock. In that firm rap, she heard the warning. The impatience of it meant she couldn't hide any longer. She pulled open the door. The bright rays of the setting sun momentarily blinded her. Then he stepped forward, the shadowy bulk of him blocking the light and casting a pall over her.

A whole herd of spiders ran up her spine, and it was all she could do not to cringe.

"The house must be bigger than it looks." A jab at how long it had taken her to answer. While Brock's lips might be curved into a jovial smile, she knew better. She recognized the glint in his eyes. The one that said he wasn't done screwing with her.

"I had to wash my hands," she lied rather than admit her trepidation.

"I'm sure you did." His tone quite clearly conveyed that he didn't believe her.

"You're early." Damned guy never missed a damned visit. Never arrived late either. He was always a few minutes early. Always showed up with that smirk that said, *I'm coming to get you.*

"Just a few minutes early because I couldn't wait to see my ladybug." He turned a smile full of charm on their daughter, and Lily felt nothing. The cuteness of it couldn't touch her anymore. Not after all he'd done. She knew it for what it was.

A mask to hide the demon underneath. Didn't the Bible condone the eradication of evil?

Give me a stake.

"I'll get Zoe." Who happened to be sitting in a kitchen with a wooden chair that wouldn't take much to break into usable kindling.

She turned but didn't move. Zoe stood at the far end of the hall, not exactly shying from her visits with her father but definitely not approaching them with a healthy enthusiasm either.

That's our fault. Zoe surely felt the tension in the air.

Pasting on a fake smile, Lily grabbed the knapsack by the door. It had become the annoying reminder that she was ordered by law to hand her daughter off each week to a bastard. According to the judge, being an asshole didn't take away his rights as a father.

"Come on, Zoe. Daddy is waiting for you." To Brock, she said, "I've packed some clothes and her Woobie." Woobie being the name of the stuffed animal with its fur worn shiny in some spots and missing an eye.

"You didn't have to. She's got things at my place. A whole room. Remember?"

Yeah, she remembered the house he'd bought. However, she'd prefer to forget that prison. These weekly visits didn't help. But she hoped to change that. Lisa, her lawyer, thought they might be able to get a new custody agreement. They just needed evidence that Brock was unfit, evidence that proved elusive thus far. Brock played a perfect game in public.

But I know some of your secrets. Thing was, did she have the guts to spill them?

"Ready, ladybug?" Brock held out his hand, but Zoe held back.

Lily dropped down and held open her arms. "Hugs." As little arms stretched to wrap around her neck, she whispered. "You have a good time with Daddy." She could fake it for her little girl. She'd faked it more often for Brock just to make sure he wouldn't get in one of his moods.

"I will. Bye, Mommy." A warm and sloppy kiss, and then her daughter skipped off to her daddy's car. Brock stayed behind for a moment. "Come with us. We're going to Mario's for pasta then a movie."

Her favorite restaurant, and he knew how she liked corny comedy flicks. He knew exactly how to placate her after he'd done something wrong.

No more. She knew better. "I'll see you Sunday."

"Suit yourself. Enjoy being alone." He spun on his heel and got into his car. He turned and leaned over before taking off, making sure Zoe was securely buckled. Despite all his faults, he did take care of his little girl.

It didn't make him less of an asshole, though.

She stood staring at the street long after Brock had left with her little angel, waving from the backseat.

Each time she worried.

Each time loneliness swamped her.

Shaking her head, she forced herself to look away, only to get drawn in by the deep purr of an engine next door. Pulling into the driveway from the other end of the street was her neighbor. Her very sexy neighbor.

The jerk.

She still fumed over how he'd treated her when they met. Acted as if she were neglectful. He was negligent—even if his yard was the most nicely tended in the whole neighborhood.

He might keep a nice lawn, but there was surely something wrong with him because what man lived alone in suburbia? And she meant *alone*. In the past week, she'd not once seen a girlfriend—or boyfriend—visit him.

Not that Lily spied or anything. She just happened to notice that his was the only car she ever saw in the driveway. It was a rather pretty car. No wonder Zoe wanted to stroke it.

I'd prefer to stroke the man.

The dirty thought had her ducking her head, even if he couldn't see her flaming cheeks from that far. She shut the door.

Locked it.

As if that would keep thoughts of him at bay. With Zoe gone, there was nothing to distract Lily. No supper to make. It didn't take long to tidy the place. Zoe still had many of her toys in boxes. The lack of furniture made it difficult to unpack. That would change this weekend. With what little money she had left, Lily was going shopping, the early kind that required a wagon and a travel mug of coffee.

What she didn't expect as she began her trek at the ungodly hour of seven a.m. on Saturday morning was to bump into her neighbor. He pulled into his driveway, forcing her to stop on the sidewalk or risk becoming his new hood ornament.

"Sure, don't worry about my rights as a pedestrian," she grumbled under her breath.

She used her indignation to justify shooting him a dark look—that subtly drank him in.

He emerged from his car, looking disheveled in his suit, his tie pulled loose, shirt partially unbuttoned. Obviously crawling in late from somewhere.

I wonder whose bed he slept in.

Not that she cared. "Doing the walk of shame," she muttered as she passed by his house.

"Excuse me? Did you say something?"

She froze mid-step, and her cheeks heated. Had he heard her?

Surely not. She kept walking.

"I think your cart is missing something."

For some reason, that made her stop and turn around to look at her empty plastic wagon. "What are you talking about?" She frowned at him.

He crossed the dewy lawn. "Is it me, or did you lose a child perhaps? Not that I really care, but I don't need her wandering onto my property because you've left her alone."

The snide remark had her gaping. "She is not wandering," Lily retorted.

"Did you duct tape her to a wall? Lock her in a closet?"

"Are you serious? You can't do that to a child. And in answer to your question, Zoe is not alone." Her back straightened. "She is at her dad's for the weekend."

His head canted, and his lips held a ghost of a smile. "Do you always take your wagon for a walk when she's gone?"

"If you must know, I was going garage sale hunting."

"Isn't that when you buy other people's junk to put in your garage until you either toss it or try to sell it to someone else?"

"It's not junk. All the time," she amended.

"True. Some items can be recycled. But most of it is junk."

"Thanks for your vote of confidence."

"What exactly do you hope to find?"

Find? She'd like to find the peace she'd been enjoying before her neighbor annoyed her. "If you must know, I'm looking for a bookcase."

"And you are going to what, transport it back in your wagon?" He eyed it dubiously. "It won't be very large if you're planning on using that."

"It's all I have, and I can't exactly carry it. As for my car…" She pointed at the blue, two-door Hyundai. "My car is too small to even try. So, I'm stuck using the wagon. It'll work." She eyed the conveyance with a critical eye. "If I lay it on top and am careful balancing it…." She shrugged. "It's worth a try."

"Your optimism is misplaced. Your plan is a disaster waiting to happen."

"Well, that's my problem, isn't it?" she

snapped, getting annoyed with his stupidly sound logic. She knew her plan would probably fail, but at least she tried.

"You're right. It is your problem. Good luck. You obviously need it." With that, the arrogant jerk turned on his heel and took his impeccable ass—which, yes, she stared at—into the house.

His mocking words kept Lily warm as she walked the next few hours, crisscrossing the streets in the neighborhood. She mumbled and grumbled. "Stupid know-it-all bastard. Thinks he's so fucking perfect with his fancy suits and cars." He probably shopped in a store, one of those new modern places, for his furniture. He probably didn't think a tablecloth over a box of books made a perfect nightstand. It worked, and that was all that mattered to Lily.

Everything was working out, and she wouldn't let that asshat ruin her day. She was going treasure hunting. She spent the next few hours hitting the garage sales. She even found some little things she needed, like extra dishes, some clothes that should fit Zoe, and a few books. But no bookcase. Or a hippopotamus. Lily hadn't given up hope of finding the book by Sandra Boyton. The one she used to read to Zoe every single day until Brock got rid of it, claiming it was for babies.

She dragged her little wagon back home, purposely shooting a dirty look at her neighbor's house. *Rotten jerk.* His disapproval had surely jinxed her endeavor.

Bringing in her meager finds, she stowed them away and had barely sat down to sip a hot lemon tea when a knock occurred. Probably a Jehovah's Witness trying to win her over. Or maybe some guys claiming they did water testing. Could she be so lucky as to hope for a cute fire inspector who wanted to give her a talk over coffee?

No cute guys. Also, there would be no buying any Girl Scout cookies. She could never just eat one.

Opening the door, surprise opened her eyes wide as she saw her neighbor. "Can I help you?"

"You didn't find any furniture." He stated, didn't ask.

She shrugged. "Not my lucky day, I guess." And how did he know? Did he spy on her?

"What's the bookcase for?"

She couldn't help a sarcastic, "Books."

"For your main living area?"

Her first impulse was to say, *none of your business*, but that kind of testy attitude wasn't Lily. At least not the old Lily before Brock. She sighed. "No, I wanted it for Zoe's room. I was hoping to find one so I could unpack her things before her dad brought her back on Sunday."

"He gets her for the whole weekend?"

"Unfortunately." Lily couldn't help the bitchy tone. A judge might have ordered it, but she didn't have to like it.

"Show me her room."

She wanted to ask why, but he pushed into her house, without invitation, and quickly strode down the hall, ducking into the pink bedroom. She scurried in after and found him regarding the space with his hands on his hips. "She only has a bed."

It brought out her defensive side. "I'm going to get her a nightstand and dresser. I just haven't had the money to. It took all my savings to put a deposit on this place. But I start my new job on Monday."

"Where?" he asked without looking at her.

"How's none of your business?"

At that tart reply, he turned and cast her a look that held a bit of a wry smile. "I can respect that." He turned back to look at the bare wall again, enough that it made her fidget.

Had she done the right thing moving her daughter here from the city? Sure, they didn't have much yet, but in time, she'd give Zoe the things she deserved.

What she deserves is a family, not feuding parents.

"What's your name?" she asked, because it occurred to her that he must have one, and it surely wasn't hot guy next door.

"That would invite a familiarity I'm not sure we're ready for."

Her mouth snapped shut.

A grin pulled at his lips. He teased her. It flustered for some reason.

"What's her favorite color?"

His query took her by surprise. "Excuse me?"

"Never mind. She's a girl. I'm going to assume any pastel color will do." He turned around and walked past Lily, narrowly missing her. The heat of him left an impression that froze her. By the time she moved and retorted, "That's pretty sexist," he was heading out the front door.

He paused only long enough to say, "I know. Deal with it," before shutting the door behind him.

She stared for a moment. *Well, that was strange.*

Also very distracting. Instead of wondering about Zoe and Brock the rest of that day, her thoughts turned to the guy next door. Why all the odd questions? And more importantly, was his chest as furry as his face? This inquiring neighbor wanted to know.

Chapter Four

I am just being neighborly. That was the lie Calvin told himself to justify his actions. How else to explain why he'd gone next door?

What the hell was I thinking? I must still be possessed.

Surely, he was sick. Coming down with some kind of mental illness. The flu perhaps? Something physical had to explain Calvin's obsession with his neighbor.

Perhaps he could blame sleep deprivation. Calvin should have been sleeping after his late night infiltrating the upper crust bar scene in town—also known as drinking high-end cocktails but managing to stay more sober than the fellow he needed information from. That required finesse and an ironclad liver—it also helped that he had access to certain chemicals that neutralized the alcohol in drinks. A little truth serum slipped into some glasses meant he obtained a wealth of information—and all without killing a single person. He should have killed them on sheer waste of time, though. While Calvin had learned a great many things—whose wife slept with which husband and, in one case, another wife. What stocks were about to dive or skyrocket. Even which horse to bet on in an upcoming race because a jockey was about to suffer an accident—he hadn't learned a damned thing about designer drugs or the kids using them.

The lack of information didn't discourage. The job would be too easy if the answer came so quickly. Subterfuge never revealed itself on the first attempt. And in a job like this, Calvin could bill for expenses. Get paid to drink high-quality booze. Mason would be so jealous.

Calvin had remained out until the after-hours clubs began to shut down. Only then did he make his way home. As dawn had crested the horizon, and he blasted the radio to keep himself awake, he had a very simple plan. Get home. Eat the giant roast beef sandwich he'd grabbed earlier at the deli. Then sleep all day.

And ignore the next-door neighbor.

He'd managed the sandwich part but not the sleeping all day. Once he ran into his neighbor on the sidewalk, all he'd managed was a powernap. A nap that had left him energized. So invigorated, he happened to see the hottie returning without a bookcase. *Because I was stalking her from the window.*

Then, due to a lack of sleep and judgment, he'd gone over with a plan to mock her.

That had failed miserably because he spent the next few hours ensconced in his workshop in the basement. Measuring. Sawing. Assembling. And finally carrying over the finished product to his neighbor's porch.

Since she didn't open the door at his arrival—*because she's not obsessed with watching me, apparently*—he knocked.

He heard movement and a muffled, "Who is it?"

"Open the door and find out."

"What if you're a murderer?"

"You know a lot of murderers who knock?" Calvin knew of one, and he currently stood on her front porch wearing a T-shirt that said *Poke Me and Die.* In answer to the question? It had happened before. It was why his secret Santa had bought it for him last year.

A series of clicks, and the door opened. The woman, whose name he'd yet to discern—because none of his databases yet showed the new occupant for this address and he wasn't about to ask Mason, who would prove too curious—eyed him suspiciously. "You again?"

The lack of joy in her tone made him frown. "You say that as if I'm over often."

"Twice in one day. Three times if we count the sidewalk."

"I promise not to make a habit of it." Even if bumping into her was proving more pleasant than it should.

"Why are you here? Need to disparage my lack of furniture some more? Perhaps mock the fact that I only have a mismatched set of dishes fit to feed two?"

"While your sarcasm is on point, I am actually here because I brought this." He waved a hand to the shelving unit he'd built, but her gaze never left his face.

"And?"

"And it's for your daughter's room."

"Why didn't you tell me this morning you had a bookcase for sale?"

"I didn't have one this morning."

The expression on her face turned downright hostile. "So you went out and bought one? You can keep it. I don't have the money to pay you."

"Who says you need to pay?"

Her arms crossed over her T-shirt that spelled in bold letters, *I'd rather be reading.* "I don't accept charity."

"For God's sake, woman. Why must you make this so difficult? I made the child a bloody bookcase. The least you can do is take it and say thank you."

"Made it." She frowned at him. "I never asked you to make it for me, and I'm really sorry you wasted your time."

"Don't be so stubborn. Your child needs a bookcase. I had some leftover wood and time on my hands. If you don't take it, it's going to the curb."

"You don't expect payment?" Her brow still wore a frown.

"No."

"If I accept, you aren't going to suddenly think you get to paw me or demand sexual favors, are you?"

Such a suspicious mind. He kind of approved. "Bloody fucking hell, has no one ever done something nice for you? Although, if this is how you say thank you, I can see why."

"People don't do nice things for nothing."

On that point, she was right, they didn't. And, usually, Calvin didn't either, so why the sudden change of heart? He didn't know, and it pissed him off, which probably explained his terseness. "Just move aside, would you, so I can put the damned thing in the child's room."

"She has a name."

"Zoe. I know. You're both rather shrill when you're outside."

"Shrill?" She arched a brow. "It's called playing. You should try it sometime."

"Is that an invitation?" He couldn't help a husky purr. He noted how she sucked in a breath at his words.

"I don't play with strangers."

At that, he grinned and stuck out his hand. "Calvin Jones. Your neighbor." Known in other circles by another name. But that one he kept secret.

Her slim fingers briefly met his for a short shake as she gave him a begrudging, "Lily."

A case where the name totally suited its owner. A delicate flower in appearance and yet stronger than expected. Since when did he wax fucking poetic?

"Nice to meet you, *Lily*." He might have given it a touch of inflection and rubbed his thumb across the back of her hand.

She snatched her hand away but not before he caught her shiver. "A displeasure, I'm sure." She tucked her hands behind her back and looked at him with a raised chin.

The spirit she showed should have sent him running. She obviously had an axe to grind with mankind, yet the very fact that she didn't cower, even as he sensed a thin tremble in her, fascinated him. A part of her sensed the predator within him, and yet, she didn't run.

"Take a picture, it will last longer." She pursed her lips as she caught him staring.

She really had the oddest effect on him. Time for him to snap out of it.

He hoisted the bookcase. "If you'll move out of the way, I'll put this in your daughter's room."

"No funny business?"

He snorted. "I don't need funny business to get laid. So you needn't worry on that account."

"Then you won't mind if I do this." Lifting her phone, Lily took a picture of him. "It's already on my iCloud so don't even think of doing something to me. My best friend knows my password."

Calvin didn't worry. Mason would pull it off for him later. "Your best friend should tell you that it's more customary to say thank you than accuse someone of being a sexual predator."

"You don't know my best friend well,

then. Jenny would probably tell me to get some action if she saw you." At her words, pink rose to highlight her cheeks.

A smile tugged at his lips. She'd inadvertently admitted she found him attractive. It stoked his ego. He forgave her suspicion. She was right about him being dangerous, and smart to be cautious. But he wasn't her enemy.

"While I do work out, I'd rather not carry this all day. So if we're done bashing my chromosome type?" He angled the bookcase in front of him.

Still looking mighty suspicious, Lily opened the door wide and held it as he carried the unit inside. It fit perfectly against the empty wall in the child's room and sat just a few inches below the window but looked rather lonely.

I should make a matching nightstand.

"Thank you." Said so softly.

The sincerity in the words warmed something in him. He found himself replying. "You're welcome." Then before he could ruin that peaceful moment by saying *I know how you can thank me*, he changed the subject to something that would kill any ardor he suffered. "When does the child, er, Zoe, return?"

"Tomorrow around dinner."

"So you're alone." He blurted it without thinking, and the guarded look returned to her face.

"I think you should go."

"You don't have to be scared of me."

Unless someone paid the right price. But even then, Calvin had some lines he wouldn't cross. Offing the cute neighbor next door was one of those lines.

"I'm not scared of you." Said with a false bravado and a tilt of her chin.

She acted so bravely, and yet he could see from the vein in her neck that her pulse raced. His presence affected her.

Good, because her existence sure as hell had an effect on him. She drew him, and he couldn't explain why. "I'll have to come back to paint it." He didn't have any paint girly enough for a small child.

"No need."

"Oh, there's a need." His gaze dropped to her mouth.

She cleared her throat. "Thanks again. I'm sure Lily will love the bookcase. Let me see you out."

Kicked out. Politely. But still…a man never liked rejection.

A man also never forced a woman.

Lily moved from the doorway, and he followed, noting she'd returned to the front entranceway and held the front door open. She expected him to leave.

But I'm not ready to go.

He had to. Had to leave her house and return to his.

Alone.

Seemed a shame for neither of them to

have a companion for the evening.

Maybe I should—

Don't do it!

"Have a great evening." He ducked out and almost ran back to his place. He would spend his evening alone. With Netflix. Chilling with the hand that never let him down.

Except, upon walking into his house, he got a text from Declan.

Check out the DJ at the train yards.

A simple message with no actual club name because this roving party circuit tended to move around. The cops kept threatening to shut them down. The problem was finding out about the next gathering. Festivities that didn't ask for identification and catered to more than just dancing and booze.

Given the tip was hot, Calvin knew he had to forget chilling alone tonight.

Even though it didn't take long to dress, Calvin bided his time before arriving at the rave. While he'd dressed in snug black jeans and a T-shirt, Calvin still stood out. Men like him didn't attend parties like this. Perhaps that was why the little twerp, in his falling-down pants, had tried to run when Calvin asked to talk to him. The little bastard dashed to the opposite end of the DJ booth, the rapid opening of the door letting in the sound.

Calvin hated it when they ran. It made him want to shoot them in the leg. *Let's see how fast you are crawling.* But he tried to refrain from shooting people in public places. The screaming caused ringing in his ears and took days to dissipate.

It wasn't hard to catch up. Calvin caught the boy with the dreadlocked blond hair, pasty white features, and gold-plated teeth. A wanna-be man-child who would one day soon become a prison B, as in bitch. Little DJ Lenny Rox was the kind of fellow who wouldn't do too well when put in the slammer with real criminals.

Slamming the twerp against the wall, Calvin smiled. "Why are you running? I just wanted to talk. I was told you're the guy with the goods if I want to deal."

"I don't know what you're talking about, man. I don't deal in shit but tunes. I'm just here to party."

"So am I, and I could use some stuff."

The bloodshot eyes of the DJ roved to the left as he lied. "I ain't got no stuff, and if I did, I wouldn't give it to no narc."

"You think I'm a cop." The idea was quite amusing. "I'm worse than a policeman." He leaned close. "They have to follow rules. I prefer to break them. Would you like me to break you?"

"You can't fucking—"

Wham. "Can't?" Calvin squeezed the hand around the guy's neck. "I can and will do whatever I like. And you can't stop me."

"Fuck—"

A few more raps against the wall and cutting off his air supply served to show the DJ, and small-time dealer, that it was best to cooperate.

"I'll talk," the DJ gasped.

"You'd better, wanna-be Lenny. I don't have much patience. I want to know who sold you the shit in the bags with the crest on it."

"I told you I ain't no dealer."

Calvin tsked. "Did I forget to tell you about my dislike of lying?" Wham. Wham. It took a few slams before the dealer remembered who'd given him the drugs. A few more slaps against the wall meant he coughed up the stash he had stuffed inside a pocket sewn into his pants.

"Is that all of it?" Calvin asked.

"Yeah." Lenny's eyes listed left.

The broken nose smashed off the wall reminded Lenny there was more in his car trunk.

Shoving the sniveling DJ from him, Calvin stood over the opened trunk and gazed at the tiny packets bearing the stamp of his old school. "Where did you get these?"

"I didn't get them."

At Calvin's growl, the twerp raised his hands. "Swear, I don't know. They just kind of appeared one day with a note about what it was and who I could sell it to."

"It came with instructions on clientele?" Odd.

"I was told to hit the rich kids who have cash for it. They told me no fronting for this shit, and no one off the streets. This stuff is high-end and fetches a good price."

"It's killing kids." He glared.

The guy in front of him didn't even try to act brave. "Not my shit. No one's OD'd on my stash."

"Yet."

"You can't blame me. I wasn't the one who made the stuff."

No, but the little shit was in his town corrupting kids. Calvin didn't like it. But he wasn't convinced that Lenny needed killing.

Okay, Lenny *did* deserve to die for being an absolute twat waffle, but killing him meant taking it somewhere for disposal, then wiping down his car.

He'd rather be drinking tequila at home. So he let the DJ live. "Leave. Don't come back." Calvin didn't add "or else," but made sure it was implied. Calvin didn't usually kill for free, but should they cross paths again…his town would be better off without this lowlife.

Spitting blood, Lenny made the right choice. "I'm out of here. This town sucks."

"And it's going to suck a hell of a lot more for your kind," Calvin muttered as he slammed the trunk shut after grabbing the bag of drugs.

The DJ fled with his wheels, and Calvin walked a few blocks to his car with the duffle. On the way, he only had to knock out two vagrants who thought him easy pickings.

Before heading home, he swung by a drop spot and left the drugs. A quick text assured that someone would get them and have them sent to a lab for processing.

This first evidence of the logo and drugs meant he'd succeeded in his mission. They were one step closer to finding out who was behind this. Cleaning up his town. It oddly had a nice ring to it.

The evening was still young, not quite midnight. The thing to do was head home and spend the rest of his Friday night on the couch relaxing with a drink.

Alone.

His fault for not asking out his cute little neighbor.

The very thought of her had him hitting a bar a few miles from his place, where he got royally drunk, so drunk, Ben—*my good friend, Ben*—came to find him. He supported a loaded Calvin back to his house. A house next door to Lily.

"She doesn't like me," he said, pointing at one of the three houses bobbing in his line of sight. He'd not taken the alcohol neutralizer, so the booze had hit him hard.

Ben grunted. "Could it be she doesn't like you because you eat too many donuts?"

"My ass isn't fat." Calvin slurred. "Is it?" Ben would tell him the truth.

"No, it's not fat, but your head will be in the morning. Since when do you get loaded?"

"I don't." Truly, Calvin didn't. Which was why it didn't take much to put him over the edge.

"Want to talk about why?"

"Can't a man just want to get wasted?"

Calvin's bed rose to smack him in the face. Fucker. He'd shoot the mattress tomorrow because, for now, the solid surface at least kept him from succumbing to the spinning room.

"Men like us should never get that drunk," Ben lectured.

"Men like us never get the girl either," Calvin muttered as his eyes shut.

"Who says bad boys don't get a happily-ever-after?"

Hadn't the sergeant warned them about personal attachments?

Didn't Sarge celebrate every major holiday alone?

All alone.

I'm just like Sarge.

He'd rather be like Harry. Harry had a wife. A family. A life.

"I'm so confused." He didn't know he'd spoken aloud until Ben replied.

"Don't worry. We'll fix that right up. I'll be sure to slather you with lube, my hairy friend, to ease your transition."

Ben just couldn't help the dirty jokes. He also couldn't help logging onto Calvin's Xbox and fucking up his stats on *Call of Duty*. Bastard. But a bastard Calvin could count on.

Who did Lily have?

And why did a part of him want to say, "Me"?

Chapter Five

I have no life.

Spending the evening alone didn't appeal. Especially once Lily saw Calvin taking off in his fancy car, looking slick in his jeans and silky-looking shirt. Where was he going tonight?

Probably a booty call.

She didn't understand the jealousy, so she tried to work it off. All the boxes were unpacked except for Zoe's toys. That they could do together with her new bookcase.

A bookcase Calvin had built.

Ditching housework, Lily told Jenny about the bookcase over a few glasses of wine. Jenny might live hundreds of miles away, but Skype was their friend. She angled her smartphone for Jenny to fully admire the bookcase the hot neighbor had built. It took pride of position in the living room because Lily had brought it out for admiration. She might have stroked it a little, wondering if Calvin had touched the same spot with his hands.

Those lovely, big hands.

She might have said it out loud. But Jenny didn't mock her. Jenny was usually the first one to notice a man's big hands.

"That's a sweet fucking bookcase," Jenny remarked, leaning back in her seat and sipping her wine. She'd chosen to use her desktop for their chat because, as a workaholic, she was never far from it.

"It is. And he did it so quick. I mean, I didn't know a man could build something that fast, and it's so nice."

"Most can't do shit, so you should nail him down and keep him."

"What?" Lily almost choked on her wine.

"Nail. Him. Many. Many times," Jenny advised. She didn't believe in any man getting away.

"You're bad!" Lily huffed, but she laughed. And it wasn't just the wine making her cheeks hot. Calvin was the epitome of sexy. Too sexy.

A good-looking guy like that would bring only trouble. Look at Brock. Pretty on the outside but nasty on the inside.

"It's not bad to want my best friend to get laid. And laid well. I want you to get some toe-curling sex, sex so good you can't help but claw him to shreds and be forced to wear a turtleneck to hide hickeys."

"Sounds unpleasant for both parties."

"Only because you've never had the really good kind."

Apparently. "I don't need sex." Lily leaned forward and poured some more wine, the cheap stuff in a carton, but after the third glass, it tasted just fine.

"Everyone needs sex. Or at least

cuddling."

"I'll visit you and cuddle."

"But I can't give you a beard rub like Mr. McHottie next door."

No, Jenny couldn't. Odd how Lily had never imagined liking a man with a beard. Beards were for mountain men and Santa. But on Calvin…would it tickle between the thighs?

She chugged her glass of wine and poured another. "I'd be crazy to get involved. What if it doesn't work? Then we'd have to live beside each other and avoid eye contact forever."

"If it gets too awkward, then he can move."

"I think he owns his house."

"Then you move."

"I have a lease. I can't just break it."

"You're making excuses," Jenny pointed out. "As a single girl now, you have to take the opportunities presented."

"I'm not ready."

"You never will be, which is why you need to jump back into the game."

"It's too soon."

"Bullcrap. It's been months. You're allowed to go on with your life." Jenny changed tactics. "What if he's the one?"

By that, Jenny meant the prince charming every girl dreamed of meeting. "He can't be the one. At best, he'd be the rebound guy. It never works out for them."

"Not never, just rarely. What if he's that

rare catch?"

"You just won't give up, will you?"

Jenny snickered as she raised her glass in a toast. "Nope. Here's to you getting laid. And soon. You deserve a happily-ever-after given what that dipshit has been putting you through." Jenny refused to use Brock's name. Said she wouldn't give that demon the power. Jenny blamed herself for not recognizing Brock was evil. Lily tried to reassure her that no one could have seen it coming.

Much like that first fist had come out of nowhere. *What do you mean you forgot?* She didn't even remember what she'd forgotten. And it happened so many times after.

"I just don't think I'm ready," Lily admitted. "I'm starting a new job. And Zoe's still adjusting to school. Plus, it's nice to kind of just be by myself." She only had herself and Zoe to care for. No extra pressure to perform. No one to please.

"Yeah, well, let's see what you're saying once you've finished watching all Netflix has to offer. You'll be bored and dying for companionship. That's when the real mistakes are made. I call Gerry my desperation phase." Gerry being serious boyfriend number three. It hadn't been a bad thing when they'd tossed him back in the clink for violating his parole.

"When I'm ready, I'll date, and not a minute before." Lily also planned to wait until Brock veered his sights away from her. Married, his jealousy often proved an issue. She wasn't sure just how far she could test it yet.

Her phone screamed, startling her with the *Psycho* theme. Speak of the devil. She flicked the notification box.

What's this I hear about a guy with a hot car?

She knew better than to ignore him. **Just the neighbor. Nobody special.** He couldn't mean anything, not with the way Brock still stalked her.

"Who are you texting?" Jenny asked, leaning forward as if she could climb through the screen.

"No one."

"Oh, hell no. You're texting dipshit. Why are you doing that? I thought I told you to stop talking to him."

"I have, but I can't completely block him when he's got Zoe." What if it was important?

"If it's not about Zoe, don't reply. You know he's screwing with you."

"I know." Lily knew all too well.

"You can't trust him." Jenny scowled.

"You also don't trust the guy at the bagel shop."

"Nobody should. I'm telling you, there's something wrong with him. No guy that hot works in a bakery. He's a plant."

"A plant for what?" Lily snorted. At times, Jenny and her conspiracy-geared mind saw things that weren't there.

"Probably something big and government related. You'll see."

"What I'll see one day is you coming over in a head-to-toe aluminum suit meant to stop the radio waves from controlling your brain."

"You know they're trying."

"For all you know, they've succeeded, and this is you playing puppet to their tune."

"Bitch."

"You only hate me because you think it might be true."

"Yes, damn you." Jenny laughed and raised her glass. "A toast to finding you a man."

How about a wish instead? About getting rid of a particular guy?

That night, Lily went to bed plenty drunk on wine, and her mind not full of worry for her new job or concern about how to deal with Brock's next push for her return.

Instead, she fell asleep wondering what Calvin did.

And with whom.

Chapter Six

Ugh. Apparently, I haven't learned my lesson.

Less than a week later, and Calvin had, once again, succumbed to the lure of alcohol with no metabolizer. Why the sudden need to get drunk? Was it because the newest Bad Boy case was at a standstill?

He'd hit a different posh hot spot each night this week, starting with Sunday. All of them a bust, although the absinthe in the shot glasses shaped like emeralds tasted pretty damned good once he realized he'd hit another dead end.

He just might never eat licorice again.

A groan escaped him as sunlight dared to stab him in the eye. Didn't it know it wasn't time to get up yet? He hadn't changed his mind when noon hit, and he still tried to hide in his bed.

Pussy. He could practically hear Sarge and that certain inflection he got when mocking the boys at the academy.

Calvin dragged his ass out of bed, but that was as far as it went. Saturday was spent hungover, which meant staying at home with nothing better to do than watch his neighbor next door. She left the house only once and returned with a few meager bags.

She didn't leave the rest of the day. Not

that he watched. He had cameras do the work for him while he spent time in his basement gym, working off the abuse he'd inflicted on himself the night before.

He still couldn't fathom why he kept acting like such a moron. If he had such a thing for the neighbor, why not go over and ask her out?

Because she was his neighbor, that was why, and she had a kid.

So what? *My parents did, too, once upon a time. Yeah, they did. Look at how that turned out.*

He could only imagine how different his life would have been if they hadn't overdosed in each other's arms. Kind of romantic, if you ignored the vomit.

Relationships were overrated. A single mom was definitely not on the approved list for pursuit. But all the reasons to stay away didn't stop him from watching.

Wanting.

Ask her out.

What if she said no? She hadn't seemed to have a problem getting rid of him the weekend before. He barely caught a glimpse of her despite the proximity of their homes. Did she avoid him on purpose?

That didn't usually happen to Calvin. Most women found ways to get closer to him— and take off some clothes. She'd yet to even undress him with her eyes.

Saturday night arrived, and he felt almost

back to normal, enough he could have hit Bruno's Club, a place he'd gone to before and found nothing, but he'd reached the point it was time to do the circuit again. Perhaps less discreetly this time. However, a phone call to get a reservation let him know it was closed for a private function. In other words, someone with money had rented it out for the night.

None of the other hot spots appealed. Especially since he'd already shaken up the dealers working in them. Calvin needed fresh meat.

He also needed some food. With Calvin deciding to spend the evening at home, he ordered—accidentally—a very large pizza. Too much for him to eat alone. It seemed only neighborly to walk over with the box and knock on her door.

"Who is it?"

"Pizza delivery." And wasn't that the start to many a male fantasy?

Lily, her hair in a ponytail, gaze as suspicious as ever, swung open the door and eyed him then the pizza. "I didn't order that."

"I did. But my buddy didn't come over." He lied. "Want to share?"

Her nose twitched. Such a cute nose. He rather enjoyed the light spattering of freckles on it. "What flavor?"

Aha. The smell of the pizza was winning her over.

"It's a meat *lovers.*" He might have put a

tiny inflection on the last bit.

"With pepperoni?"

He nodded.

"I can't stand pepperoni. Sorry." She slammed the door shut, and he stared at it.

Click.

Rejected.

Again.

A man couldn't help but develop a bit of a complex. *Why doesn't she like me?*

Was her dislike of pepperoni a euphemism? Is she talking about sausage? Was it a subliminal message that she didn't like dick?

A shame for mankind, but fucking hot if she was into women.

Why did he care? Her rejection was for the best. Let her abject dislike of Calvin—and hatred of savory sausage—cure him of his obsession.

For the second time in as many days, Calvin got drunk and passed out until after lunch the following day. His pounding head meant he wasn't in a good mood, so when he saw the car arrive next door, parking sloppily, he was ready to spill some blood.

Who is that guy visiting Lily?

Did it matter?

I could totally take his ass out.

Forget could, he should.

Sitting in his attic, gun pointed at the window, Calvin's finger itched to pull the trigger. It would be so easy.

And traceable.

First rule of being a killer, don't work from home. A rule he stuck to, but there were times he was tempted to break it. Like with those last tenants. Thinking they could toss cigarette butts onto his lawn.

They'd fled the state to avoid paying the numerous city fines that had suddenly showered them.

But the new neighbor wasn't annoying—unless cuteness was a crime. It should be because her adorability was why he resorted to spying.

Not spying. Keeping an eye on my neighborhood.

Sitting on his haunches, his rifle held shoulder level and his eye trained on the gun sight, Calvin swiveled slightly to follow the swagger of the asshole, who missed the driveway when he parked his car and had two wheels sitting on the grass. Not his grass, or the prick would already be fertilizing daisies. As it was, the fellow only lived by a thread—and because there was no profit to his death.

I don't know, there's a lot to be said for personal satisfaction.

All assassins of repute worked for a fee. Perhaps Calvin should offer a discount to take the guy out.

A guy who arrived with a little girl.

Zoe and her dad.

The ex.

Calvin hated him on sight.

The fellow reached the front door and leaned on the doorbell. Calvin couldn't hear the insistent ring, but he could imagine it. *Bing bong, bing bong.*

Except, oddly enough, he could hear… *Dring. Dring.*

The old-school telephone ring that he used for notifications distracted and tore his gaze from the scope. Someone had news. He rolled onto his back, flipping his phone over him to check the text.

The shit was clean.

It seemed the latest stuff he'd pulled off a drug dealer a few days ago wasn't of the tainted variety. It also didn't relinquish any decent prints or leads. Nothing to tell Calvin and the boys who was feeding these lowlifes the drugs.

Someone had to be supplying, and surely it wasn't for free. Somewhere, someone had to be making a profit. But who?

The case is what I should be working on. Not spying on the neighbor and her domestic issues.

Getting to his feet, Calvin removed the rifle from the tripod and moved it to the gun rack he'd affixed to the attic wall. The whole top floor of his house was converted into one big gun closet. He hung the weapon and stood back to admire his arsenal.

Some might wonder at his decision to leave his guns out in the open. To that he'd say, if law enforcement ever made it to his attic, then he had bigger problems than them wondering why he had enough weapons to start a mini-war—and win.

Despite his being nowhere close to the window, he could hear the voices outside, one of them a male timbre raised in anger. Calvin also clearly heard the word, "Bitch."

Perhaps the guy talked about a dog and not his ex-wife.

Pivoting, Calvin peeked out the window and noted Lily stood, arms crossed, in front of her door, chatting with her ex. The little girl appeared to have vanished indoors.

The voice of the guy next door rose. Loud and intimidating. Though dwarfed by the larger man, Lily stood her ground, and he couldn't help but admire the courage it must take. Good girl. Also, not his business.

He left his office and hit the main floor. It was recycling day tomorrow, so he had a good reason to carry his bin to the end of his driveway. It was quite by happenstance that, on the way back, he noted the man wedging himself in the doorway so that Lily couldn't close the door.

Her face looked pinched and angry.

The man appeared rather threatening.

It brought back memories of a childhood he preferred to forget. Calvin didn't appreciate it. He also didn't like bullies who took out their anger over their small penises on women.

Before he could talk himself out of it, Calvin marched over and, when he was close enough, introduced himself.

He also started a fight.

The day was looking up.

Chapter Seven

There's going to be a fight.

From the moment the first text arrived the previous night—and then kept coming—Lily had known today's drop-off would be bad. The texts didn't stop. Asking if she was cheating. Attempting to guilt her into coming home. Threatening Lily if she didn't.

Forget keeping a record of them to use against Brock. The messages always disappeared as soon as she read them, making her wonder if she'd lost her mind. Did Brock really send those vile things? Or did she imagine it? At times, she wondered.

She'd tried using another camera to screen shot the text. But those were thrown out as being fabricated. The police department seemed to accord her a hell of a lot of confidence in her artistic skills. She didn't know how to remove red eye, let alone edit photos to look like real texts.

No one believed her. They accused her of making up stuff, and Brock kept getting away with the harassment.

As six o'clock and drop-off time approached, she tensed and clenched her fists by her sides. Her teeth ground together as she heard the sound of an engine. The insistent ring of the doorbell signaled the start of the cage match.

It started out innocuously enough. "Hey, ladybug. So glad to see you," Lily said to Zoe, who immediately hugged her tightly.

A small hand held up something fluffy and pink. "Daddy got me a new stuffie." Zoe's weakness. Brock could get away with a lot of things by bribing his daughter with plushy new friends.

"Say thank you and goodnight to Daddy," Lily said, doing her best to keep things on a polite level.

Brock knelt and held out his arms. Zoe did a slow about-face and marched into the embrace. She hugged him, no hesitation, but it didn't have the same enthusiasm as the hugs given to Lily. It made her wonder what exactly happened during those two days Brock had his daughter. Lily knew Zoe spent lots of time at Brock's parents because he sometimes had to work. But what about when he didn't?

Zoe squirmed free of her father and dashed off. "I'm gonna show her to Morty." Her stuffed crocodile. Zoe slipped into her room, and the door closed. Probably escaping the coming battle because drop-offs often turned into shouting matches. Her little girl might only be a child, but she was bright for her age, and this in spite of the fact that her father was an ass.

Brock didn't leave. "I'm going to swing by Wednesday to grab Zoe and take her for a bite."

Ding. Round one was about to begin.

"That's not part of the custody agreement."

"Are you really going to be such a cow? It's one lousy dinner."

"It's you disrupting her schedule on purpose."

"I have a right to see my daughter."

"You get her every weekend."

"That isn't enough." Brock wanted a true fifty-fifty split, but the commute to bring Zoe to school would have screwed with his shifts. So Lily got Sunday evening to Friday night.

"Good night, Brock. I'll see you next Friday."

He still didn't leave. "I am taking her to dinner."

"And I'm saying no. According to the court document, you can't force it. Just like you can't just show up here and bully me."

"There you go, being a bitch again. You just can't help picking a fight."

She blinked at him. Ding. Round two. "You need to leave and not come back until it's your appointed time." Having a backbone felt great and terrifying at the same time. On the one hand, saying no was liberating. He couldn't tell her what to do. On the other hand, saying no instead of placating him didn't sit well. Brock could get nasty.

"I will show up whenever I damned well please." Brock leaned in. "Zoe is my kid. And you are my wife."

"Ex-wife."

"Wife. We promised until death do us part. We are tied together, wife. Which means if I want to fucking come see you or her, there isn't a thing you can do to stop me."

In a sense, he was right. She'd tried to have him stop stalking her. He posed a clear and present threat, yet no one would help her. Like many women caught in this situation, Lily couldn't get anyone to listen because Brock hadn't done anything yet. Nothing she could prove, anyway. So she received no protection.

All the dirt she had on him, and she knew some big secrets, bigger than the fact that he cheated on his taxes, did her no good. She couldn't use them to blackmail him. He had one big piece of leverage against her—Zoe. No matter what, Lily had to look out for her daughter.

"I can and will stop you. I have your visitation rights in black and white. Don't make me enforce them."

"I can't believe you're being such a fucking bitch. Get the fuck over it."

"You get over it. I'm done with you." She wished so hard that she wouldn't have to see him again. Unfortunately, he'd yet to get hit by a bus.

"You'll never be done with me, Lily. I will be around until the day you die. Let's just hope it's not anytime soon for you."

The threat boiled her blood instead of chilling it. How dare he threaten her? "Who says you won't die first." She spat the words and saw she'd managed to surprise him. Meek little Lily from their marriage was gone now. She'd spent too many years cowing to his ego. No more.

"Have you forgotten what happens to mouthy girls?" He didn't threaten, but she recalled nonetheless.

The urge to touch her cheek meant she tucked her hands behind her back. From time to time, the cheekbone ached, the ghost pain a constant reminder of what he'd done. That had been one of his worst outbursts, and also the last time he'd laid a hand on her.

When it had happened the first time, when his palm cracked across her cheek, she'd made excuses for it. He'd had a shit day at work. Or he'd had a few too many at the bar and came home feisty. Then the taps—"love taps" he sometimes called them—became a habit. And still, she didn't blame him. Only herself.

She should have made sure she didn't start dinner too early, thus drying it out.

She should have known to wash and iron the shirt he'd tossed in the wash the night before after she'd gone to sleep.

So many things she'd done wrong. He pointed them out, each and every one.

Not anymore. Never again.

She crossed her arms. "You can't threaten me."

"Who you going to tell? The cops?" he said, his smile a touch too wide. "Go ahead. Let me know what they say."

Frustration boiled inside her. She already knew what they would say. They'd said it to her the last time she went to the station asking for some kind of protection: "Can't help you." Because here was the thing. Brock had never directly done anything. Even his threats were veiled. If someone asked him what he meant when he asked Lily what happened to bad girls, he'd probably wink and say, "They get a bare bottom spanking and a tickle." Then they'd all have a laugh and talk about women who took shit too literally.

Brock never got caught doing a damned thing. The times he did lay hands and bruised her, he had a ready explanation.

Guess what, though, she had an excuse ready, too, for the day she finally snapped and stabbed him with a knife. "He deserved it."

Given she'd heard all Brock's rants before, Lily tuned out the implied threats. The problem with constant abuse was, at some point, you got numb to it.

"Why can't you just go away?" She tired of this circle of arguing.

"Give me Zoe, and maybe I will."

At this absurd request, her frustration boiled over. Lily snapped. "Zoe is not a toy or a trophy. She is a child."

"And I am her father. It's my right to be with her."

"Perhaps you should have tried being a father before. A real father spends time with their kid on a regular basis. Doesn't suddenly cancel plans with his little girl at the last minute because it's inconvenient to his life. A father is someone who doesn't forget her birthday." Although, according to Brock, that was also Lily's fault, even though they'd been divorced six weeks at the time. "A father is supposed to be there to support his daughter. Not use her as blackmail."

"Maybe if somebody hadn't left me, I'd be able to do those things. Whose fault is it I can't be there for Zoe?"

She couldn't help an incredulous arch of her brow. "You are a piece of work. Get out." She shoved the door, but he wedged himself in the crack.

"We're not done talking."

"Yes, we are. So leave, please, before Zoe sees us arguing again."

"You're the one arguing. I'm just talking. Don't you think our daughter would like to see her parents together for the evening?"

Before she could tell Brock one more futile time to depart, Calvin arrived, looking angry, and yet his face remained smooth. So why did she think rage simmered beneath his placid expression?

There was something in his eyes. Something...dangerous.

Is this the same man?

Calvin didn't appear as a tame businessman in a suit. On the contrary, he looked big and burly in his snug jeans and black T-shirt.

He didn't sound metrosexual either as he threatened Brock. "Hey, asshole. Yes, you. I think the lady said no. To which, I'm sure you'll tell me to fuck off. I'll continue the cliché by saying pick on someone your own size. You'll snarl and tell me to stay out of it or else. At which point, I'll laugh as I beat the hell out of you and win the day. That's option one. Or, you can save yourself the embarrassment and leave now before your daughter sees her daddy sniveling on the ground like the little bitch he is."

He did not just say that!

Lily didn't know whether to be horrified by Calvin's words or start clapping. People did not often argue with Brock. When they did, he didn't react well. So with Calvin challenging him, in front of Lily no less, Brock turned his full ire on her neighbor. The explosion was all too predictable.

"What did you say?"

"Are you fucking stupid, too? I said, lay off the lady before I rearrange your face."

It truly was a beautiful sentiment and such a bad idea. Brock often acted like a guy on 'roids. Always angry, super temperamental, and Brock especially didn't take well to being threatened.

He took a step toward Calvin.

Calvin didn't budge.

What a stark contrast. Her ex-husband appeared rather unimposing compared to her neighbor. Brock might be tall, but Calvin was taller by at least two or three inches, putting him probably around six feet to six-three. A very nice height. Where Brock had a blocky, wide, football-player build, Calvin was slimly built with broad shoulders that led to a wide chest. The shirt clung enough to show off hints of a six-pack. His jeans hung on his hips below his lean waist. Brock had short, curly, blond hair and Greek features with a sharp nose and chin. He always sported a clean-shaven jaw. Calvin, on the other hand, with his close-cropped beard and trim hair that begged for a set of fingers—hers—had a bit of an untamed presence to him now that he didn't wear his suit. One could even say he looked dangerous, especially given the uncompromising look in Calvin's eyes.

"I don't know who the fuck you think you are, but this is private business. So shove off." Brock didn't let a thing like a bigger guy stepping in stop him.

"Private business?" Calvin smiled, but it wasn't a smile that reached his eyes. "The whole fucking neighborhood can hear you screaming about your *business*. It's disturbing my peace."

"I'm going to disturb you if you don't back off, asshole."

"Oooh, I'm shaking in my shoes," Calvin mocked. He crooked one set of fingers. "Let's go, big boy. You obviously think you're a big shot. Hit me."

"I'm not stupid. I'm going to guess you've got cameras watching. Everybody does nowadays. Why don't you throw the first punch?"

"All words, no action. I should have guessed. You're only good at picking on women." The barb hit deep.

Brock's features twisted. "You need to stop talking. Do you have any idea who I am?"

"A douchebag?" Calvin offered while Brock's lips tightened. "Asshat of the highest order?" Brock growled. Calvin's lips stretched into a smile. "Or, how about I don't give a fuck who you are, but I will make you a promise: either you leave now, or you'll regret it."

Given the high level of testosterone hinting at violence, Lily knew she should step in. Should say something. Anything. Calvin didn't know whom he threatened. But at the same time, seeing someone stick up for her, so unafraid of the consequences, so strong…

She selfishly enjoyed it.

"You'll pay for that," Brock threatened.

"No, I won't." Said with casual confidence just before Calvin lunged forward and wrapped Brock in a headlock. Calvin twisted him so that his body was dragged up against his. "Say goodbye."

"This is assault."

"Is it? See, the thing about owning the cameras watching is that I get to decide who sees what's on them."

"There's a witness."

She might have derived a good bit of satisfaction in replying. "I saw nothing."

"Bitc—"

The word was choked off as Calvin proceeded to drag/frog-march Brock to his badly parked car. It must have occurred to Brock that he'd met with someone stronger than him. He didn't struggle, and yet, she could tell by the press of his lips that he fought a mighty rage.

That's not good.

Too late to change things now.

Her neighbor wrenched open the car door and shoved Brock at the opening. Brock, however, wasn't about to go so easily. He whirled, and even from the porch, Lily could see his eyes blazing. Brock practically frothed at the mouth like a rabid dog.

"You'll pay for this."

She didn't hear Calvin's reply as he leaned in close to Brock. Brock, however, heard every word, and the color drained from his face. Without another word, he slammed into his car and took off.

This wouldn't end well.

She crossed her arms tightly over her chest and glared at Calvin marching back toward her. "You shouldn't have done that."

"If you ask me, it should have been done a while ago. Is he always that obnoxious?"

"Yes."

"And you haven't killed him yet?" He sounded genuinely surprised.

"The thought has crossed my mind." More than once.

"Is Daddy gone?" The little voice came

from behind, and Lily peered back to see Zoe looking hesitant, peeking from her door.

"Yes, he's gone, baby girl."

Her daughter ventured out and shot a giant beamer of a smile at Calvin. Mega-watts slammed into him, and Lily almost laughed as his jaw dropped. Poor guy, he didn't know what hit him.

Zoe took her gleaming grin and entered the living room, her favorite stuffie, a little jaguar, bought for her as a baby, tucked under her arm. "What's that?" Lily heard her daughter ask.

Lily pivoted to see Zoe in the living room pointing at the bookcase.

"That, my little bug, is something to store your books and toys in. Mr. Jones, our neighbor next door, built it for you."

"It's mine?" Such breathless wonder. Big, big eyes turned his way. She could see Calvin being treated to the full effect of those baby blues. "Thank you." Pronounced with only a hint of a lisp. "I love it."

"Um."

While Calvin coped with little girl cuteness in what seemed like his very first time, Lily entered the living room and grabbed hold of the bookcase. "Let me bring it back to your room. I was just showing it to Jenny last night."

"I've got this." As Calvin brushed past Lily to grab it, he murmured, "Showing off my work, were you?"

Yes, which was embarrassing in itself, but

not as mortifying as being caught by him.

He repositioned the case in Zoe's room, and her little girl proceeded to put Fluffy Pink Puff—her newest friend—on a shelf. Lily left her to it and almost ran into Calvin in the hall. He stood much too close, invading her space.

It disturbed her, but not in a creepy, being-stalked way. More as if he made her body aware of him. Much *too* aware of him, in a way that made her feel like a woman. A female with needs.

Stay strong.

"Thanks again for the bookcase."

"You're welcome. And my pleasure for getting rid of that moron, too. Let me know if he harasses you again."

"He will, but you can't come over each time. It will just make things worse."

"Maybe you should try calling the cops. They have a thing called restraining orders, you know."

She almost sighed in reply. "I do know. Restraining orders are great if you can get one. Unfortunately, Brock knows the law a little too well."

"Then stop following the rule of the law."

A part of her had begun to contemplate it. If Brock wasn't going to fight fair, then maybe she shouldn't either.

But how far am I willing to go?

She stood by the open door in clear message. "Have a good night."

He walked past without stopping. "Lock the door when I leave," was his parting reply.

Then he left, and he didn't look back.

For the rest of that week, Lily didn't see him—at least not in any meaningful way. The previous week, she had started her new job at the law firm. Week one was spent mostly in a fog, learning everything and adjusting to a new schedule. So much happened every day. At first, it proved overwhelming, but by the end of the week, she'd fallen into a rhythm. By the following week, a sense of satisfaction filled her as she remembered what it was like to be something other than a mother and a wife. Those were meaningful jobs, but along the way, she'd lost herself. Finally, she started finding herself again.

Smiling, too.

Working a cliché nine-to-four meant she bustled, leaving before eight a.m. so she could get Lily to school and then drive herself to work. Since the firm had many lawyers working late nights, they offered two receptionist positions. The first shift was the nine-to-four one, while the second shift was a late four p.m. to eleven, at which point, the company insisted everyone go home. The hours worked great for Lily, especially since she still had to run around after picking up Zoe from daycare. One night she didn't make it home until almost seven. Groceries and other errands had to be done. A certain pair of golden arches made a hungry child happy, and Lily heartily enjoyed the crunchy fries.

The days during the week flew by, but she also got her downtime—her *me* time—daily. By eight o'clock, eight-thirty at the latest, Zoe was in bed, arm tucked around her worn Woobie, eyes drooping. Lily never could resist stroking her baby's hair when she slept so peacefully like this. Every night she remembered why she couldn't screw up.

Bedtime accomplished, Lily always spent a few minutes tidying up. It didn't take long. By nine, she was ready to relax, and yet, before sitting on her couch, she always took a peek outside. Always snuck a look at *his* house.

Wondered what he did.

Wondered if he thought of her.

Wondered if all recently divorced women were as pathetic as she was. So pathetic, and yet she couldn't quell this insane curiosity she had about him. Who was he?

And why do I crave him so badly? She couldn't have explained it, couldn't seem to quench it, so she settled for chocolate ice cream and watching television.

The week passed, and Friday arrived, but instead of elation at the coming weekend and a chance to maybe sleep in, her tummy clenched. The countdown to swap time with Brock had begun.

Despite his threat, Brock didn't appear that week to take Zoe for dinner. He didn't text or call either.

No contact. It should have been a relief.

Lily fretted because she knew what this meant all too well. He simmered with rage. It brewed and bubbled under his skin. Once started, it wouldn't leave until he got a chance to blow up.

Lily would have to be very careful. She made sure she was out on the front lawn with Lily when Brock arrived. The more witnesses, the better.

A part of her hoped he wouldn't come, that they could be free of him. Not for the first time, Lily wondered how she could let Zoe go with him. What if he was one of those fathers who snapped?

The cops didn't care about her gut feeling. Without proof, she couldn't ban him from his daughter's life according to the law.

Are they waiting for Brock to kill her?

How could anyone force her to do this?

Lily braced herself as Brock got out of his car.

Expecting a war, she was surprised when he greeted them both with a wide smile. "Hello, Lily, you're looking well." A brief, courteous greeting. No snark or name-calling. He didn't even sport a scowl.

I don't trust it.

The smile he tossed wasn't aimed at Lily but someone shorter. Brock dropped to his knees and opened his arms. "There's my ladybug. Give Daddy a hug."

Zoe hesitated for a moment, and Lily clenched her fists, wanting to hold her back.

He's her dad. He's never done anything to her. Never hurt her.

Her mommy sense screamed at her.

Zoe skipped toward Brock, her sneakers lighting on each step. Lily looked away as they hugged. Seeing them together like that always hurt.

Glancing at Calvin's house—*because, hey, I'm outside. It's not considered stalking now*—she probably imagined the twitch of the curtain at the window.

Brock tucked their daughter into the car, chatting amiably. He waved goodbye to Lily. Smiled while doing it. Didn't mouth a single profanity. The perfectly civil hand-off, and yet she didn't trust it.

She stood watching a long time after the car was gone.

I should follow him. Because that wouldn't look crazy in court.

I should have never let her go. If she refused, he'd just tear Zoe from her because the law was on his side.

I should have. I should have. I—

"No problems this time?"

The deep voice startled her since she'd not heard him approach. The damn man should wear a bell. She whirled. "Were you watching?" Had he seen her watching him?

He looked entirely too deadpan as he claimed, "A man never admits to stalking."

"A man should never stalk next door to

home. Doesn't that make you a lazy stalker?"

The beard made it hard to see the more subtle twitches, but she caught the hint of a smile when he replied, "I see it more as being frugal with our planetary resources."

She blinked.

He smiled. "Stalking close to home means no burning fossil fuels following you around."

A snort left her. "So you're saving the world by choosing to stalk me. How noble." She teased him, and yet she found it oddly exciting he pretended the same fascination with her as she had with him.

"Noble as in a hero?" He made a face. "That's just mean."

"Would you prefer to be the villain?"

"For some, it's a role that fits. And doesn't the villain always get the girl?"

"I thought that was supposed to be the hero."

No mistaking the distaste on his face. "Who wants to be a hero? They have to follow the rules all the time."

"I'd say a better question is, who aspires to be a villain?"

"A boy with visions of high-tech gadgets and hot women."

For some reason, this prompted her to ask, "What do you do for a living?" He wore a suit to work. Owned a nice car. She assumed he owned his home. He certainly kept it well maintained.

"Guess."

"Accountant."

He snorted.

"Banker?"

"I like money, but no."

"Programmer?"

He winked. "Too well dressed for that."

True. He had more of a Bond air about him than a pencil pusher. She threw something oddball at him. "Spy?"

"Not a spy but an assassin. An incredibly good one, too, I might add."

She laughed. "I see someone watched the John Wick movie this past weekend."

"You don't think I'm a killer." His lips curved, and she snickered louder.

"No, I totally believe it. But you obviously have a cover. What are you? Lawyer? Teacher?"

He winked. "Actually, given I travel a lot because of my work, I have a job as an international real estate broker."

How utterly mundane and boring. It totally didn't jive with her perception of him living on the edge. A pity he wasn't really the assassin he claimed to be. She could have used one.

"How did you learn to wrestle?" Because she'd recognized the submission hold he'd subdued Brock with as something she used to see during those fighting matches Brock liked to watch on television.

"I learned everything I know in school."

"That's some kind of school. Our gym teacher usually made us walk the track."

"Not run?"

She made a face. "Running was for real athletes who didn't have two left feet. I was more of a bookworm."

"I am the opposite. I love sports. The private academy I attended was big on all kinds of athletics."

"Private school?" She eyed him up and down. "I can't picture you wearing a uniform."

"It was a place for juvenile delinquents to rehabilitate themselves. I graduated. With honors."

A reformed bad boy. Did he seriously do it on purpose to make himself more attractive?

Stay away. He obviously fed her a line. *I mean, look how easily he fed me the lie about being an assassin.* He'd said it with such ease, as if it was the truth. The man couldn't be trusted.

"Nice seeing you." She turned to leave, but he stopped her with a question.

"Do you have plans for the evening?"

"No," she answered without thinking. How pathetic did that sound? Friday night and nothing to do. Nothing but worry and hope for a text from Zoe.

"Would you care to accompany me tonight to dinner and a round of billiards?"

It took a moment to process. When it did, Lily rounded on him and stared a moment before asking slowly, "Are you asking me on a date?"

She bit her tongue before she screamed "yes." What happened to not trusting him?

What happened to not even giving a person a chance?

And hello, "Did you say dinner?"

Chapter Eight

"Yes, I said dinner." Was Lily asking about the involvement of food because she happened to be one of those girls who wouldn't eat in front of a man? If that was the case, then he'd best cut his losses.

"Sorry, I can't." She shook her head.

"Did you already eat?"

"No."

"You do eat, right?"

Her lips curved. "I do. I just can't afford to eat out right now. Ask me again in a few weeks when I've got my bills all squared away."

"You're not paying. The dinner would be on me."

"I still can't go."

"Why not? I just said you didn't have to pay."

"Exactly, which now makes it look like I was asking. Which I wasn't." She shook her head and actually looked horrified.

"I'm paying because I have this silly notion that if a man asks a woman out, he pays."

"Because he's expecting something in return." Another shake of her head.

"You're right. I do expect something. Something kind of spy-ish."

"Role playing?" She arched a brow.

"Role playing is fake. This is real. I need you to play the part of my girlfriend. Tonight we're going on a reconnaissance mission to retrieve information, but we must do so discreetly." The amusing thing about telling the truth was the fact that she never suspected it.

"You want me to pretend to be your girlfriend? Don't you have a real one you can call?"

"Is this your subtle way of asking if I'm single? I am, by the way."

"I really don't care if you're dating anyone because I have no interest in you."

"Then where is the harm in coming?"

Such distrust Lily showed. It didn't take a genius to see she'd been hurt. He thought it entertaining how he told her the truth and she treated it as a joke. Yet Calvin actually had asked her to go in part because he thought she'd make a great cover for him. The other part was because she was cute, and he couldn't stop thinking about her.

It was stupid, as stupid as messing with her by actually telling her the truth. Why would he do that? What if someone listened? Then again, if anyone had ears on him, then he'd failed as an assassin to secure his neighborhood.

"Before you say no again to being my covert companion in the field, let me try and bribe you with the thought of the best shareable appetizer menu you've ever tasted."

"How good is it?"

He wanted to purr, "so good," but he manned up and instead said, "Are you coming with me or not?" And he wondered if she caught how dirty that sounded.

In a second, she'd probably blast him. Tell him he was a pig. *I'm dirty, and not just because of my job.* She inspired the lustiest thoughts in him. Probably best she not go.

"Okay," she said.

What? She'd agreed. How unexpected. He recovered quickly. "Excellent. It's sixish now. What do you say I grab you around eight? Wear something swanky. The place we're going is a little high-end, so no jeans or yoga pants."

"Any other requests?" she asked, leaning against the door, her gaze amused, the curve of her lips taunting.

Probably too soon to ask her to go commando. "Since you're taking orders, how about letting your hair down?"

"I might be able to arrange that. And what about you? What will you wear?"

Again, saying he'd like to wear her probably strayed into getting-slapped territory. "Probably another suit."

"I like the suits." As if she'd not meant to say it, her head ducked.

"What about what's in the suit? Do you like that, too?" Was he flirting? Like fuck. He shouldn't flirt with his neighbor. He also shouldn't have asked her out or told her the truth.

She raised her gaze. "Is that a corny way of asking if I like you?"

How bold of her to ask. And yet... "You avoided answering."

"Do you want me to tell you that you're pretty?" She arched a brow and grinned.

"I'd say that part was obvious."

"What makes you think that?"

"You did say yes to a date."

"I'm saying yes to free food. Oh, and to kicking your butt at pool for money. I could use some cash to do a good grocery run."

"You think you can beat me?"

"I know I can." Her smile emerged wicked with promise.

"You're on." Let her bring it. He was pretty slick with a cue.

As promised, Calvin picked her up by eight. Seven forty-five, actually, because he was ready and ridiculously impatient.

It turned out she was ready, too, and looked scrumptious with her hair down. It went just past her shoulders and framed her face in soft waves. He couldn't help but reach out to touch it.

"I like this."

"Thanks." She fidgeted, her hands clutching a small purse.

The walk to his car proved quiet and weird. For some reason, he found himself tongue-tied around her. Him, a guy who'd sweet-talked his way out of a firing squad death. Then killed the guy who spared him. He would add that he did the world a favor—and filled his offshore account.

The inside of the car proved a close atmosphere, especially since she sat stiffly looking ahead, her hands clasped in her lap. She obviously regretted saying yes. He could feel the trepidation rolling off her. Why did she fear him so much? He'd done nothing to inspire that level of disquiet.

Maybe she's finally beginning to believe I'm the bad boy she should stay away from.

Problem was, he didn't want her to go.

"Are you ready to slip into your role?" he said lightly.

"Are we still pretending to be spies?"

"No pretense. We'll have to play it right if we don't want to look out of place."

"And what's playing it right?" she asked, the tension in her easing the more they spoke.

"Well, we're obviously infatuated with each other. So that means no staring at other men." He'd hate to have to kill them later.

"That goes for you too, then."

"I'll do my best to not ogle the men."

She laughed. "Eyes off cleavage and butts."

"What about legs?"

"Do you want to blow our cover?" she teased.

He'd blow if she touched him. "You'll have to laugh at every joke I make."

"That should be easy. You and your delusions are entertaining."

A smile teased his lips. "Or perhaps I really am telling the truth. I am an assassin."

"And I am a covert Russian agent."

"Not likely. Your accent is too American, and your coloring screams more Italian."

She looked over at him. "Next time we play, maybe you should pretend to be a bear shapeshifter. You are hairy enough to pull it off."

"Next time?" He caught the slip of words. "Are we already planning a repeat?"

"Let's see how this evening goes."

The evening would go perfectly. He would allow nothing less.

The club he took her to was high-end and linked to a golf course. A swanky place that required a membership, mostly to prove you could afford the tab. No one was gauche enough to use actual money. Everything was done out of sight and discreetly.

In Calvin's case, the membership was done through the company. Never knew when he'd have to wine and dine someone with money who wanted to buy property. Because, yes, in order to maintain their guise, they did wheel and deal realty. Usually to others of their ilk, who could afford it and needed a travel alibi.

The maître d' recognized Calvin. "Nice to see you again, sir."

No shit. The Bad Boys were known as excellent tippers. Calvin held out his hand and, as he shook Francis's palm, greased it with a few bills. "The lady and I would prefer a table in the back."

"But, of course. If you'll follow me." The maître d' set them up in the farthest corner. The table was covered in snowy-white linen, while the chairs were polished wood, the seat and back upholstered and cushioned for comfort.

"You weren't kidding about this place being upscale." For some reason, Lily whispered. "I don't know if this was a good idea."

"Is this your way of reneging on playing billiards with me?"

"I—" Lily looked around and then down at her hands, hands with short, blunt nails and no polish. "I shouldn't be here."

"But you are. And you're going to eat and play with me." He meant that in the dirtiest way possible, and he caught the hint of pink rise in her cheeks.

A waitress appeared and took their order. While they waited for it to arrive, he draped his jacket over the seat and rolled his sleeves before he grabbed a cue from the rack on the wall. "Ready to play?"

For a moment, Lily hesitated. He saw the moment she made up her mind. Her back straightened, and her chin lifted.

"Are we playing for money?"

"I couldn't take money from you."

Her lips curved. "I was hoping you'd say that, since I don't have any. But who says you'd win? How about a friendly wager?"

"What will you give me if you have no money?"

"How about a kiss?"

"What happened to no sexual favors?"

"No expectation of sexual favors," she corrected. "This is my offer. One kiss if you win. A five spot for me if you don't."

"I'll give you five dollars right now for a kiss."

"Play me and win it. If you dare." She arched a brow and looked so cute he was ready to dump his wallet on the table if he could toss her onto the pool table.

"I dare." He pulled a fiver from his clip and placed it on the carved wooden rail. No fake pressed wood or vinyl for this moneyed place. The felt top on the table was a deep burgundy, the pockets woven leather strips. He racked the balls as she chose a cue.

He gestured to the neat triangle of balls. "Ladies first."

"If you insist."

That first game, he got to put away five balls before she beat him. The second game, he got three. By the fifth quick round, she smirked as she snared the ten spot sitting on the bar. She was still wagering kisses for money. He'd yet to get a single peck.

"Play again?"

Given she'd already cleared him of forty dollars, he thought a break was called for. He signaled the barmaid as he headed back to their table.

"So much for my cover as a pool shark," he grumbled, though good-naturedly. Yes, he'd gotten beaten badly. He'd like to say he held back, but she'd spanked him.

Good thing he'd managed to fluster her once or twice, or he'd have completely lost his Bad Boy Inc. membership.

"Are you going to whine about losing to a girl?"

"What happened to us looking like a couple to keep our cover?"

She grinned at him from across the table. "I made it look real, I thought, when I grabbed your ass."

"As I was taking a shot. You made me scratch." Eight ball down, and she'd crowed in victory.

He'd called foul, and yet hoped she'd do it again.

She can grab any part of me that she likes.

Their little table at the back gave them a good view of the place. With their departure, the pool table acquired new players. It would give them something to watch. They also had a view of the far end of the bar. This early in the evening, it wasn't packed shoulder to shoulder. It would get a little busier the later it got, and yet would still be less packed than most public bars. Privilege kept it exclusive, which was why the parents of rich kids loved to play here.

Once her initial surprise was over, Lily didn't seem impressed by his choice of venue, but she certainly fit in. She didn't wear a dress—pity, he loved legs—but the dress slacks with the flare at the bottom somehow showcased her hippy nature. The silk blouse, also in black, ghosted close to her skin, at times molding it and then hiding. It distracted Calvin, especially when he got hints of her brassiere underneath. Some men got turned on by naked images. He preferred it subtly hidden, making the reveal all the more special.

The waitress had left them a platter of edibles, as well as fresh glasses of wine. He took a sip and let the liquid roll around on his tongue. What ambrosia. In a place like this, the palate was expected to cater to a higher echelon, hence nothing in a brown bottle. Any kind of beer arrived in a glass, chilled and with only a hint of foam on top.

His pool shark of a neighbor liked wine with a hint of rosé. She handled a few glasses well, only the flush in her cheeks and the brightness in her eyes giving away her slightly tipsy state. She smiled at him often now, completely at ease and still thinking he bullshitted her about the assassin thing.

If only she knew. She'd probably run screaming.

Then he'd have to break one of his cardinal rules and shoot her.

Sentimentality got people killed. The

sergeant had taught them that.

Given she thought he lied, he didn't understand her motive in agreeing to come out with him. Then again, he still questioned his decision to ask her.

Since when did he mix his personal life with his professional one? Since when did he tell anyone the truth?

When did I get tired of always living a lie?

He needed to smarten up. He'd come here tonight to gather information. Bringing a woman along wasn't part of the plan. She shouldn't belong in any kind of plan, and yet there she sat across from him. Entertaining to talk to. Spirited to play. And so sexy he wanted to drag her out of here and hope he made it to his place before tearing the clothes from her and making her cry out his name.

His constant state of semi-erection obviously addled what wits he had. He should try eating more red meat to up his red blood cell count.

A brief glance at the bar gave him a slight reprieve. Perhaps he should make an attempt to at least try and achieve what he'd come here for tonight. Scanning the faces, one drew his eyes. He knew that face. It was in a stack of pictures he'd memorized earlier as possible drug connections.

"I should check on our drinks," he said, standing from the table.

"Is that code for completing the mission?"

"Actually," he said with a grin, "it is. I

have to talk to a guy. It shouldn't take me more than a few minutes."

"While you're saving the world, oh mighty double-oh-neighbor, I'm going to visit the ladies' room. All kinds of action to be had in there. Hopefully, I won't run into any bad guys."

"Watch out for bathroom ninjas. They're deadly with a tube of lipstick." He winked, and she laughed as she rose from the table.

They headed in opposite directions, and as Calvin got closer to the bar, he couldn't help but feel he was going the wrong way.

The target is at the bar. Dealing with him wouldn't take long. Harry expected results, and Calvin always succeeded.

"Tony." Calvin clapped the short guy on the back, but didn't manage to knock him over. The fellow had more than a few pounds to keep him steady.

"Do I know you?" Beady eyes perused Calvin. Tony "Stubby" Clemons Junior was a several-generation mutt living off the money his daddy had made in the mattress business. Calvin had seen him around but never paid him much mind. He didn't associate with lowlifes.

"You don't know me, but you know my buddy. Daryl Rose." Everyone knew Daryl. Rich playboy who prided himself on never being without the influence of something.

"Daryl I'm familiar with, but I've never met you."

"I guess I didn't make a great impression,

and I haven't been around in a bit. You know how it is. Work. More work." He shrugged.

The shorter fellow dressed in an ill-fitting shirt let out a noisy laugh. "Yeah, I do know."

"Speaking of work, I don't suppose we can do business?" Calvin leaned against the bar and noted his table was still empty. Then again, Lily was a woman. She'd probably take a while. Women had this strange ritual when it came to bathrooms. Fixing their face being the one he didn't quite get. Were they secretly aliens readjusting their noses?

"We can do business. Why don't we go step into my office."

Had to love the clichéd nature of every drug dealer he'd ever met.

Tony led the way to the men's room, and it occurred to Calvin that he would probably run into Lily on the way. It wouldn't look odd at all for two guys to go toward the bathroom together. Not strange in the least to anyone who knew Tony. But what would Lily think?

She still didn't believe he was a spy of sorts.

Why did he care what she thought? He didn't know, just like he didn't know why he couldn't wait to get back to her.

I am enjoying myself. And his business with Tony interfered with that.

Let's get this over with.

Calvin didn't encounter Lily at all on the way to the men's room, and entering, he quickly noted it was empty. The handful of stall doors open, the urinal vacant. The door to the hall swung shut, cutting off some of the noise. As Tony babbled and reached into his pocket, Calvin grabbed him. He pushed Tony up against the door, hard enough to make him grunt.

An arm over a throat pinned the guy while Calvin grabbed the baggie out of his hand. He held it up and shook it, recognizing the symbol on the little packets. He might have found some of the tainted product. Only tests by Benedict would say for certain.

He waggled it. "Where did you get this?"

Tony didn't seem to grasp the trouble he was in. "Give it back. It's mine."

"No, it's mine."

"You don't know who you're dealing with."

"Oh, I know what you are. You, on the other hand, have no idea just how much shit you're in. So you'll have to trust me when I say don't fuck with me. Now I'm going to ask you again, who gave you this?"

"Fuck you, asshole."

Slam. The door, a modern metal thing of brushed nickel, dented slightly as Tony's head smashed into it.

"Motherfuc—"

Now that was just profane. Wham.

"Let's try this again. Who." Whap. "Sold you this shit?" Calvin held Tony up so that they were eye level, which meant Tony's feet dangled off the ground. He wouldn't be able to hold it for long—the guy ate way too many donuts for that—but it always impressed opponents when you dominated them like that.

A pity Lily wasn't there to admire his strength. Speaking of whom, he really should get back to his date.

"I don't hear you talking." He sang the words while rapping Tony's head off the door in time to the beat of the music being piped through speakers.

The man finally broke. "I don't know his name. The guy who dropped this off to me is not my regular dealer. I tried asking him, but even he doesn't know who's giving it to him. He's just a hired hand."

Layers upon layers of mystery. "Are you cutting the stuff with anything?" Dealers had a tendency to do that to increase the profit margin. People often argued against legalization of certain drugs, figuring it would addict and kill people. They didn't understand addicts were already dying because they had to deal with two-bit a-holes who didn't mind mixing their drugs with powdered cleaner if they could get a little richer.

"If you're talking about the tainted shit, then that wasn't me. I swear. I had nothing to do with it."

"You say that, yet you also just admitted to selling this"—a baggie shake—"from some unknown source."

"Because it's good shit."

"Shit that kills."

"Only some of it."

"Don't you have any kind of remorse for possibly killing kids?"

"Wasn't me."

"Are you going to say you didn't know any of them?" Calvin leaned in close.

"I knew one, maybe two. But definitely not the Asian kid."

Lee Huong could have gotten it off someone who did deal with Tony, but chances were if someone were disseminating the stuff all over the place, there was probably another dealer, or two, or more out there still peddling the stuff.

"Who else runs dope to the silver spooners?" It took a few more whacks for Calvin to get two names and locations. By the time he was done, there had been a few impatient knocks and shoves at the door.

Time to leave.

He dropped Tony. "Nice doing business with you. Now, a word of advice. Find a new place to live, or the next time I run into you, you'll find yourself living here permanently. Six feet under." These kinds of sleazy lowlifes annoyed him. It was past time Calvin took a moment to clean up his city.

Calvin exited the bathroom to see the corridor empty and a chilly swirl of outdoor air dissipating. Some guys probably used the alley when they found the bathroom occupied.

He finger-combed his hair and headed

back to his table. The empty table. His date hadn't returned.

A quick scan around, and he realized that either she was still in the bathroom, which seemed rather unlikely, or she'd disappeared.

Ditched? Surely not.

I was only gone a few minutes. Did she use that time to make her escape? Perhaps she faked having a good time.

If she did leave, though, she wouldn't have left her sweater behind. He looked at the knitted sweater still draped across the back of her chair.

She'd probably not yet returned. Didn't women complain of lines in their bathrooms?

He slid into his seat and waited. He kept peeking in the direction of the hall for the washrooms. He couldn't help but recall at the far end of it, displayed in garish, red-lighted letters, *EXIT.* An exit he knew had recently been open.

Just folks going for a pee or a smoke in the alley. Happened all the time.

A tug in his gut said he should check.

He resisted the temptation to free the gun from his ankle holster—people saw a weapon these days and started screaming. He did, however, slide a hand into his pants pocket and curl his fingers around the garrote he kept in there. Because a man never knew when he'd need another tie for a neck.

Someone else's neck.

As he pushed the matte black-painted bar to open the exit door, he wondered if he'd have to use it.

Hopefully. And maybe then Lily would start to believe him.

Chapter Nine

I can't believe Calvin's still playing that game.

Although Lily did find it kind of cute how his assertion they were on a mission kept their date lighthearted and fun.

Total fun. As in she hadn't smiled this much and hard in ages.

When he'd opted to check on their drinks, under the guise of pretending to talk to a man, she didn't just use the washroom as an excuse to escape. A few glasses of wine meant nature called—urgently. But when done, she took longer than needed, mostly because she wanted to try and figure out what was happening here.

I'm on a date and enjoying it. But how far was she willing to let things go?

As she washed her hands in the bathroom sink, Lily stared at her reflection in the mirror. She'd left her hair loose as he'd requested, but only at the last minute. She'd meant to pin it up, out of the way. Armor against his charm, just like her pants and long-sleeved blouse were meant to show him that she wasn't falling for his flirtatious game. Yet, even as she told herself to guard against him, she couldn't help but enjoy, make that *crave*, the warmth of his gaze, the smooth tickle of his voice.

She blamed his velvety tone for the fact that she'd said yes to going on the date. What had happened to her theory that men were evil? Where along the way did her plans to be independent vanish?

Weren't the real questions, how long should she stay alone, and when would she learn to trust again?

The split from Brock had happened over nine months ago. Nine months of first living in a cramped woman's shelter, then a one-bedroom apartment that the group for abused women helped Lily find.

Because I can't ignore it anymore. I was abused.

Keyword being was. She'd escaped taking nothing but a bag of clothes and Zoe, and once in a safe spot, with the help of the group, immediately filed for divorce.

Despite all his protests, Brock settled out of court. She made it easy, she asked for nothing. Nothing except a chance to escape, and now the divorce was now going on its third month. It was over except for Brock whining and cajoling.

What she couldn't understand was they were no longer a couple, so why did she hesitate to move on? She couldn't hide forever. Being alone should never be anyone's goal in life. But she feared moving too fast.

Jenny didn't seem to think it was too fast, and Lily knew other people got into new entanglements sometimes faster, but…

But what?

Would it really hurt to try? Maybe Calvin wasn't Mr. Right—even if he certainly ticked all the right boxes when it came to looks and personality. She could do worse than getting back into the dating game with a nice and decent guy—with a ton of arrogance.

Did a truly arrogant man build a freaking bookcase from scratch for a little girl? She'd never even managed to get Brock to fix the broken screen in their house—which meant flies every time she opened the window for air.

What if this date was Calvin's way of getting paid for the nice gesture? He'd better not think he was getting a piece of her. This place was a heck of a lot more expensive than expected when she'd accepted his offer of dinner. Sure, he'd beaten his chest and claimed "I am man, I will pay," but that could just be clever acting. Perhaps he thought he could ply her with a few drinks, tickle her taste buds with good food, and then get her panties off.

Good luck with that. She was wearing a full-bottomed granny pair. Good for funerals and first dates with hot guys next door.

Someone grumbled behind her about a princess taking her sweet time. It seemed a line had started for the sinks while she woolgathered. Even swanky places had issues with women. She'd spent enough time stalling. Lily couldn't avoid her date forever. Nor did she want to. Being with Calvin was the most fun she'd had with a man in longer than she could remember.

She exited the bathroom and was about to head back to their table when she noted someone she recognized coming her way. He hadn't noticed her yet, intent on his phone.

Oh, hell no. *He can't see me here.*

Whirling, she noted the exit sign and walked quickly to it. She shoved at the bar and spilled out onto a metal staircase. She clambered down the steps, causing a noisy clanking even with her multi-function black flats. At the bottom, people milled around, having a smoke, not all of it tobacco.

She went to walk past them, only an arm shot out. "Well, well, if it isn't the former Mrs. Fitzpatrick. What are you doing here? This isn't your kind of hangout." The voice made her stomach sink. She knew that voice.

A turn of her head and she saw the familiar countenance of Dillon, a close friend of her ex-husband's. "Just having an evening out."

"An evening that ends in an alleyway? Don't tell me you've taken up a new line of work?" Dillon tugged her away from the smokers, who didn't seem inclined to interfere as Dillon moved her deeper into the shadows.

Lily refused to panic yet, but it did creep in slowly. Surely, if she screamed, someone would act.

I hope. Dillon wouldn't dare be so brazen as to try something here.

"Wait until the rest of the gang sees who I ran into."

There were more of them here? She didn't need the gang mentality. "I've got to go." She pulled at his grip, only Dillon tightened it.

"You can't leave yet. We were just getting started."

The door to the club briefly opened, bringing sound and life for a moment before closing. Lily couldn't help but hear the steps vibrate as someone bounced down them.

Her hope for rescue was dashed as Zach, another of Brock's buddies, joined them. "I thought I recognized the lying whore inside."

"I am not a whore." With a sharp yank, Lily pulled her arm from Dillon's grip. "Leave me alone."

As if it would be so easy.

"You know you really hurt Brock's feelings going to court and lying about him like that."

"It wasn't lies, and you know it," Lily retorted. To think, she didn't even tell them the worst of what Brock had done. Some things she preferred to keep to herself.

Zach hooked his fingers on his belt loops. "Brock always did say you had a rude mouth on you."

"I told him how to fix that," Dillon snickered.

"Leave me alone." She went to walk around them, but they formed a wall. Whirling to go the other way meant Zach grabbed her in a grip tight enough to make her cry out.

"You need to let the woman go." The low warning sent a shiver through her.

She knew that voice. Lily glanced over her shoulder to see a rather grim-faced Calvin standing there.

Tell him to go away before he gets involved, before he gets hurt.

Dillon stepped in front of her. "Fuck off. This ain't none of your business."

"Actually, it is. This lady is my date."

She could have killed him for saying it out loud because both Zach and Dillon took the news with too much interest.

Zach squeezed her arm tightly enough to bruise. "Date? You're already dating? I know someone who will find that very interesting."

As for Dillon, he snickered. "He'll especially enjoy when we tell him how we beat up his wife's new boyfriend."

"He's not my boyfriend," she muttered.

"And I'm not that easy to beat up," Calvin added. He followed those words with a sharp left-handed jab that snapped Dillon's head back.

Dillon bellowed in pain, and Zach snarled, "You fucking ass—"

Whack.

Another quick fist, and Zach was the one reeling. Sensing the moment, Lily snatched her arm free and took a few steps back. Then another as Zach flailed at Calvin, and he dodged the blows before landing a few of his own.

She didn't try to stop the fight. Why

would she?

Zach and Dillon had asked for it. And look at that. Calvin knew how to bring it. He might wear a suit and push paper for a living, but the man possessed some smooth moves. Slick enough that, despite it being two to one, they never landed a blow. Calvin, on the other hand, kept hitting them with unerring, flesh-thunking accuracy.

When it was all over, Dillon was stumbling away, Zach supporting him, the pair uttering vague threats of, "You'll regret this."

She agreed. "You shouldn't have done that. They won't forgive you and will try to get revenge."

"Let them. I can handle those punks."

"Those *punks* could have really hurt you."

"Not this assassin." He winked. "I've got the right moves."

He did, but there were things he didn't understand. "They don't play fair. You do realize they're going to tell Brock. They'll come back with reinforcements."

"You think they'll tattle to your ex?" He smiled. "I should hope so. I planned on it."

"Are you trying to cause trouble?"

He grinned. A panty-wetting whopper of a grin. "Yeah. Maybe I am. Care to join me?"

He held out his palm, a dashing still-mostly stranger, who didn't hesitate to step in and prove chivalry wasn't dead. She wanted so much to take his hand. To let herself see where that grin would go. Instead, she tucked her arms tightly around her chest.

"I think I should go home now." Alone, before she did something crazy. Like, let herself fall in love again with a rakish smile.

Chapter Ten

The date had failed miserably. Sure, Calvin had managed to obtain the information he'd gone looking for, but the rest of his evening was a failure because, while he'd been roughing up Tony, someone was roughing up his date.

And now said date tried to placate him with, "It's not your fault."

"I shouldn't have left you alone." A woman alone around men drinking? Might as well drop a gazelle amidst a herd of lions. The a-holes in the alley had culled her from the crowd and moved in for the kill. He just didn't know why she'd entered the alley in the first place. Did she have a secret vice?

"You were taking care of our drinks. You couldn't have known my ex's friends would accost me. Don't worry." She patted his arm. "Even if you hadn't shown up, I would have handled it."

"I could see how you were handling it." Trying to look brave but appearing so small next to the guys.

She needed protection. A guard. A bodyguard like him.

No, what she needs is a gun. He even owned one just the right size for her hand.

"Dillon and Zach are mostly talk. Since the divorce, they seem to think it's their job to harass me for dumping Brock."

"How about I harass them for harassing you?" Why oh why couldn't he keep his mouth shut around her? What happened to his calm and cool persona? He was the guy with the patience of a rock. He could sit on a stakeout for hours. Lie flat on a rooftop, even in the rain, eye to the scope, waiting for the money shot.

Seeing Lily get grabbed by another guy? He'd almost strangled both of the men in the alley—and that would have caused some shit. Especially as there were quite a few witnesses he would have had to silence. Law enforcement— and Harry—tended to frown on mass killings.

Why couldn't this evening have gone like he wanted? *I had a plan, dammit.* In his plan, he'd figured to take the neighbor out on an easy date. He'd learn she was an annoying or boring housewife with ex-husband issues. She'd be desperate and bitter. In other words, easy to get out of his system.

His plan had failed in epic fashion because he was more enthralled by her than ever. Look at her, sitting prim and proper in her seat, hands folded neatly, lips pressed. He couldn't help but want to pull the car over and yank her over the console into his lap.

He wouldn't. Not just because she might say no, but because his car really wasn't built for that kind of make-out session.

But my bed is.

The chances of getting her to visit his bedroom? Probably slim to none at this point.

He pulled into his driveway, and she didn't wait for him to come around before opening the passenger side door and stepping out.

"Thank you for the evening." She shut the door with a resounding thud and walked away. For a moment, he stared at her before scrambling from his car. Things couldn't end like this.

A certain Bond fellow wouldn't allow it, and neither would he.

She whirled as she heard him approaching. "What are you doing?" He could hear the fear in her tone, see the trepidation in her gaze.

What happened to the trust they'd built?

"A gentleman always walks a lady to the door."

"I can walk myself."

"Why are you mad at me?" He asked the question bluntly, having noted her coldness since the altercation. "Is it because I used violence to quell those guys?" Some people couldn't handle it. Best to know now given his employment.

"I don't care what you did to them. You did what you had to. Violence is probably the only thing Dillon and Zach understand, but in doing so, you put yourself on their radar." She shrugged. Small defeated shoulders. "For that, I'm sorry."

"You're worried about me?" He couldn't help a note of incredulity. "You do recall I handled them with ease, right?"

"Yes, but they'll be back. They won't let you off the hook."

"Retaliation?" He laughed. "They can try." He'd shut them down rather fast. "You do realize, with my mad skills, death is only one of the tools I have in my arsenal. I could probably beat them to a pulp with one hand tied behind my back." A training exercise at the academy.

"You shouldn't joke about this. It's really serious."

"So am I." *About you.* He managed to hold back the words.

They reached the front step of her house, and she paused. "Even though things ended ugly, I did have fun tonight."

"And by fun, you mean cleaned me out because you're a pool shark."

She smiled. "That will teach you to underestimate a woman."

"You're right. It will." Because he kept underestimating her charm. Her impish smile begged him to do something more than talk.

She pulled out her keys, but paused with her hand on the knob. "Goodnight, Calvin."

She turned the knob, and the door opened a crack. She hesitated, probably because he'd not yet moved. Probably because he knew he was on the cusp of something. Something that had him reaching to cup her head, drawing her close, leaning down to meet her when her tiptoes didn't reach high enough.

Their lips brushed, a soft sensual slide that wrought a shudder in him and a soft sound from her. He pulled her closer, meshing his mouth more firmly. Truly wanting to taste her lips.

She melted into him, her body molding to his. His free hand reached down to cup her ass. Her lips parted, breath panted. Arousal rose and swirled between them, hot and heavy—

The squeal of tires and the rev of an engine saw him tearing his mouth free. As he whirled to look at the street, he noted the bright, blinding glare of a car using its high beams as it sped close. Instinct, honed over the years, screamed, "Danger!"

He shoved Lily down just in time.

Gunfire erupted, a single blast from a shotgun spraying pellets only feet from where they stood!

Like hell. Not on his turf.

The hunter within awoke, and it wanted blood. First, though, he needed to protect Lily and get rid of possible witnesses.

Then…this assassin would play.

Chapter Eleven

Oh my God, someone is shooting at us. Lily's hands scraped on the concrete front porch as the realization hit. The first name that came to mind was Brock. The psychopath had finally snapped. Probably because he saw her kissing another man—and what an epic kiss.

Her lips still tingled, her body ached, but the pleasure didn't take away the fear. *Someone shot at me.* But would Brock really indulge in something so impersonal as a drive-by? *He'd want to kill me up close and personal.* The very fact that she believed it made her wonder again why she bothered listening to the lawyers and didn't just take Zoe and run.

Because he'd find me. There was only one way to stop someone like Brock.

The taillights brightened as the car braked in front of Calvin's house. It sat idling, just a few feet off the curb, a hovering and menacing presence.

Boom.

The streetlight in front of Calvin's yard exploded, and a pocket of darkness fell, highlighting the evil red eyes of the car. The lights got larger as the car rolled backwards. Closer.

Calvin snatched the keys she'd dropped

and used them to quickly unlock her door before he opened it and pushed her inside. "Get in and stay down. Even better, move to the back of the house."

Good plan. Move away from the guy with the gun. Lily ended up crawling down the short hall, hands and knees slapping the floor as Calvin slammed the door shut. She made it to the edge of the kitchen linoleum when she realized she didn't hear or sense him behind her. She cast a glance over her shoulder, only to see the hall and entrance empty.

Don't tell me Calvin didn't follow me in? Is he crazy?

Maybe he'd ducked into the living room for a better look at the shooter. He could risk himself if he wanted. She liked her body without any holes, thank you very much. Given she didn't want to bleed, why was she heading back up the hall?

No, you idiot. Move to the back. The back is safer.

The rebuke didn't stop her. She knew she should move fully into the kitchen away from the front, and yet instead, she sidled back up the hall and sideways into the living room. Calvin wasn't there, so she kept going until she reached the window. Holding her breath, she peeked over the ledge.

Red brake lights still glowed where the car sat parked on the street in front of her house. She ducked back down and heard the boom of a gun firing. Another boom, and the living room got darker as another street lamp died.

Since her windows remained intact, Lily braved another peek, hoping she wouldn't see Calvin dead on the front lawn.

The meager porch light illuminated enough that she could see the lawn remained body free. She didn't spot a single sign of her date. But she did hear a slight popping sound. *Pop. Pop. Pop.* More shots were being fired, but not the same shotgun blasts from before. These were more focused and determined. The red lights on the car went out, one by one.

The porch light went next.

Darkness fell so thickly and suddenly, she blinked. The weak porch light across the street didn't extend its illumination far. A single pop and, a moment later, it died too.

Pure darkness blanketed the world outside. As did silence.

What had happened? Who shot at the car? Was it Calvin? Another one of the neighbors?

A sudden rev of an engine and the car, no longer sporting any lights, squealed as it took off, the sound of its engine fading as it left the neighborhood. She slumped to the floor and heaved a shuddering breath, wondering if Calvin had chased them off. Even if he had, how long before they came back?

This was Brock punishing her for moving on. She was certain of it, which was why, when Calvin suddenly appeared in the living room and flicked on a light, after she finished blinking, she jabbed a finger in his direction and said, "Out. You need to go. Right now." The date was wrong. Getting involved with anyone right now? Wrong and selfish. It stopped now.

"You don't have to be scared."

"Out." She kept pointing and wouldn't look at him lest she give in to her hormones again.

"Don't forget to lock your door."

No begging to stay and protect her. No telling her everything would be all right.

He left.

The loneliness hit her hard, and she tucked her knees to her chin. She rocked and hugged herself tightly, mostly because she wanted to run after him and beg him to come back. To just hold her for a little while and tell her everything would be okay.

Instead, she did what she always did. Protected others. Protected him.

Stay away from me.
It's for the best.

Chapter Twelve

Lock your door? Really? That was all he had to say to her? Calvin couldn't help but be disgusted with himself. Lily sat on the floor terrified. Shaking. He should have been reassuring her; instead, he left.

Striding back to his house, Calvin cursed under his breath. What else could he do? He couldn't blame her for telling him to get out. How many dates did she have that ended in shots fired?

Despite all his precautions, someone had found him.

Calvin yanked out his cell phone and unlocked it with his fingerprint. It took only a ring before someone answered. "I need you to run a plate for me."

Mason didn't ask questions, although he did grumble. "Why can't criminals work at a decent hour?"

Because dirty deeds were always done under the cover of darkness. "Someone shot at me."

"And missed? That wasn't too bright of them."

No kidding, because Calvin wouldn't miss when he got a chance. He'd hoped to disable the car enough to get to talk to the driver, but they'd taken off like cowards, despite the flat tires. They wouldn't get far. "I want a name and address."

"I'll call you back when I get results," Mason replied. He wouldn't do something stupid like try and talk Calvin out of it. Academy boys didn't let any slights pass them by. Strength and the appearance of power were everything.

The moments it took for Mason to get an answer gave Calvin the time he needed to make it into his house and up to his attic. He flicked on his screens and pulled up the programs that ran his cameras. He'd placed a number around his property for security. If a mouse so much as twitched a whisker in and around his place, he'd know.

His phone rang. "I got the info you wanted on the plate."

Calvin envied Mason the speed he could pull info. While Calvin had access to a great many things, police databases and DMV records were harder to crack since they'd upgraded their security yet again. Then again, Calvin preferred hands-on tasks, whereas Mason was more of a technology kind of guy. Together, they made a good team.

"Hit me with it. Who's the owner? Gangbanger? Drug dealer?"

Or perhaps the incident was related to something more personal such as an ex-husband, or, more specifically, the friends Calvin had humiliated. They obviously hadn't learned their lesson.

"Actually, the owner has nothing to do with the drive-by at all. The vehicle we're talking about was reported stolen less than half an hour ago from a convenience store. Someone hopped into it while the guy was buying gum."

"Someone stole a car to come shoot at me?" Evidently wanting to hide their tracks, but also risky given that they'd have to ditch the vehicle soon so the cops didn't nab them.

"We don't know that they were after you. This could have been a simple crime of opportunity. If the information I'm now reading is accurate, whoever stole it abandoned the car already."

"Are we sure it's the same vehicle?

"Not entirely. Someone called in a partial plate and description. Apparently, the car is on fire." Sirens wailed in the distance, and Calvin's lips pursed. Those sounded close.

Too close.

Whoever had driven and ditched the ruined car was now on foot. Or had they acquired new wheels?

His camera watching the north end of the street beeped, and he tapped to enlarge the video feed. He didn't need to see it, though, to mark the arrival of the cops. Hard to miss their presence with the red and blue swirl of lights illuminating the darkness and managing to color the inside of his attic.

A peek outside, and he marked the

location of the cruiser, sitting in Lily's driveway. Someone had called 911. Not surprising. A few windows on the street had lights on, and he'd wager faces were pressed eagerly against the glass in order to inhale the sudden action happening on the usually quiet street. Gun blasts in suburbia weren't an everyday occurrence.

They shouldn't happen at all in his neighborhood.

It offended Calvin. This was his castle. His home. Which meant he'd have to do something about it, but only after he dealt with the cops. Once done talking to Lily, they'd surely end up at his place asking questions. Then he'd have to lie, just enough to make them think the attack was random and had nothing to do with a benign real estate broker.

I wonder if Lily believes me now when I say I'm a killer.

She certainly understood he wasn't a regular kind of guy. Regular guys didn't get shot at.

Since Mason had already promised to keep an eye on whether the burning car coughed up any clues via forensics, Calvin shut down his command center—also known as his sweetest computer setup yet.

He couldn't have told you what it ran in bytes and RAM and shit. Mason had been the one to completely score him a state-of-the-art system. All Calvin knew—and cared about—was that the computer itself ran fast, and if anyone other than he or Mason touched it, it would have a complete and utter meltdown. The security was just that good.

The stairs leading up to the attic were easy to fold, and the entire trapdoor lifted, sealing it off. The coolest thing was, if anybody pulled the cord and peeked, they wouldn't see a thing. Holographic technology covered the attic's use by displaying insulation, wooden support beams, and other things one would expect to see when looking through a trap door. Anybody who'd ever loved a good spy or contraband movie would appreciate the clever design of it.

Trotting down the stairs to the front hall, Calvin could still see the red and blue lights casting strangely colored, moving shadows. He bent and pulled his holster off his ankle and tucked it in a safe spot hidden under the console table in his front hall. Custom-made, of course.

A lot of his furniture had been designed with extra functions. He ordered the stuff from a specialty shop. It might cost a bundle, but the people knew how to build. Given his line of work and his paranoid nature, Calvin had hiding spots all over the house. He also had safe houses around the world. The apocalypse could hit at any time. He was ready.

Peeking through the curtains, Calvin took stock of the disco strobe of the cop lights, which illuminated the outside enough for him to see that nothing moved between the houses. He fixed himself a drink and waited, waited while scrolling through some stuff on his phone, replaying video footage of the attack. None of it gave any clues. The car had been stolen and thus wouldn't lead back to anyone. The grainy footage, because the shadows were so thick on the street, meant he only got one view of the driver, and the…

"Fucker is wearing a balaclava." Or some kind of face-covering hood with basic holes for the eyes and mouth. Hiding his face. Simple drive-bys wouldn't bother.

Rewind. He watched again. And again. He took a sip of his drink and frowned at the image.

He rewound it and played it slowly. The driver remained an expressionless blob behind the wheel, but what was that?

There. In the back.

He paused, rewound, and played the video even slower, frame-by-frame, and noted a passenger in the back seat. Also wearing a head covering and almost missed but for the movement and sudden outline of a profile before the lights went out. There were two people in the car.

Important but not as important as the fact that the car slowed down in front of Lily's place and began to fire. Not *his* house.

Were they stupid? Did they miscount? Did they see Calvin and Lily and jump to the assumption that it was his house?

Am I even the target?

There was a slim chance it had nothing to do with him. Perhaps it truly was random. A crime of the moment.

Maybe they were after Lily.

They'd better not be.

Taking another sip of his drink, he wondered when the cops would get here and get his statement over with. He had better things to do—like march back over to give Lily a proper goodnight kiss. And then convince her to let him spend the night.

What?

Shock had him spewing his drink because, what the hell? Why the fuck would he go over there? The date had failed miserably.

But the kiss...

The kiss had ended in near bloodshed.

He finished his drink and drummed his fingers on the armrest of his chair.

Are those cops ever going to get here?

It occurred to him that perhaps he was looking guilty by not showing more curiosity. After all, in suburbia, wasn't everyone's business the hottest topic around? Perhaps he should show an interest. After all, the shooting had happened during the failed date. He moved to the window and twitched the drape aside.

He was just in time to see the police car, the lights flickering off, driving away—without talking to him. Ignoring a witness.

That made no sense.

What had Lily told them? Surely she'd said something about Calvin. They were together. Hell, she'd figured out the whole shooting was his fault and told him to leave. Because of him, she no longer felt safe.

To his surprise, an odd sense of chivalry rose and insisted he do something about that. Figure out who was behind the drive-by and take care of them because this was his house. His turf. Nobody was going to fuck with that.

And they need to stay away from Lily.

To protect her, he needed to know what had happened with the police. Had Lily placed all the blame on him, accusing him of bringing a criminal element into their midst? Would the police return with a warrant? That would suck. He'd put down a good chunk of money on this house and poured a ton of sweat equity into it, as well. Changing personas and relocating didn't appeal.

I doubt my next place will have a hottie next door. A hottie who might have ruined his gig. What had she told the cops?

Let's find out. He slid on his shoes and headed outside. Forget overthinking the brilliance of it. He rapped on the door before he could change his mind.

No answer.

It called for another firm tap. "Lily. We need to talk." Never ask a question. He remembered hearing that rule somewhere. He just wasn't sure if it applied to women or children.

Creak.

"Are you really going to pretend you're not behind the door?" He sighed. "I'm not leaving until you talk to me."

"It's late."

"It is, but you're not sleeping, and neither am I."

The door opened a crack, and a single brown eye peered at him. "I would be in bed if you went away."

Bed. What a nice idea. He wouldn't mind that at all.

He reeled his mind out of the gutter to focus on important business. "What happened with the police? I saw them here." No point in pretending he hadn't.

Still from the small crack she'd opened. "Someone called them claiming they heard gunshots. I gave them a statement, and they went away."

No more details appeared forthcoming. "And?"

"And what?" The door swung open a little farther, revealing her whole face. Features wan, she shrugged and offered a weak smile. "According to them, it's just a random act of violence. Probably something to do with the previous tenant since I moved in so recently."

"Are they filing a report?"

"Why bother? No one got hurt. The property was not really damaged that they could see. Why waste everyone's time?"

It sounded so coolly logical even if her voice trembled. It surprised him that she would blow this off. Guns should always be taken seriously. "Did you tell them I was with you?"

Another shrug. "Again, why bother? It wouldn't have changed anything. As far as they know, I got home, there were gunshots, I ran into the house. I saw nothing."

"Saw nothing?" He couldn't help but repeat with a touch of incredulity. "What are you, mafia?" Because her story seemed a little too pat. As if she'd lied to authorities before. How unexpected and yet utterly beguiling.

Her lips pulled down. "Not mafia. Worse. Which is why you need to leave. Like now. I just want to go to bed. I'll pack in the morning."

"Pack? Why would you pack?"

"Because I can't bring my daughter back here." She said it with a *duh* tone.

She's afraid. The violence had come too close, and she wanted to run. Run to protect her little girl. That made sense, yet he didn't care for it. The thought of her leaving didn't please him at all.

So how to fix this?

How to make her feel safe again? He couldn't exactly send her a video of him killing the two guys in the car. Lily was too gentle and sweet. She would never condone the kind of violence he believed in. However, she didn't have to see it to feel protected.

"You shouldn't go on account of one bad incident. If the cops are right, then it was a random thing."

"Random violence doesn't make it any less

real."

"Moving doesn't mean you'll be safe. This is your home now. Make it your fortress." It could be done. Calvin was doing it. Giving himself a safe place. It would be safer by the time he was done cleaning the city. *Betcha Mason would give me a hand culling some of the crime.*

"A fortress needs guards. Is this your way of telling me to get a dog?" She arched a brow.

"I prefer cats."

"Are we seriously talking pet choices at just past midnight?"

"No, we're talking about the fact that you need to stick around."

"I don't want to run. But it's not just about me." Her head ducked. "I can't allow anything to happen to Zoe. She's my life."

The words struck a nerve with him. His own parents hadn't been around much when he was growing up. Their absence was the main reason Calvin had ended up in and out of foster care. As with many kids in the system, he rebelled. It was how he'd ended up meeting his new family at the academy.

A family he could always count on.

"What if I said I knew some people who could look into this?"

Her head lifted, and she tossed him a sharp look. "What do you mean by look into this? Like private eyes? I don't have money to hire anybody."

"No cost. Just a few friends doing favors."

Calvin was owed more than a few. Time to call some in and make promises for others because he was declaring this part of suburbia off-limits to criminals. Lily didn't know it yet, but this area was about to become crazy secure.

I promise to make you and your daughter safe.

Calvin couldn't help but take a step closer to her. He couldn't have said why, except the space between them offended him. He stood close enough that his hand couldn't resist sinking into her hair, the long darkness of it like silk in his hand.

"What will those favors cost me?" Her eyes stared, big and beguiling. Hesitation in their depths but also a faint hope.

Cost? "No cost." Because didn't she realize yet that he needed to do this? Needed to… Threading his fingers to cup her head, he drew her close, close enough that his words hit her lips. "I'll keep you safe because I want to."

He would. It seemed important that she know this. He dipped lower, and his mouth brushed hers.

Soft and trembling, her flesh met his. Her breath caught as he slowly rubbed his lips over hers. He tugged at her lower lip with his teeth, and a tremor went through her. His free hand curved around her waist and tugged her close, close enough to mold her to him.

A low sound rumbled through her, a moan that only heightened his awareness of her as a woman. Desire rushed through him.

He deepened the kiss, parting her lips that he might slide his tongue along hers. Teasing and stroking. He crushed her tighter. Tasted her. Felt the excitement in her body, her sweet trembles, and naughtier undulations.

It occurred to him that they kissed in the middle of her front hall, the door still wide open at his back.

Dumb and dangerous. He shuffled them backwards, enough that his foot hooked the door and shut it.

Click.

She froze.

Her hands then pressed on his chest, and she said something involving goodnight, but he could barely comprehend beyond the incredulity.

She's telling me to go away.

Chapter Thirteen

"Thanks for coming to check on me. Goodnight."

"Goodnight?" He looked perplexed, and with good reason.

That was a mighty fine kiss. Better than fine. Stupendous. Panty wetting. She'd *felt* it.

Which was why she'd ended it.

The kind of fire igniting between Lily and Calvin would burn out quickly, and for what? A few minutes of heaven? Was the brief pleasure worth the possible pain? And she didn't mean the break-up kind.

Tonight, the stakes had gone higher than ever. If it were Brock's doing, then Calvin was right about one thing. Running away wouldn't work. He'd find her, and the next time would be worse. She needed to take care of this problem between her and Brock. She needed help.

But from whom?

I don't know how to fix this.

She needed someone with connections and know-how. Someone who could get the job done. Hadn't Calvin just claimed he knew those kinds of people?

"Those friends of yours, just what can they do?" She knew better than to ask him if he knew of any hitmen for hire. She couldn't be entirely sure the house wasn't bugged. She wouldn't put it past Brock. So far, she'd not done anything that crossed any lines, but the moment she did... Brock would use it against her.

I can't let that happen.

"My friends have varied skills, so they can do just about anything. They're very good at—" He paused for a second. "—solving problems."

"Yeah, but this is a big problem. I mean, you saw what happened tonight. Brock will stoop to any level."

Putting it out there, it didn't surprise Lily to see his face go blank. He took a moment to process her accusation. "You think that shooter was after you because of your ex?"

"Obviously. Brock wants to scare me into going back to him." Brock didn't want her dead. Killing Lily, a mere woman, would make him look weak. He'd prefer to see her go crawling back to him.

Never.

"Can I kill him?" Calvin said it so seriously. It just about melted her panties right off.

No man should ever look or sound so sexy. A pity he didn't mean it. A dead Brock would solve many problems. Except for one. "I can't kill Zoe's dad."

"You wouldn't have to." His lips stretched, and his teeth pearled between them. If a shark smiled, it would have looked like

Calvin—with a beard.

She really needed to go to bed. Before she began hallucinating he could change into an actual animal like those guys in romance novels sometimes did. Men becoming moose and wolves and bears. Lily didn't get the appeal.

"You should go." She needed to sleep and figure out a game plan in the morning.

"I will, but only because I've got some phone calls to make." He tilted her chin with a finger. "Sleep tight. I got this."

"Whenever Zoe says that, it results in stuff getting spilled."

His lips curved. "Funny thing, but that's usually how it works for me, too."

"You're a strange man, Calvin Jones."

"Not strange, more like multi-layered. Keep peeling, and perhaps you'll see the real me." Before she could wonder what that meant, he dropped a kiss on her lips and left.

For the second time that night, he was gone, and yet she didn't have the same despair as before. She shut the door and locked it, leaning against it for a moment.

What was it about Calvin that made her feel safe? He made it seem like he truly could handle anything. But he sold real estate for a living. Real estate. Like, seriously. What could his friends do? Call the IRS on Brock? Wreck his credit rating?

She needed a plan to deal with Brock. One that didn't involve a gun or a manacle attached to a cinder block. What about arsenic?

Would Brock notice rat poison in his coffee? Probably not since he'd never noticed the laxatives she gave him when she wanted petty revenge.

Much as she might joke, though, she couldn't kill him. She didn't have the guts to do it. If only she knew someone who did.

Chapter Fourteen

Despite it being Saturday, it wasn't unusual for the boys of Bad Boy Inc. to pop into the office. Harry was there, along with Mason and Ben.

"Just the fellows I want to see." Calvin dragged them all into the secure boardroom before he laid it out for them. The idea had come to him the night before, and he'd had hours now to plan his argument.

He started with a presentation of newspaper articles he'd pulled and then had Mason compile into a slideshow. Crime after crime happening in their town. Going unpunished. Calvin said nothing as he clicked from slide to slide, just let them absorb it all before he began his speech. "Our town's gone to hell."

"What town hasn't?" retorted Ben.

"It goes further than regular crime. And it's more than just this case we've got going with the drugs and deaths. A house in my neighborhood was targeted in a random act of violence."

"Was it random?" Harry asked, a devil's advocate in a three-piece suit.

"I don't know, and it shouldn't matter. We should not be allowing this kind of shit to happen in our town."

"Is it really our town, though?" Ben leaned back in his chair and laced his fingers over his abdomen. "I mean, don't we all have another life waiting for us in a new location should this one go to hell? I just negotiated a sweet deal for a house on the Riviera."

"How about not letting hell take over in the first place? I don't know about you guys, but I like my house. I want to stay in it. And eventually…" He said it in a quick rush of words. "I might have kids living in it. Those kids should be safe."

Mason spewed his coffee. "Holy fuck. Since when do you want to become a family man?"

"I don't." Or so Calvin used to think. Then he began watching Lily and her daughter. It was probably just as creepy as it sounded, but he couldn't help himself.

In them, he saw something he didn't have right now. Something he'd never had as a child. Something he craved.

A home. A family. A woman to call his own. A child he could teach and protect.

It seemed like an impossible dream for an assassin. Calvin was a man who worked on the wrong side of the law. He killed people. Many of the people he took out had connections and money, which meant revenge was something to watch for. Not everyone understood that Calvin just did his job.

As such, Calvin always watched for the hit. Always kept an eye on his back. A suspicious nature meant cameras everywhere, not just inside and outside his house, with motion detection and infrared. He had cameras discreetly placed in the neighbors' homes, as well—including Lily's. When she'd left for work, he had plenty of time to install a few extra ones and check out her place. In the name of research, of course, to make sure she wasn't working for any of his enemies.

He didn't like what he saw. She hardly had any dishes to fill the cupboards. All of her labels for cereal and canned goods were generic brands, and often in multiples from a bulk buy. She didn't have cable, but she did have a few novels on her nightstand. Horror stories for the most part and one suspense. He also discovered she liked to wear full-bottomed underwear.

Yes, he'd looked, but he didn't sniff or keep any. That would have been weird—or at least weirder than looking in the first place.

"Did you get a girl pregnant?" Mason asked, still on the subject of Calvin admitting he might want a family. "I didn't even know you were seeing anyone."

Pregnancy would require sex with someone other than his hand. He'd been a tad busy of late. "No one's pregnant. However, look around, we're all getting older." He'd passed the big three-oh, and while a ways from forty, it was time to start thinking ahead. "What's wrong with ensuring a spot for our golden years?" He wasn't just proposing a city cleanup for Lily. This would benefit them all.

"My golden years will be somewhere with no winters and topless men," Ben grumbled. "But I hear what you're saying. I'm living downtown in the good part, and yet Mrs. Grossinger, who makes those excellent gingersnap cookies, got mugged. She's gotta weigh a hundred pounds soaking wet, and I doubt she's got two extra quarters to her name."

"Not the cookie lady!" Jerome, a man with a serious sweet tooth, rubbed his stomach. "We must avenge her!"

Harry interjected. "You're talking about working for free."

Expecting that argument, Calvin had an answer. "We'd be working for ourselves. It's different."

"Damned right it's different. It means possibly exposing who we are and what we do." Harry frowned, but Calvin could see the gears turning in his head. Harry already had a family. Kids. A legacy to protect.

Calvin kept pushing. "Maybe other cities have let themselves get overrun by the lazy and criminal—"

"Aren't we criminals?" Ben pointed out.

Harry replied most indignantly. "Academy graduates aren't anything so common. We are pros. Belonging to a long line of professionals."

"Who do things that are against the law."

"But we follow a set of rules," Jerome

added. Rules that those academy-trained adhered to, such as keeping their dual lifestyle a secret.

"We might live life our own way, but we still pay our taxes." Calvin hated the IRS, but he did his part.

"An ungodly amount of taxes," Harry grumbled. "Which is why I don't get this sudden altruism."

"Don't you ever want to be more than just a guy for hire?" Was he the only one who wanted a little more meaning to his life?

Mason got it, and his brows shot up. "Holy fuck. You want to be a bloody hero. Whoever this chick is, she must be hot."

Very hot.

"I can't believe you're proposing we turn our city into some kind of Gotham protected by academy boys."

"And girls." Mustn't forget Kacy.

Harry's expression turned pensive. "If I were to say yes to this crazy idea, what are you proposing?"

"First, we deal with this drug thing that's happening." Because drugs were a huge part of the criminal element. Take out the dealers, and crime would drop.

Ben raised his hand, drawing their attention. "Speaking of drugs, I've got a source that's saying our problem goes deeper than the police department. If they're right, then there are tons of folks involved. Guys in high places. We keep digging, and people are gonna notice and get pissed."

"I don't care how high up they are if they're crooked. We need to clean out the corruption."

"Someone hand Calvin a cape," Mason snickered.

"While your sense of justice is noble, we can't start killing cops," Harry pointed out.

"We aren't cop-killers. But, perhaps we can try and handle them in a way that will effectively dissuade others from following their example," Ben offered.

"Sticking it to them on the sly. I like it," Mason said with a grin.

"In order to decide a course of action, first we need to figure out who's dealing the shit." Harry brought them back on topic.

"We're getting close to figuring that out." Surely, by now, word had begun to filter down that someone was messing with the dealers. Soon, people would come looking, and when they did…

Bad Boy Inc. would be ready.

The meeting adjourned with the tentative consensus being that they'd handle the drug thing and reevaluate. That had proved easier to negotiate than expected. Now, if only Calvin could convince Lily. Saturday night loomed, and he wondered what it would take to get her to spend it with him.

I don't think tying her to a chair and forcing her at gunpoint is going to work. This would require a little more finesse—and bribery. *I wonder how she feels about chocolate.*

As the boys filed out of the boardroom, Calvin signaled to Harry. The boss hung back, but Calvin waited until the door had shut tightly before broaching the sensitive subject.

"What's it like to be married with kids?"

To his credit, Harry didn't spew his coffee, laugh, or fall over from a heart attack. He leaned back in his chair and assumed a pensive look. "It's amazing."

Calvin felt the tension easing in him.

"Sometimes frustrating. And often, scary as shit."

The tension returned, and a frown formed on Calvin's brow. "You aren't exactly selling it."

"Because it's not something that should be sold. Listen…" Harry leaned forward. "When I graduated from the academy, I never expected to be where I am today. I was a field agent." A damned good one, too, by all accounts. "I spent my time running from mission to mission, not giving a damn about anything but the next score. I got pussy like that." Harry snapped his fingers. "I didn't need the baggage of a wife and kids."

"What changed?"

"I ended up in a cell."

"You got a glimpse of mortality and decided to scale things back." Losing his or her nerve took many operatives out of the game. You couldn't show or feel fear. Fear got you killed.

"Not exactly. I was still a wild dumbshit after that. What changed was I met Sherry while in that jail."

"As in your wife, Sherry?"

"Best damned covert operative you ever did see." Harry smiled. "She was working in the area when one of my contacts asked her if she could lend me a hand."

Calvin couldn't help but snicker. "She saved your ass."

"I saved my own ass, thank you. I had just busted out when she walked in, carrying a semi-automatic shotgun. We took one look at each other and…*bam*."

"Love at first sight?" Calvin couldn't help a skeptical note and yet…hadn't he found himself obsessed with Lily from the very beginning?

"More like annoyance mixed with lust. She was a mouthy thing, and I was full of myself. But we couldn't keep our hands off each other. After that mission, we stuck together and went on a few as a team. Diamond and Dust."

His eyes widened. "Dust was Sherry's code name?"

"She had a reputation for not leaving anything behind." A fond smile pulled at Harry's lips. "When we decided to have kids, she wiped herself clean and has been doing an excellent job maintaining our cover."

"But don't you get worried someone will find you? And what about your kids?"

"I'm a father, so of course, I worry." Harry's face turned serious. "Every day I worry someone will recognize us from our field days.

That someone with an axe to grind with Bad Boy Inc. will come hunting us. If they do, they'll regret it." No mistaking the flinty hard tone. "But…" Harry shrugged. "Here's the thing about fear. You can't let it dictate your life. Sure our jobs are dangerous, so is walking down the street. Even schools aren't safe anymore. Kids bringing guns and knives. Danger lurks everywhere. We can't live life wondering what if."

"Do you ever regret settling down and leaving the field?"

At that query, Harry shook his head. "No. I rather enjoy the micromanaging of the missions. And if you're wondering if that's the only option that would allow you to have a family and a home, then the answer is no. I know operatives who continue to work after marriage and kids. Some spouses never know about the double life their significant others lead."

Harry's words stuck with Calvin as he puttered around his office for a few minutes. A part of him couldn't even believe he contemplated it. A life with someone. Maybe children and a legacy.

A few weeks ago, he would have scoffed, but now…now he wanted more than just his regular existence.

Heading down to the parking garage, he exited to find the shadows thicker than usual. A few of the lights were dark. It happened, bulbs burned out, but the glass on the ground suggested something a little more nefarious. Especially since none of those lights had been broken when he arrived and parked.

Excellent. Someone thought to play with him.

Bring it.

Whistling and swinging his briefcase, he shoved a hand in his pocket as he sauntered to his car. Just a real estate agent without a care in the world.

A scuff of footsteps from behind and to the left. A movement of shadow to his right. Calvin slowed his step before reaching his car. He didn't want to scratch its paint by accident. He chose to stop by the trunk of a silver BMW. Ben's car and not as nice as Calvin's, of course.

He pretended to look for his keys, head ducked, completely oblivious. The thugs took advantage, stepping out from between cars and out of shadows to surround him. Four guys plus… "Douche nozzle, imagine running into you here."

"You weren't hard to find," Brock said with a sneer.

"I should hope not, given I never tried to hide. To what do I owe the pleasure? Looking to buy some property? I know of some lovely swampland perfect for disposing of your body."

"Such a fucking comedian," said another voice.

"I see you brought some friends." Two of them still sported bruises from the previous night.

"Word has it you were seen with my wife."

"Ex-wife because she was smart enough to dump your ass."

Brock came close, feeling brave with his friends at his back. Calvin tried not to smirk and let Brock advance.

The smaller man bared his teeth as he growled, "Stay away from Lily."

"Or what?" Calvin asked.

"How about a lesson you won't forget?"

"Apparently, you forgot what I told you. You were supposed to leave Lily alone." Or else. Apparently, Calvin would have to teach Brock what "or else" meant.

"Make me." Brock threw a punch, which Calvin blocked, meaning his hand was occupied when Brock's friends rushed, a pair on each side to hold him.

Hold him for a sucker-punch. Brock hit him hard in the gut. Hard enough that Calvin coughed. But he didn't lose his smile. "Is that all you've got?"

Before Brock could swing again, Calvin's foot shot out and hit Brock in the stomach, propelling him back. At the same time, Calvin flung out his arms, taking those holding him by surprise, so that when he dropped, he tore free of their grip. His foot swept in an arc, cracking at least one ankle and toppling another attacker.

Coming out of that floor spin, he sprang to his feet and began to throw out jabs, his fist hitting and cracking against flesh. His blood heated, and he got into a rhythm that saw the thugs attacking getting bruised and bloodied.

A certain coward thought to ruin it with the barrel of a gun pointed at his head.

"Move away from him," he told his friends. "I think poor Calvin here is about to become the victim of a mugging."

"Move away from my car." Ben spoke from behind Brock, but the real emphasis in his words came from the weapon resting against the back of Brock's head. "I don't want to get your brains all over the paint."

Brock lifted his hands and turned to see them both. "Who the fuck are you guys?"

Being a bit of a smartass, Ben handed him a business card before tucking his gun away. "Bad Boy Inc., the best damned real estate firm in town. I would suggest you get your asses out of here before you find out if we're something else."

"This isn't over," Brock warned, backing away from them, his limping friends by his side.

"You know where to find me," Calvin called out. "If I'm not home, then I'm probably in Lily's bed."

It took all of Brock's friends to drag him away.

Shaking his head, Ben sighed. "You just had to piss him off even more."

"Well, yeah."

"I hope you know what you're doing."

Calvin didn't, but that wouldn't stop him

where Lily was concerned.

Chapter Fifteen

I don't know what to do. Lily had run out of chocolate ice cream and was too lazy to run out and fetch more.

What a pathetic way to spend her Saturday. Watching furtively from windows, under the guise of cleaning, spying on her neighbor. She blamed him for that. Last night's excitement had left her confused.

Do I want him? Why would I want him?

One thing she knew for sure was that being with him made her feel alive. Calvin had a way of engaging all her senses, and he knew how to kiss a girl breathless.

A kiss that shouldn't have happened. But she had a hard time regretting it. How could she regret something that made her feel so good?

How did he make her feel so safe? The guy had a mundane job selling property. Yet, in the face of someone shooting at them last night, he'd kept his cool.

Because, according to him, he's an assassin for hire. His fantasy world was amusing, and she would admit, he'd played well upon the trope during their date. Made her laugh too many times.

He oozed confidence, but he wasn't a dick about it. He also flirted shamelessly. It stroked her wounded ego, healed it enough that she wondered what a true stroking by his hands would feel like.

A part of her totally wanted to see where things with him could go, but the rational part of Lily realized it as being the worst idea ever.

I'm not ready to get involved with anyone yet. The thought terrified her. She didn't trust her judgment anymore. Look how wrong she'd been with Brock.

She needed to stay away from Calvin, any man for that matter, until she managed to figure out some things. A great plan, which didn't explain why Lily kept watching for a glimpse of Calvin, spying so often through windows that she noticed him leaving his place wearing a suit, that crazy string tie, and his cowboy boots, briefcase in hand. His car reversed onto the road and paused for a moment in front of her house. She rolled away from the edge of the window and flattened herself against the wall.

Is he looking? Did he find himself imbued with a crazy need to see her, too? *You certainly kept me awake last night.* Insomnia sucked. She'd tried counting sheep, but after a while, the sheep had ended up being Calvin, running and jumping over a fence because Brock chased him.

I really should do something about my ex.
Kill him.

I can't. If Lily got caught, then Zoe would have no one. Part of the reason why Brock had managed to hold on to her for so long was that

Lily had no one. Her parents had had her late in life—early forties for her mom, fifty for her dad. By the time she hit her teen years, Dad was dead of a heart attack. Her mother followed a few years after. It left Lily alone and vulnerable. Brock seized on that.

Now, Lily paid the price. No matter how much she hated him, she could only suck it up and endure it for the sake of their child.

It didn't mean she liked it.

Argh. She scrubbed hard at the kitchen counter and sink. As if cleaning would free her of her frustration. It didn't. She tired of having to live like this. Afraid. Angry.

What if Brock never stops? What if he never moved on? Would she not be allowed to ever find a little peace and happiness?

Brock has to go.

So I can have Calvin.

The thought didn't completely shock. How could it when she couldn't stop thinking about him? If he touched her again, chances were they'd end up in bed. The attraction was just too strong.

But sleeping with Calvin might open a great big old can of worms. As in if Brock found out, he'd flip. Without a doubt.

So no Calvin for Lily, which meant she was alone—with her thoughts.

Her thoughts were really annoying.

Those thoughts kept her cleaning while Calvin was gone that day. Vacuuming with the old upright the landlord provided. She'd bought the mop with a foam head earlier that week. She vigorously gave the worn linoleum a good scrub. Sweating and unrelenting, she cleaned the floors first, and then she hit the windows and the sills with glass cleaner. Inside and then out.

He arrived while she stretched to get the top part of the bay window at the front of the house.

"Are you a cat?" Calvin asked, his low baritone not a surprise given she'd seen him arrive in his car. A peek to her left, and she saw him strolling across the small strip of lawn dividing their driveways.

Balanced precariously on a kitchen chair, of which one leg insisted on sinking and tilting the whole thing, she sprayed the window while shifting her weight to keep the wobbly chair from falling over. "I wish I had nine lives. The trick is to fall in a tuck and protect the face."

"Given your knowledge on this matter, I'm going to assume it happens often."

"I used to be pretty clumsy. My dad taught me how to protect myself when it happened."

"How come he hasn't taken care of your ex-husband?"

The blunt question startled her, and she lost her balance. A pair of strong arms caught her.

"I think you might still have issues with gravity."

She smiled at him, mostly so she wouldn't groan. He'd caught her sweaty, hair caught in a messy tail, and wearing her paint-spattered track pants. The T-shirt with the superhero logo sported an epic grape juice stain.

It was also damned comfortable, in direct proportion to how it was extremely ugly and unsexy. *Please tell me my antiperspirant is working.*

"Maybe if you didn't distract me I wouldn't need help."

"But I like distracting you. It means you notice me."

"Why do you need me to notice you?" She noted that she stared at his lips and veered her attention elsewhere. He still hadn't put her down. It brought them so close, and her body reacted, heating and relaxing. A part of her wanted to do a sinuous stretch like a cat.

She chose instead to tuck her head down lest he read her naughty—and yet pleasurable—intentions. Bad move getting closer to him. While she might reek, he smelled all too good, his cologne a soft tickle that made her want to nuzzle his skin.

He shifted her around, and she had to extend her legs to brace her feet as he stood her upright. Placed her down, but didn't let her move away. Their bodies touched, a soft sway of flesh covered by clothes.

It still made her much too aware of him. She chose to look at his chest, the pale blue linen buttoned but for the top two, the tie pulled to hang loosely. The hollow at the base of his throat begged for a kiss. "You're looking overdressed for the weekend." She said it too fast. The giddiness was very real.

Madonna had been on to something when she sang *Like a Virgin*. This could have been the first time Lily had ever interacted with a boy. Her body woke and blossomed. It ached for his touch.

"I agree." He looked down. "I am wearing way too many clothes. Want to help me strip?" He smiled, slow and sexy. He also winked.

He might as well have clobbered her with Lily-kryptonite—her resolve melted, and she was pretty sure part of her panties did, too. Heat rushed to her cheeks. "Is there something I can do for you?" *Ask me to do you. You might be surprised by the answer.*

Could she at least make an attempt to hold him off for a little while?

"Do you have plans for the night?" She threw it out there. A chance to spend time with him.

"Depends. What are you doing?"

She knew what she wanted to do. Keep unbuttoning those little plastic discs until she could see what he hid under that shirt.

It was such a horrible thing to think. Treating him like a sex object. She tried to feel castigated. She mostly felt hot. He needed to go away before she did something stupid.

"I just remembered, I'm busy tonight. My friend Jenny is coming over for wine." Calvin didn't need to know that she'd just decided it and that the coming over part would be via Skype. Getting drunk while listening to Jenny get mad at her for not taking a chance on getting some action was the smart thing to do. "I gotta go." She fled to the inside of her house, leaving behind her cleaning equipment. Shutting the front door, she leaned against it, but it didn't quell her racing heart, cool the heat in her skin, or dull the excitement adrenalizing her body.

She could try and fight this attraction with Calvin all she wanted. With each meeting, it just got stronger. Each time she saw him, she found herself drawn to him. He had a certain calming stability to him, a rock solidness that said he'd stand fast no matter what.

How long would that stoic resolve last once Brock started to really go after him? When the incidents began to happen? Lily had gotten used to the annoyances she had to deal with when Brock got angry. Was it fair to pile it on someone else?

She leaned against the door, hating her life. Hating that fear controlled her.

Why must I be afraid of happiness?

Why did she keep letting Brock win?

Because he held the power. She needed to find a way to shift that.

Given her disreputable state, which did reek more than she would have liked, she took a shower. Before she jumped in, she tossed a frozen pizza in the oven. Singles dinner at its finest.

For some reason, she shaved in the shower. Shaved that Sasquatch downy fur on her legs and the tufts under her arms. She even trimmed between her thighs. It had gotten a little too seventies for her liking.

It had nothing to do with her interest in Calvin.

Snicker.

Okay, so she still couldn't help but wonder if perhaps she should give the guy a chance. What was the worst that could happen?

You'll become a sad headline in a newspaper. Psycho Husband Murders His Ex-wife.

She frowned. The timer dinged, and she had to rush, given she still dripped and wore a towel. A few minutes later, she rescued the pizza before it turned too brown on top. She cut a few slices and tossed a tablespoon of butter on the side to dip the crust in. Sometimes she liked that part better than the middle.

The plate went on the makeshift living room table she'd made with boxes. Sturdy boxes that she'd decorated with a cloth on top. It worked.

She sat cross-legged by it, her large robe, while worn, still long enough to tuck under her when she sat. The towel on her head, wrapped around her hair, kept the wet mop out of her face. Before eating, she propped her phone on the table and called Jenny.

The first thing Lily said was, "I think you were right. I should have sex with him."

Chapter Sixteen

Sex with who?

Calvin almost spat out his beer when he heard the admission. Yes, heard. He'd been kind of keeping an eye on Lily in her place ever since the drive-by incident. Just a few cameras and microphones hidden here and there for safety.

Not because he was a creepy stalker or anything. No cameras went near the bathroom or her bedroom, and Zoe's room remained clear, too. He wasn't a pervert, but he did have cameras in her front hall, living room, and kitchen.

He justified it as making sure she didn't run into trouble with her ex or anyone else who thought a single woman was an easy target.

Such bullshit.

Mostly, he watched her and learned all kinds of neat little things, such as her obsession with peeking out windows. He'd also discovered she liked to hum to herself. Short and cute little pieces of music. Some popular, some classical.

Fascinating.

She parented her daughter with a firm yet sarcastic tone.

Zoe: "I hurt myself."

Lily: "Want a Band-Aid?"

Zoe: "No. It hurts too much." Spoken

with a huge wail.

Lily: "I'll get the axe."

Zoe: "Feeling better." And off the child ran.

It was a spellbinding skit that repeated, and he didn't tire of it.

He couldn't stop observing their day-to-day life. Envying it. Wishing he could be a part of it. Calvin knew how to spy all too well, which meant he knew an awful lot about Lily, except for one thing. *Who's this guy she wants to have sex with?* And would anyone notice if that guy disappeared?

"About time you got back on that horse," a woman squealed. "Is it a big horse? Or thick?"

"Don't get too excited. I haven't done it yet. I might have even screwed up my chances."

"What did you do now?"

"Turned him down for another date."

Hold on a second. Lily talked about him. Calvin might have spun in his chair and fist pumped. Yes, that excited him, but he'd deny it if asked and pass any lie detector test. The academy taught them how to cheat.

"Why did you say no?" The other woman sounded utterly incredulous.

Calvin understood. He couldn't fathom it either. Why did she turn him down if she wanted him?

"For one thing, he lives next door."

"And? It will keep babysitting costs down if he can just pop over around Zoe's schedule."

"Speaking of whom, there's Zoe." Lily

took a big sip of wine. "She's the biggest reason why I shouldn't. I don't want her to think I'm replacing her daddy."

Really? Because the guy was an ass. Calvin could think of many other men who would make a much better father. Though he'd kill them all to be first in line.

"Zoe will be fine if you take some time for yourself. You have needs, too."

Yes, she did, and Calvin was more than happy to meet them.

"I guess I could keep him away from Zoe so she doesn't get attached until this thing I have for him runs its course."

Runs its course? He frowned and leaned his elbows on his desk. Did she truly think their passion so fleeting?

Hadn't he wondered the same thing himself?

The fact that she hesitated meant he spent a moment staring at Lily on the screen. She fought so hard to push him away. Was her rejection what pulled him so hard?

Could this just be a short-lived infatuation? Was she right? A few rolls in the sack and, presto, they'd both go back to being happily single.

Except… A part of him didn't believe it. Something about Lily was different. Made him feel different. *With her, I want things I never imagined.*

Her friend crowed. "Now you're talking. Set him up for a few booty calls. See if he's good in bed or not."

As if there was any question.

Lily shrugged. "Maybe."

"What do you mean maybe? Keep in mind, if he's bad, he can be taught."

Taught? Hello, he knew his way around a woman's body.

Lily made a face. "How am I supposed to know if he's bad? Maybe it's just me. Maybe I just don't get the whole sex thing."

"The fact that Brock was selfish doesn't mean all guys are. When it comes to sexual games, it should be tit for tat. It will make you both happier in the long run."

A snort escaped Lily, and Calvin, who'd heard worse dirty banter, smiled. He rather liked the reciprocal policy.

A sigh left Lily. "He is so freaking hot."

Yes, he was.

"And, if I indulge with him now, then when the real guy for me comes along, I'll have gotten the rebound thing out of my system."

Whoa. Hold on a second and back up. What was this about the *next guy*? The real guy?

What's wrong with me?

"What makes you think he's not the one?"

Why couldn't he be the one?

"Well, for one thing, he's a pencil pusher. I mean, can you see me with a guy like that?"

"Nothing wrong with a man who shuffles paper for a living."

"I guess." Lily shrugged and took a bite of

her pizza, chewed, and swallowed before replying. "I don't know. I get the impression he's not into kids."

"He built her that bookcase."

"Yeah, but you should have heard him the first time we met."

In retrospect, perhaps Calvin had come across harshly. But she'd stood her ground against him, and he respected her for that.

"All great fathers start out as bachelors."

Lily leaned back against the couch, the robe she wore slipping partially off a shoulder. She took a sip of wine, the liquid clinging to her lips. "Zoe won't ever have a stepfather. Brock will never allow it."

"Brock doesn't need to know."

"Brock always finds out." Lily shoved her hand in the pocket of her robe and pulled something out. "Check out what I found when I stripped Zoe's bed to wash the sheets."

"What is it?" asked the woman on the phone.

As he listened, Calvin managed to trap the signal for the Skype conversation and with a little bit of reverse engineering—known as an app Mason had installed—had a name and address for one Jenny Harrison, living in Kentucky, several states away. He'd been ditched for a video call.

"This"—Lily held up a tiny device—"is the camera that I found in Zoe's latest bear. He had a fucking camera watching us."

"Had? Did you disable it?"

"What do you think? I put it in a glass of cola then microwaved it." Lily dropped the device on her table. "It just goes to show, he won't ever go away."

Oh, but he could. Calvin was good at making folks like Brock disappear.

"Call the cops."

"Again?" Lily's brow arched. "Why? What's the point? You know they won't do anything. No one will do anything." The frustration in her tone boiled over before she slumped. She sipped from her glass. "I just want to be happy."

"I can make you happy." Calvin said the words aloud, but Lily couldn't hear him.

"Your day will come, Lily."

"Not while Brock's alive."

I could do something about that.

"Don't give up," Jenny said.

"I'm trying not to, but it's hard. What do you wanna bet that Brock will have a new camera somewhere in Zoe's stuff when he drops her off?"

"How do you know there aren't some more in the house? He could have planted some while you were at work."

No, there weren't because Calvin would have noticed. *The same way I noticed the one in the bear?* He had to wonder if the hidden camera had caught him during his own bugging of the house.

"I cleaned the house top to bottom today. I didn't find any more cameras. What I did discover was they used an awful lot of tape to hold the wallpaper accents together at the seams. If it wasn't such a big job, I'd peel it."

"It's a rental. I wouldn't bother."

No, don't do it because some of those supposed pieces of tape were actually Calvin's cameras. And no, the hours of feed he recorded did not make him creepy. He acted to keep her safe.

"Are you sure there aren't any more cameras?" the woman on the phone asked. "Last thing you need is to have your naked ass on the Internet. Knowing Brock, he'd make it look like you're some Internet peep-show star and use that to screw you in court."

Mouth full of pizza and chewing, Lily shook her head. She swallowed before saying, "I couldn't find any, but who knows for sure. I sure as hell hope he doesn't."

Wink. The power in his place stuttered, enough to make his lights flicker. The backup generator kicked in right away, though, the stored solar energy providing instant electricity. His screen remained dark, the reboot having caused him to lose his video connection to Lily.

Calvin stood from his workstation and peeked out the window. The whole street appeared dark. He didn't like it. Power outages happened for a reason, storms being the main culprit. No precipitation fell, however. The air hung heavy and still. Not a breath of wind whistled. The night was clear.

Had a transformer blown? He'd not heard any explosions.

Did some idiot drive into a pole? Possible. There weren't many reasons a neighborhood would go dark.

Just in case it proved nefarious in nature, he loaded up. He tucked a gun into the back of his pants—safety on so he didn't shoot his ass off. A knife went into a pocket, the blade sheathed to avoid accident. He wrapped a garrote around his fist. In certain situations, silence was golden, especially in an ambush where numbers worked against a target.

Why do I keep assuming this is intentional?

Because assassins didn't live to a ripe old age without a heavy dose of skepticism—and a trail of bodies to warn off threats.

Calvin hit the main floor of his house in bare feet. He'd left only the light over his stove on, but given his generator only pumped juice to certain parts of his house, he found thick darkness. He didn't waste power on lights or appliances. Only his security system and secret lair got the benefits.

Knowing every inch of his place, Calvin moved without bumping into anything. The floors didn't creak. He didn't brush anything in passing. Not a single sound other than a lone bark of a dog broke the heavy silence.

The green light on his alarm system touchpad remained steady. Nothing had disturbed any of its zones. And yet…he didn't completely trust it. Electronics could be hacked. He'd know. Mason did it all the time, and he'd infiltrated more than his fair share of supposedly secure places. Eschewing the front door, he peeked out a kitchen window to his yard. A privacy fence made of chain link and established hedges all around kept it pretty secure, and yet, he didn't trust the shadows.

A pair of shoes by the door went onto his feet. A small remote in his pocket responded to a pattern of clicks. Five quick clicks to disarm the back door. He eased open the sliding door with one hand, standing to the side. Nothing happened. He exited and shut the door behind him, and knew his alarm system had just rearmed itself.

Outside, there was a little more noise. That damned dog barking again, the hum of a car engine a street over. Even a neighbor yelling, "It's out across the way, too."

Using the shadows, Calvin ghosted around to the front, his eyes adjusting enough to make out shapes. The crescent moon provided a semblance of illumination.

Nothing marred the serenity of the night, and yet, something nagged at him.

Reaching his front yard, he noted small pinpricks of light here and there behind windows. Candles and flashlights as residents adjusted to the loss of power. No one liked to stay in darkness for long.

Calvin didn't mind. Even before the

academy, he'd found comfort in the hugging embrace of shadows.

Did Lily fear the dark, though?

He made his way across the median separating their driveways, driven by an impulse to check on her.

He knocked. Three firm raps.

He heard banging and reached for his gun, only to relax as he heard her cursing.

"Stupid wall."

He had his hands tucked behind his back when she opened the door, phone in hand, using it as a flashlight.

"Everything okay?" he asked because surely this was the neighborly thing to do.

"I'm fine. Why?" Her brows drew together. "Is something wrong?"

"No. Nothing wrong. I just thought I'd check on you since we lost power."

"I'm fine. Bruised, but I'll live. I don't suppose you have candles."

Did flares and flashbangs count? "Not even the birthday cake kind."

"Oh. That sucks. I never even thought to buy some or a flashlight."

"I doubt it will be out for long." Look at him being all reassuring.

"Thanks for checking on me." She ducked her head. "Did you want to come in and wait for the power to come back?"

Yes, he did! However, academy training held firm. No relaxing until he'd ascertained the cause of the outage. Probably nothing, but a man could never be too sure. The academy used those who got complacent as an example to those who came after. Johnny Bonneville had assumed that guy really worked for the company. Johnny got barbecued. Calvin avoided gas entirely because of that tale.

"I'd love to come in, but give me a few minutes. I'm going to check things out first."

"You think this is intentional?" Fear entered her gaze, and her fingers curled around the edge of the door.

"No. Probably a squirrel chewing through a wire, or a pot farm drawing too much juice. But just in case, lock your door and don't open it until I get back."

"You're coming back?" He didn't miss the hopeful lilt.

He couldn't resist dropping a kiss on her lips. "Damned right I am."

He waited to hear the click of the lock engaging before heading out. More and more he didn't think there was anything to worry about. Surely if this were a hit, he'd have seen something by now. *Don't be Rory.* Rory had thought the cable guy working out front of his house was normal, too, until the guy blew his brains out.

Calvin slid from her property to the next. He became one with the shadows as he slid down the road, house to house, looking for suspicious activity. He saw a few neighbors out on their porch, their soft buzz of conversation, the red pinpricks the tips of cigarettes.

He kept moving east because studies of the neighborhood showed it as the most likely point of entrance if someone wanted to plan an ambush.

Seeing nothing at the corner, he crossed and returned on the opposite side, keeping to the darkest pockets, alert for anything out of place.

A full circuit and he didn't find a thing.

No strange cars parked. No signs of unusual activity. No cries for help.

He found himself back in front of Lily's place, noted that she'd yet to find a light source, and wondered how she fared. Had she changed into something more comfortable as she waited for him to return?

It occurred to him that he should grab the flashlight he kept in the front hall for scaring off the raccoons—they loved to try and get at his garbage cans.

Only instinct made him duck as something fired from the shadows. The small knife whistled past him and hit the sapling by the curb. It fell onto the grass.

Missed me. My turn.

Pulling out his knife—a much bigger one—Calvin ran in the direction of the thrown weapon, knowing he perhaps had only seconds before another came flying, or the culprit took off.

Don't run. I want to say hello.

This wasn't some random kid or adult

playing pin the assassin. People didn't throw knives in suburbia, not unless they were looking for a quiet kill.

Another thing the academy had taught him? Hit your fucking target. A second weapon flew past, and he narrowly dodged it.

There was no third attempt as Calvin dashed the last few yards and tackled the figure that stood with arms wide, ready to receive him, yet another small knife clenched in a fist.

In the movies, fight scenes tended to be long, drawn-out affairs. Lots of slugging and wrestling. That only happened if your opponent had some skill. This moron didn't. The itty-bitty blade never even came close. Calvin, on the other hand, knew how to wield his. His knife went in under the man's chin, sharp enough that he didn't need to apply too much pressure to slide it into flesh. The body went limp.

One down. Was there another? If this were a crime of opportunity, then no, but somehow, Calvin doubted it. He pulled the body out of sight beside the garage. Time to hunt for others.

Rounding the corner of his house, Calvin ghosted to his yard and saw two targets at his back door with a pry bar. They'd wedged it against the door and frame, trying to snap the lock. When the sliding door didn't budge, they whacked the pane. A waste of time. Calvin had had it custom-made out of bulletproof glass. Again, only in the movies did people live in homes with shattering points of entry.

"Looking for me?" He drew their attention and made sure they saw the knife he tossed from hand to hand. Let them focus on the blade, which wasn't the real threat. So long as Calvin breathed, he was the most dangerous thing they'd ever meet.

"Get him," grunted one of the attackers.

How original.

Also, his last words.

Thunk. Calvin tossed the blade and buried it in his throat.

The other guy took a moment to round his mouth in surprise before snarling, "Motherfucker. You killed Jory."

"Don't worry, you won't be separated long." Running at the other guy, Calvin easily dodged the wildly swinging crowbar. Someone had sent amateurs after him.

That was their first mistake; the second one was coming after him, period.

A solidly thrown fist took the man in the gut, causing him to double over with a gasp. The garrote slipped from Calvin's wrist and, look at that, found its way around the neck of the fellow.

Fingers clawed at the rawhide. Useless. Sturdy, black, braided leather wouldn't shred. Great for strangling people and making a fashion statement. He even had a clasp for it in his pocket that contained a small amount of explosives. Never knew when he'd have to blow some shit up.

The choking fellow didn't need much encouragement to go to his knees. His eyes bulged, very white in the darkness. The wheezing noises didn't reveal any answers, but then again, Calvin had yet to ask questions.

Such as, were there any more incompetents running around the neighborhood that needed to be taken care of? "How many with you?"

The eyes said, "Fuck you." Calvin's grip on the necktie said otherwise.

The guy's face turned purple, but he raised two fingers.

"There's the first smart thing you've done today." Calvin loosened the tension. "Who sent you?"

"Dunno."

He tightened the garrote.

The fellow bucked, and his fingers clawed at skin as the leather pressed into his flesh.

"I'll loosen it when you stop dicking me around. Who sent you?" Calvin eased the tension enough for a reply.

The guy first sucked in a few wheezing breaths. "Dunno."

Calvin growled. "Is that your final answer?"

"I don't know. I swear." The guy's words emerged in a frantic rush. "Someone dropped off some money at Johnny's place and left a note with an address, saying there'd be more if we scared you."

"Scared me from what?"

"I dunno. Just that they didn't care if you got hurt in the process."

Did someone really think this puny trio would stop him? Obviously, whoever had sent these imbeciles didn't know whom they were dealing with. "When and where are you supposed to get the other half of the money for the job?"

"The note didn't say."

The ineptitude kept mounting. For a man academy-trained, it was almost painful to listen to. "Do you always obey notes from strangers? You know what, don't answer that." Because it was obvious this douchebag was just a disposable peon meant to send a message. One that said, we know who you are and where you live.

Epic.

Whoever thought to mess with him on his turf had just made it personal. Calvin decided to send a message back.

He wrenched the garrote one last time until the life left the eyes. One less scumbag roaming his town. But three bodies to dispose of. Pulling out his phone, he fired off a quick text. **Got three cords of wood by the side of the garage ready for burning.** Soon after, he keyed in a string of numbers and sent a payment.

Only those starting out with little cash to burn ever disposed of the bodies. True assassins let professional cleaners take care of their messes.

Calvin tucked the phone away before grabbing the bodies and carrying them around to the side of the building. The guy he'd knifed had bled onto his grass, meaning he'd have to hose the area down and drop some fertilizer. Not that the cops would come looking. Those who cleaned the bodies tended to burn them thoroughly, as in even dental records wouldn't apply.

Through it all, the neighborhood remained dark. No shouts of alarm. No sirens. The three bodies didn't rise and walk again, and yet Calvin couldn't shake the sense of something still wrong.

Did another incompetent thug lurk in the shadows? Calvin didn't think so. His unease didn't prickle and indicate that eyes watched from the shadows.

Was anyone else a target while the lights were out? Criminals did so love to lurk in the dark. He glanced over to Lily's house. Had someone seen him at her door? He'd been very stupid showing her attention before securing the area. If these thugs had been sent to scare him, then what better way than to mess with the woman he'd shown interest in?

I should check on her. He used that as his excuse to head over instead of making another neighborhood check. A few yards from her concrete porch, he immediately noted the front door slightly ajar. She didn't seem like the type to do that unless she meant it as an invitation.

Is this her way of telling me to come right on in?

He wanted to. The thought of her waiting for him, possibly wearing little to no clothes, made him want to rush in. He hesitated, torn between his academy training and this woman. This woman who made him a little crazy.

I should make sure there's no more danger.

What if she waited for him in bed? Naked.

What if there's more thugs out there?

What if she was being held at gunpoint by her ex-husband or one of his friends?

I really should make sure she's all right first.

Pushing at the door with his fingertips, he listened. Not a sound emerged, but that prickling sense of danger intensified.

He didn't speak, not yet. Advantage came with surprise. He took a step in, and his hand curled around the grip of his gun, pulling it forth. He held it steady, ready to act, especially when he saw a shoe. A slipper really.

A woman's slipper left alone in the front hall.

The sense of wrongness deepened.

He moved quickly, peeking into the living room shrouded in darkness. No Lily. A sudden flare of brightness drew his gaze up the hall. It extinguished a moment later, and he could smell smoke. Cigarette smoke, yet Lily wasn't a smoker.

Another flash of light, and then a steady glow that flickered. Someone had lit a candle.

Remaining flat to the hall wall, Calvin slunk down the length of it and walked into the kitchen, gun raised high enough for a headshot.

He froze.

The man with shockingly short blond hair

took a drag from his cigarette while the knife at Lily's throat dimpled her skin. "About time you came back. Someone has a message for you."

Chapter Seventeen

I don't want to die.

Lily had only herself to blame if it happened. She'd answered the door when someone lightly knocked.

I thought it was Calvin.

Wrong.

When she'd answered the door, much too quickly and eagerly, she'd stared for a moment at the stranger. Tall, thin, and with shockingly white, spiked hair.

"Can I help you?"

"Just the lady I wanted to see."

"I'm afraid you're mistaken." She went to close the door, but the stranger proved faster than her, shoving his way in, sending her stumbling back. Before she could cry out for help, she noted the glint of a knife.

The sharp tip of the blade pointed. "Be a good girl and keep your hands where I can see them."

Raising them over her head, she tried to understand who this man was and why he was here. "What do you want? I have no money."

"You think this is a robbery?" He looked down at himself then her. He shook his head. "Do I look like a man who needs money?"

"Then why are you here?"

"Because someone has been sniffing around places he shouldn't. I was sent to warn him off."

Her blood froze as the words penetrated. "You're here about Calvin?"

"Indeed, I am. I don't suppose he's the bloke who was just here smooching you?"

She nodded.

Pearly white teeth gleamed in a rapier smile. "Excellent. And if I heard correctly, he's coming back. Naughty boy. Thinking he's going to get a piece."

"Listen, I don't know what Brock told you—" Because who else but Brock would send some lowlife creep to threaten her and Calvin?

"You talk too much. Which is why I always carry this." This turned out to be a roll of duct tape. Dull gray and wide, it sealed her mouth shut, and wound around her wrists, it kept her hands immobile in front of her, which meant she couldn't move away from the knife at her throat when Calvin appeared in her kitchen.

Holding a gun!

Why does he have a gun? And why didn't he look more freaked out? He also sounded quite firm when he said, "Move away from the woman."

The punk at her back didn't ease the pressure on the blade. She feared swallowing, lest the tip dig deeper.

"No hello? That's rude, and after I was

kind enough to wait for you before I started carving up pieces of your girlfriend."

"Harm her, and you will die screaming."

"Oooh. I'm just fucking shaking. You've got an awful lot of balls. Threatening me when I'm the one in charge."

"What makes you think that? I've got the gun."

"And I've got the knife. One wrong move and…" The point pressed deep enough to pinch, and she felt warm liquid rolling down her neck. Lily couldn't help but whimper. This wasn't supposed to be happening. She'd gotten away from Brock. How could she be embroiled in something just as deadly? "Drop the gun or I kill the girl."

"You do realize I don't need it to kill you." Calvin said it, and yet the gun hung limply from his grip, dangling from a finger before he tossed it to the floor. The loud thump of it as it hit did nothing to reassure.

Unarmed, Calvin didn't stand a chance. She didn't stand a chance. *We're going to die.* Brock might have wanted to scare them, but Lily feared the worst. The guy at her back was deranged.

"To think, the boss said you were fucking dangerous." Her captor snorted. He dropped his cigarette on the floor and ground it out. She stupidly couldn't help but wonder if the landlord would notice the damage to the linoleum and bill her.

Assuming I get out of this alive.

"Who are you?" Calvin's voice emerged quite steady. He showed nerves of steel. Unlike her. Lily was pretty sure she'd wet her panties. Hard to tell given she also sweated something fierce.

"Is it time for introductions? But what if I like the mystery? Perhaps I'm not ready to meet the world."

"You're going to meet my foot up your ass if you don't stop fucking around." For the first time since the encounter began, Lily noted Calvin beginning to lose some of his cool.

"I'm the guy you've been looking for, apparently. Rumor on the street has it you've been asking questions about our operation."

Looking for? Lily didn't have to feign confusion because the words made no sense. She'd assumed the punk was here because of Brock and his jealousy issues. Since her ex didn't dare get his hands dirty, she thought he'd sent someone else.

"Are you the a-hole giving out the drugs?"

"And if I am?"

"Then I'm telling you right now, you need to close up shop and move on."

"I sense an *or else* here, Calvin. You don't mind if I call you that, do you, or do you prefer Sicarius? My boss says you work under two names, which is really strange if you ask me for a guy who supposedly sells real estate."

"No *supposed* about it. I'm one of the best international brokers around. But real estate isn't all I'm good with. Or did your boss forget to mention that? You really don't want to mess with me."

"Threats? And here I thought we'd be friends. Your girlfriends wants to be my friend, don't you sweetheart?"

Despite her wrists being taped, she could raise them enough to grab the tape across her mouth and tear it free. "Leave us alone."

The grip on her tightened. "That's not very nice. And here I thought we were getting along."

"Get out of my town." Calvin's tone dropped to a low menacing level.

"*Your* town?" The tip of the knife dug in, and Lily's eyes widened. "I think you're the one who needs to relocate, Calvin. Time to find yourself a new place to live. I'm here to tell you to stop meddling in our business."

Large chunks of the conversation eluded Lily, but one thing was clear: Calvin wasn't who he claimed to be, and she was in the middle of something bad. Really, really bad.

"Who is your boss? I want to talk to him."

"And yet my boss doesn't want to talk to you. Why do you think he sent me?"

A smile curled Calvin's lips as he cocked his head. "I think he sent you because you were considered expendable. You've already admitted you're the one handing out the drugs, which means you're the person I've been hired to find. My client will be pleased."

"Tell your client to piss off."

"You killed someone close to him."

"I've killed a few people in this town. You'll have to be more specific."

"You do realize you won't leave this house alive?"

"More threats. You do realize I'm the one with a knife at your girlfriend's throat?"

Calvin made himself comfortable, leaning his backside against her small kitchen table tucked against the wall. "I did notice and will say I find it really rude. But before I teach you why that was a bad idea, let me ask you…ever play Fruit Ninja?"

"What the fuck are you talking about?"

"How well do you slice?" Calvin suddenly threw his arm forward, the apple he'd palmed from the bowl she kept on the table flying straight at the other man's face. The knife moved from her neck in an attempt to deflect, and the apple speared itself on the tip with a sound that had her swallowing hard.

With a snarl of annoyance, the guy waved the knife away from him, looking to dislodge the fruit.

Calvin took that moment to lunge, but he didn't aim for the thug holding Lily. Instead, Calvin went after the candle and snuffed it.

Chapter Eighteen

Something happened to people when sudden darkness hit. Some found a calm serenity in it. He rather liked the dark—and the things he could do in it. For Calvin, it manifested as a cool, flowing force that rendered him hyper alert.

Others feared the darkness. The loss of their sense of sight meant panic clawed at them. The fear tended to blind them more than the murky shadows.

The a-hole who dared to threaten Lily was the kind who didn't thrive in true darkness. In a voice threaded with anxiousness, he yelled, "Don't you fucking move."

A part of Calvin wanted to ghost to the dickwad's side and whisper "Boo," in his ear. Want to bet the a-hole would scream like a girl? He dearly wanted to find out, and maybe he would after he ensured Lily evaded the knife.

"This is your last chance to let the girl go and get your ass out of here. I'm going to count to three…" Calvin said as his eyes acclimated to the gloom.

"Don't you fucking move. Orders or not, I will kill her."

"One." The word hung in the dark kitchen, and he wondered if Lily paid attention.

Would she know to act when her chance came?

"I mean it. I'll slit her throat."

Calvin began to doubt it. This mouthpiece was just a braggart without balls, even more inept than the thugs Calvin had dispatched. "Two." The word caused the a-hole to drag in a hitching breath.

"You're fucking nuts."

This from the guy holding a knife to Lily's throat? A compliment because, of the two of them, Calvin probably was a little crazier.

"Three." He didn't move. He didn't say anything at all.

This was the fun part.

A shuffle of fabric. "Where are you?" The query came and hung in the air.

It hung without an answer.

Calvin held in a grin so his teeth wouldn't gleam.

"If you hurt me, my friends will come after you."

Let them. Calvin planned to rout all the rats from his town.

He moved closer to where his senses claimed the a-hole stood. His eyes were adjusting to the gloom, and he could see shapes inside the shadows. He also saw the outline of the knife, a faint glint giving it away. A shot to the hand holding it might cause it to dig, so instead, Calvin chose to lash out with his foot, cracking it against a-hole's shin.

He dutifully screamed, and the hand

holding the knife jerked away from Lily's neck. A scuffle erupted, with Lily shoving away from dickwad. But the guy recovered faster than expected, and his loose hand shot out and grabbed her by the hair, jerking her back toward him, causing her to emit a sharp cry.

Oh, hell no.

Fuck patience. Waiting was no longer an option. Calvin lunged for the a-hole, aiming for the bulk of his shadow, but the guy managed to evade, lunging to the side.

The lights flickered on, just for a second, enough for Calvin to see Lily's wide and frightened, pain-filled eyes. To note the panicked gleam in the a-hole's, and then the lights went out again, leaving them all blind.

But Calvin had a better idea of the guy's position. He lunged and grabbed the arm of the man's knife-wielding hand. As he held it away, his knee rose and delivered a blow to dickwad's midsection. They grappled, Calvin mostly holding the fellow's knife hand so he couldn't inadvertently strike at Lily.

Calvin didn't dare get too violent, not with Lily so close by. As he tried to smash the guy's hand to drop the blade, he felt Lily flailing beside him, still caught by fingers tangled in her hair. He shouldered the other guy, trying to throw him off balance, but the fellow proved more solid than expected. It didn't help that Lily, in an attempt to aid, landed a blow—right in his sac.

Ouch.

The other guy took advantage and shoved at Calvin. He reeled back and lost his bearings for a moment.

Grunts and a few harshly sputtered exhalations accompanied soft, meaty thuds. Who was hitting whom? Did it matter?

I am supposed to be the professional here. He should try fucking acting like it.

Closing his eyes, he felt at the space around him. In many ways, his training at the academy in the Box—what he and the other boys called that dark, locked room they trained in—reminded him of young Luke's training. He let his other senses test the air.

There.

He darted forward, hands once again lunging. He caught fabric, thick cotton fibers, and fisted it.

"Get back here," he growled as he yanked. Instead of resisting the pull, the a-hole moved toward him with a cry of rage. It caused them to go off balance.

Calvin's back hit the hard floor, and his head snapped hard. *That will leave a lump.* He couldn't afford the pain dulling his senses.

Never give in to the pain. Hesitation would kill.

Instinct made him fling both his hands outward in time to catch a thick wrist. Want to bet it held a knife?

How exciting. Calvin rocked to his left, hoping to roll them, but the body over him went only so far before jamming. Damned counters were in the way.

They weren't the only things getting into his path of victory. Lily seemed determined to help—also known as hinder.

He could hear her muttering. "Get off him. What is wrong with everyone? Why can't you leave me alone?"

Did she chastise the dickwad?

Calvin managed to tuck his knees up, enough that he could heave the guy off him. Once again, Lily cried out, but more in annoyance.

"Why won't you just go away?"

No. Don't go away. Stay. He still had questions.

Calvin got to his feet just as something hit him. He grabbed at the body, trying to avoid flailing limbs. Delicate ones. "Is this how you're going to thank me?"

"Calvin?" The fighting stopped. She leaned into him, but he didn't have time for that.

There was still a man to find. He moved toward the back door, the sliding panes as dark as the rest of his house, and yet his assailant couldn't hide the whisper as it slid open, nor prevent the cooler breeze from wafting in.

He ran in the right direction—hopefully, or else he stood to face-plant in a wall or glass door. If he was really wrong, he'd hit the table and bag himself. He'd prefer to smash his face.

The fresh air of the yard hit him in the

face, and he slowed his step. Out in the open, he could see a little bit, shades of shadows created by the few stars shining in the sky, bare pinpricks that provided a touch of light. Enough that he could see the whole yard, one side with hedges, tall and thick, with chain link running through, the border to his yard. The rear boasted weathered plank things, eight-feet high and stained some strange orange-brown color. For the third side, more wooden fencing, the grain gray and the tops ragged.

Which way had the a-hole gone? *Come back. I'm not done talking to you.*

He turned in a circle, trying to figure out where he'd run.

How dare he think to attack Lily. This is because of Harry's investigation. Someone didn't like them poking. *Isn't that too fucking bad.*

Of more concern than the warning was how someone had managed to trace him and, even more astonishing, knew his secret identity? Whoever had hired the lowlife had told him his other name, his assassin name: Sicarius. But how did they find out? Calvin was always very careful about hiding his tracks, and Mason, along with Sherry, ensured the rest.

I've been compromised. The general rule of thumb when that happened was to leave. Clean out and move away to start over. Except Calvin had been here a while. Longer than anywhere else in his life.

He liked it, and kind of wanted to keep it.

Creak. The sound was pretty quiet. Nothing sharp or attention grabbing, and yet, he stiffened. Calvin whirled and saw the body straddling the top of the fence.

There you are. Calvin ran toward him, long strides that thudded in the dark night. A face briefly turned his way, the eyes wide, the obscene gesture clear. The middle finger salute disappeared from sight as the guy finished his climb over the fence.

It took too long for Calvin to reach it. He vaulted it, his hands gripping the top edge when he leaped, hoping the creaking and swaying section would hold. He hit the other side feet first and in a crouch.

Pounding steps showed a-hole racing down the side of the house, his feet hitting the pavers hard. Calvin sprinted after him, hands ready to grab.

A motor grumbled, and lights lit the road ahead. Calvin pumped harder, only a few yards behind. The car squealed to a stop, the door opening even as it still moved. Dickwad's face briefly shone in the feeble overhead light as he dove inside. The door hadn't even finished shutting when it took off with a squeal of tires.

Memorizing the license plate, Calvin didn't hold much hope. Chances were they'd stolen the vehicle.

Fucker had escaped him. How embarrassing.

He returned to Lily's house, opting to use

the front door. The lights came on as he strode down the hall to the kitchen. The sudden brightness had him blinking. But that wasn't why he frowned.

Lily stood at the sink. A knife sat on the counter alongside the tape she'd managed to remove from her wrists. One of her hands clutched the counter's edge, the other pressed to her neck. Her bloodied neck. The red stain reminded him of how close she'd come to getting permanently hurt.

Hurt because of me.

He wouldn't accept that. This couldn't be allowed to happen.

I'll kill that little bastard. Him. His boss. His brother. Anyone who thought they could hurt someone he cared about.

"Are you okay?" Him, the suave guy who'd mingled with high society, stuck asking a stupid question. Of course she wasn't okay. Someone had just threatened to slice her throat.

"I'll be fine. It's just a scratch."

"It's not fine. You're hurt. And it's my fault." Which really pissed him off. This was why he'd never mixed pleasure with business in the past. This was why he didn't have ties.

"It wasn't your fault." Her chin ducked as she shook her head. "I shouldn't have opened the door. Safety rule number one when you're a single lady. Always check who's knocking first."

"You shouldn't have to check. The neighborhood should be safe."

"Nothing is ever truly safe." Her lips turned into a wan smile.

"It should be. I want it to be. I'm working on it."

"Working on it how?" Her left brow arched. "By shaking up the local drug dealers so they come looking for you?"

"They shouldn't have been able to find me."

"You're a realtor. Your face is probably on park benches and the sides of buses. How did you think they wouldn't? You should leave the crime fighting to the pros."

"I am a pro. Assassin, remember?"

Another ghost of a smile. "I do remember, and you obviously know how to take care of yourself. But wanting to be a crime fighter and truly fighting it are two different things. You seem like a good guy, Calvin, but you're dabbling in things you shouldn't, with people who aren't afraid of violence."

"I'm not afraid of violence." As he said that, he grabbed his gun off the counter and waved it.

For a moment, fear shone in her eyes.

He didn't like it one bit. He tucked the gun into the back of his pants. "Don't be scared."

"I'm not afraid of you." Lily turned away and reached to turn on the tap. She leaned for the paper towel and grabbed a couple. She wet them and then pressed them against her bloody neck.

It only served to remind him of his failure.

It should have been grounds for them to go their separate ways. He'd brought this danger on to her. He was responsible.

Walk away.

Never.

Life was dangerous. But so was he.

"I never want you to be afraid of me."

She dabbed at her neck, wiping the drying lines of blood. "You say that, and yet, I can tell you right now, sometimes that changes. People change."

He knew whom she referenced. "Please let me kill him."

"No."

"It would solve so many problems."

She leaned against the counter and stared at him. "I never know if you're joking or not when you say things like that. I mean, it's almost as if you want me to believe you're capable of murder."

"And if I were? There are some individuals that pose such an inherent danger to others. Some people who are irredeemable. In those cases, the best course of action is elimination." But he should add that not all those he killed were bad. Sometimes, his targets simply stood in the way of something someone else wanted. Those jobs tended to give the best return.

"Killing for the good of mankind? Is that what you're saying?"

"I don't kill to be a hero. I offer problem-solving when other solutions fail."

For some reason, his words saw her face shutting down, her expression tight. He could almost see the rigid armor encasing her, and the cold radiating from her body.

"You're a freaking cop, aren't you?"

For a moment, he stared at her dumbstruck. "A cop? What the fuck?"

Her lips pursed. "It would explain a few things. Are you trying to trap me into saying…no, I won't even say it out loud in case you are recording this. Knowing him, he'd edit anything I said to make me sound worse."

"I am not a cop. And I am not trying to trap you into saying anything. Why the fuck would you even think that?" Did she not see he truly wanted to help her in the only way he knew how?

"Then why do you keep pushing me? Why keep telling me and teasing me about Brock? Do you think I enjoy having a lunatic ex-husband? I mean, you saw what happened with him. He's a loose cannon."

"All the more reason to let me take care of it."

She shook her head. "No. Much as I want him out of my life, I would never advocate murder."

"Fine. He lives, for now." Said darkly, and she noticed.

"Why do you even care? I'm nobody to you. Just a lady next door with a shit-ton of baggage."

"No one should live in fear."

"Yeah, well, sometimes life sucks." She turned away from him, and he could see the tightness in her frame.

"It doesn't have to suck," said the king of eloquence. "I could help you. Let me help you. I've been watching and—"

At that, she spun. "You're spying on me?"

"Says the woman who's always peeking through her windows."

Pink blotches appeared on her cheeks. "I'm allowed to look outside."

"You are, just like I'm allowed to look out, too. Don't forget, I'm an assassin. Observation is something we do."

"No, what you do is mess with drugs. I knew there had to be something wrong with you. That's why that guy was here waiting for you. Are you part of some rival gang?"

"I don't deal drugs. But I am trying to disband a group of people who are."

"Because you're a spy in a real estate agent disguise." She rolled her eyes. "God, would you drop the act already. It was cute at first, but now it's getting us both into trouble."

"It's not an act. Assassin is my true title, but parts of that include espionage."

She shook her head but didn't ask him to leave. He noticed she'd changed since he'd seen her from her robe into thin track pants and a sweatshirt. She wore one slipper only, and her hair haloed from her head in a half wet, half dry, tangled heap. Bedraggled and forlorn, yet he still wanted her.

A high-pitched laugh emerged from her. "Why is it I want to believe your fairy tale? You, an American James Bond, and me, the femme fatale by your side. Absolute make-believe."

"It doesn't have to be."

"If only." She shook her head. "You should have gone into acting. You're good at making me want to believe."

"And you're stubborn. I am telling the truth." Because, for once in his life, he wanted to build something with a woman. This woman. And he didn't want it to be based on lies.

"If you are, then what makes you think it appeals? What woman would sign up for life with a criminal?"

"Professional bound by a code of conduct instilled in us at the academy."

"An assassin's code?" Again, she laughed. "Oh, Calvin, you just don't give up. But here's the thing. I've lived a life rife with violence. I'm done with that. I deserve a quiet life."

"Quiet? You don't look like someone who enjoys being passive all the time." A hidden fire hid inside Lily. He'd seen it partially stoked. It wanted to roar to life.

"Maybe not all the time, but for now, I have to because of Zoe."

"It is because of her you should not settle for just getting by. It's because of her you shouldn't let your ex bully you. A daughter takes cues from her mother. She watches you. Emulates. What kind of woman would you have her grow up to be?"

"That's not fair."

"What isn't fair? That she looks to you?"

"I know she does, and I want to show her the right thing to do. But sometimes, the right thing can hurt people. It can…" Lily paused and bit her lip.

He couldn't help but move close and place his hands on her hips, drawing her near. "Sometimes, the right thing is the wrong thing. Sometimes, we have to be selfish."

Her hands flattened on his chest. They didn't push away. "You should go." The words sounded uncertain.

"Forget should. What did I just say about sometimes being selfish? What do you want?" He knew what he wanted. He let himself sway into her, and their bodies brushed. Did she feel the same electric awareness when it happened?

He sank his fingers into her hair, feeling the dampness of it, the fragrance soft and light, just like her. He cupped her head, pulling her closer.

"We shouldn't do this," she murmured, leaning up on tiptoe.

"Says who?"

"I don't want to fuck up," was her soft reply, a hot breath of words against his lips.

"How can something that feels this right

be a fuckup?"

"It's hormones."

More like fate. "This is going to happen." Inevitable from the moment they met and sparks flew.

Forget the shit show that just happened. Forget protocol like calling in the incident to his team because anything that affected one of them could hurt them all.

Instead of doing a great many things, he kissed Lily. He slid his tongue between her lips and tasted the grape of the wine she'd drunk before this had all started. Felt the soft pressure of her hands against his back as she embraced him back.

All of her melted into him. A sense of rightness made him hum. He could kiss her all night.

Hold her forever.

And he'd kill whoever interrupted. He broke the kiss and held in a snarl of annoyance, pulling the gun he'd retrieved from the waistband of his pants and aiming it toward the kitchen hallway arch just before the footsteps entered.

Mason held up his hands. "Don't shoot. I'm here for that beer you promised me."

Not exactly true. As soon as Calvin had put the call in for cleanup, Bad Boy Inc. would have gotten a notice. That was why Mason had shown up.

Lily put more space between them. "I have to go."

"Go where? This is your house."

"Elsewhere. Excuse me." A red-cheeked Lily took that moment to excuse herself and flee. He heard a door slam as she hid in her bedroom.

Calvin almost chased after her. But Mason stared at him. Stared enough that Calvin scratched his balls to show his utter nonchalance. "What do you say we go back to my place for that beer?"

He let Mason exit first and ensured the lock on Lily's front door engaged before pulling it shut. He then led the way over to his place, but Calvin waited until they were inside before he said, "My cover is blown."

"Was that the girl?"

"What girl?" Even as Calvin pretended, he knew Mason saw right through him.

"The girl who's got you thinking about kids." His friend snickered. "Holy shit. No wonder you want to go all avenging hero on the city. You found yourself a muffin."

"Muffin?"

"The one you want to take home instead of the cupcake. She's still just as sweet, with a moister interior and yummy little bits of fruit goodness to keep things interesting."

"What is your obsession with comparing stuff to food?"

"I've been taking cooking classes."

"And you haven't made me anything?" Calvin inquired, fingerprinting the tablet he kept in the kitchen and loading up any warnings. The systems showed an *All Clear* in all his zones. A few taps, and he noted the cameras in her place showed all the main rooms empty.

"Spying on her?" Mason asked, leaning over his shoulder.

"Trying to keep her safe."

"You took care of those thugs."

"I took care of some thugs. The one who hurt her got away."

Mason, in the process of grabbing a beer, paused. "Got away? As in you didn't kill him? What the fuck, man? You losing your touch?"

"No. I was distracted." Worried about Lily and forgetting his training. "How did you know I was over there anyhow?"

Mason waggled his phone. "Did you forget Harry had us chipped?"

Ah, yes, chipped much like a pet so the office could track them when they were out in the field and mount a rescue if needed—or notify next of kin.

"Yeah, well, your timing sucks."

"And the title of best cock block goes to…" Mason grinned and held up his beer.

"I hope you get crabs," Calvin said with a glare.

"Now that's just mean!" Mason huffed. "And to think I dropped everything I was doing to check on your ungrateful ass."

"Sorry. It's the blue balls talking." A state that hurt more than it should. "Since I've got you here, run a plate for me, would you?" Calvin recited the numbers and letters he'd memorized. It turned out to not be stolen. However, the rental company information on the driver turned out to be fake—the whole thing paid for in cash.

As for the bodies he'd had the cleaners dispose of? The pros submitted a report to the office along with a bill for their services. They actually had identities for the thugs Calvin had killed. Street thugs with lengthy rap sheets, mostly for assaults, thefts, and weapons charges. He saw no link to them and the drug trade in town. What Calvin also didn't understand was why the two separate attacks.

"Why send those three idiots to attack me and also send a dude to threaten Lily?"

Mason shrugged as he downed his beer. "Hedging their bets? Could be a question of the left hand and right hand not knowing what's going on."

"We must be getting close, though." Why else warn unless the criminals were getting worried?

From here on in, things would get more interesting. The battle lines were drawn. The war begun. Lily, the prize to be protected, even if she didn't believe there was an assassin next door.

But Calvin soon hoped to change all that and hold the title of lover.

Chapter Nineteen

Lily spent Sunday flinching at every single noise. It kind of matched how she'd spent her Saturday night after Calvin left.

She no longer felt safe in her home. Then again, she hadn't felt safe before the break-in.

How much longer am I going to live in fear? Lily had a way of solving that trepidation. A way of taking a stand and refusing to stay a victim.

Calvin's right. Zoe is looking up to me, and I need to present a good example.

Brock's sneer when he dropped off Zoe only reinforced that belief.

"How was your evening?"

"Fine."

"Really? What's that on your neck?" Brock pointed to the scratch.

"Why don't you tell me? I'll bet it was one of your friends that came over to deliver that warning."

"What are you talking about? I don't know nothing about no warning. Zoe and I spent a lovely evening watching *Ice Age* movies."

Despite his denial, she wasn't fooled. She knew how well he could lie. "I won't be threatened." She stood tall.

For some reason, Brock smiled. "No one

is threatening. Are you imagining stuff again? Perhaps you should think about going back to the doctor."

"I'm not crazy. I know you're behind the stuff that's been happening."

"Prove it." Those were his parting words.

And the thing was, she could.

By Monday morning, after lots of soul searching, Lily knew what she had to do. She cornered her boss and blurted, "I have information on the drug operation happening in this town."

Lisa didn't choke on her coffee, but she did set it down carefully. "Would you repeat what you said and add a bit more context?"

"I said I know about a certain underground drug ring, and it goes pretty high." A ring that might be related to what had happened on Saturday. After thinking it over, it had occurred to her that perhaps the drive-by was related to Calvin and the drugs, too.

If that silly man had indeed gone poking his nose where he shouldn't, then chances were he was in a lot of trouble, and by extension, since he owned the house next door, she was in trouble.

Fleeing wasn't an option, and not just because of her custody arrangement. The landlord wouldn't release her from the lease agreement, and she had no money to go stay elsewhere. That left only one option: get rid of the problem. And by get rid of, she didn't mean

Calvin. Nope, she wanted to take the bigger step of completely getting rid of the drugs. Break the ring, break the cycle of violence.

"Why bring this to me?" Lisa tapped her pen against the notepad on her desk. "I practice family law, not criminal. Shouldn't you go to the police with this?"

"I can't."

"Why can't—" Lisa's eyes widened. "You can't because they are involved."

She nodded. "They won't help, and I can't have Zoe getting hurt because of what I know."

"Then why come forward at all? This is the kind of information that gets people killed."

"I know." Lily ducked her head. "But I don't think I can avoid it anymore. And by looking away, aren't I part of the problem? Thing is, who do I tell? Who can I trust?"

"Maybe the FBI or…" Lisa trailed off, and she looked worried. "If this goes high, then our local branches could be compromised. You're right. This is dangerous stuff."

"Surely there's a way to break it up. A way to bring it to light, along with those responsible." Make her neighborhood safe again. *Make Zoe and me safe.*

Lisa's gaze stared off, and she took on a pensive expression. "You know what, there may be something I can do. Well, not me, but I know people who might be able to help. Give me a few days. Let me talk discreetly to some folks."

"You won't mention my name?"

"No, but if they agree, they'll probably want to meet you and hear firsthand what you know."

"Can I trust them?"

Lisa stared at her, and there was something in her friend's gaze, something flat and hard that she'd never seen before. "They know how to keep things quiet. And get the job done."

As Lily returned to her workstation, she could only hope that something panned out with the people Lisa knew.

The week passed, and Lily went about her life. Work, sleep, Zoe.

And Calvin. A man who seemed determined to run into her.

She emerged Monday morning to find him putting air in her tires because, he claimed, "The passenger side was getting low."

Tuesday, he met her as she pulled into the driveway and carried groceries inside.

On Wednesday, he put out her garbage.

Each time he said only a few words to her. It was very strange.

Thursday, when he mowed the lawn, she finally asked him, "What are you doing?"

"Mowing the lawn."

Shirtless—which should really come with a warning.

"But why? You know I can't pay you."

"No payment. I want to help out."

"Why?"

He dropped a kiss on her nose. Light and

teasing. "Take a guess."

She was guessing, and that guess wanted Lily to believe he courted her. Did men even do that anymore?

Friday came with coffee and donuts left on the top of her car. The note scribbled in pen on the cup said, *Think of me this weekend.*

That arrogant phrase distracted her all day and helped her not focus on her anxiety as six o'clock approached. Brock arrived at the top of the hour on the nose and took Zoe without uttering a single snide remark. Sunday night's drop-off was just as eerie and pleasant. No fighting. No name-calling. Just a happy Zoe home once more with a new stuffie.

The stiff peace meant nothing. That night, while her daughter slept, Lily dropped the camera sewn behind its eye into a glass of water. Brock was still up to something. The genial outward appearance didn't fool her.

After a weekend of no Calvin—and yes, she was aware how pathetic it was she kept watch—Monday after work, she came home to Calvin outside her place, a drill in hand, doing something to her door.

She didn't know whether to be happy or mad that he'd finally deigned to show his face.

Where has he been? What was he doing?

Don't you mean who was he doing? She wasn't used to the green monster rearing its head, and for a man who didn't even belong to her.

But he could. He kept hinting at it. She was

the one who kept rebuffing. Putting him off. Worried about so many things, the drugs, Brock, Zoe, but most of all, she worried he'd break her heart.

Lily no sooner opened the rear passenger door than Zoe immediately ran to Calvin, skipping up the front steps, a bright smile on her face.

"Calvin!" Zoe hollered his name, not showing any kind of restraint at all. "Whatcha doin'?"

"I'm installing a few safety features for your mom. I should have done this last week, but certain parts had to be ordered."

"I didn't ask you to do that." She frowned at him, especially as she noted her door stood partially ajar. *I locked it. I know I did.* Had he broken in?

"You didn't have to ask. You need it. A single woman like you should have some extra security."

"And you thought you should install it without asking first?"

"Yes." No apology for the misogyny.

It was hard to be angry, especially given she kind of wanted any extra help she could get. Brock's unnerving niceness had her on edge. The man was up to something, and she'd bet it wasn't giving her a permanent tic. To soothe her paranoia, she'd begun placing booby traps by doors and windows. Anyone trying to get in would make noise.

If they did manage to get inside, then that was where the two-by-four she'd borrowed—ripping it out of the crawlspace and removing the nails—came into play. She kept it stashed by her bed at night, waking at every sound.

It wasn't a way to live. Trying to pretend she didn't want Calvin also wasn't working.

"So what exactly do we have going on here?" she asked as Zoe inched past him into the house, probably headed for the bathroom. Her daughter had a gerbil-sized bladder.

"Installing a peek hole"—he pointed at the metal sleeve partially poking outside the door—"so you don't just answer to anyone." He slammed it in. The solid front door now boasted a silvery eye. "I also put on a tether chain."

"That won't stop someone from coming in," she noted. She'd seen enough police shows to know a solid kick would snap it.

"No, but it does give you more warning and time."

"You think someone is going to come after me again."

"Whether we intended it or not, you're now associated with me. Assassins have enemies."

"So do divorced women."

"Your ex doesn't scare me." Crouching, Calvin tucked his tools back in a portable box. He shut and snapped the lid before standing.

"You say that now."

"It won't change. I'm not afraid."

"I am." She wanted to be that girl who always acted strong and sure. But, in truth, Lily was tired and scared. She didn't want to fight alone anymore.

"Don't be frightened. You've got someone in your corner now."

But was he? How could she know if she could trust him?

Somehow, she found herself close to him. Or had he moved?

Did it matter?

His big hand cupped her cheek. He drew her close. So close she stood on tiptoe. Lifted her lips. Felt his breath against her flesh. Their mouths. It never failed to electrify her senses.

Her eyes closed, and she melted into him. Let his mouth rub over hers, claiming it with heated sensuality. His other hand flattened over her lower back, pulling her tighter to him. Helping her stay on tiptoe, within reach, and—

"Mommy, why are you kissing Calvin?"

The innocent query tore them apart, her much more quickly than him. Heat filled her cheeks, and her mind stammered for a reply.

He answered first. "I think your mommy is very nice."

"Me too. She makes me pancakes."

"It's fascinating that you say that." He dropped to his haunches, bringing himself to Zoe's level. "Because I would totally love it if she made breakfast for me."

Lily could have died, mostly because she

grasped his hint. He wanted to spend the night.

God help her, she wanted the same thing.

"Mommy also makes good supper. Tonight we're having orange pasta and bacon. With apple juice." Perhaps not the most nutritious thing, but Zoe was picky. And hey, it hit the food groups—pasta for grain, apple juice for fruit, bacon for protein, and powdered orange cheese mixed with milk and margarine for dairy. Dinner of champions—and single moms.

"Sounds delicious. I can't wait to taste it."

Taste it? His words penetrated, and Lily waved her hands. "No. You can't eat that."

"Why not?"

"Because it's…"

"It's mac 'n' cheese with a side of bacon. Sounds perfect to me. Although, I'd prefer mine with a beer. I'll bring a six-pack over in about twenty minutes. Is that enough time for you to change from work?"

"I—" Lily couldn't think of a reply. The logical one—no—just wouldn't pass her lips.

"Yay, Cal is coming to dinner. You can use my Olaf plate," her daughter replied, and it was then Lily grasped Zoe had given him a nickname. When had the pair become friends?

Good God, we're not really strangers anymore. Another reason to keep him at arm's length evaporated.

Lily panicked. *I don't know if I'm ready.* As Zoe skipped off, she hissed, "You can't be serious about coming over."

"I am totally serious. It's about time you and I went on another date, Lily."

"I can't go on a date. I have to watch Zoe."

"Exactly, so I am coming to you for our date. We'll do supper at my place tomorrow. How does Zoe feel about tacos?"

"We are not dating."

"We are."

"We can't be—"

"Before you say anything, keep in mind that I am confident Zoe will be fine with it."

"Leave Zoe out of this."

"I can't. You're obviously a package deal."

He'd noticed—and didn't run.

"Why are you doing this?"

"Doing what?"

"Insisting on getting involved with me. It's been nothing but disaster each time."

"Disaster seems a tad harsh. I would have said more like invigorating, and exciting."

"Crazy."

"Perhaps, but admit it, you liked it."

She liked him, and that was a problem. At least until she got her life sorted out. "You need to go." She shoved him toward the door.

"Only because I'm going to clean up and put my tools away. Wear something comfortable. Braless is fine by me."

Shove. "You are unbelievable."

He stepped over the doorsill but turned to say, "Twenty minutes, Lily."

"I won't answer."

She meant it. She shut the door as soon as he left and locked it. Chained it, too. She then put a pot of water on to boil as she went to change.

Changed because she wanted to. And, yes, she tossed the bra to the side, but not because he'd asked.

She started the bacon while Zoe watched some cartoons. The entire time, she couldn't help but watch the clock. Tick. Tock.

The minute hand crept. Each minute closer and closer to his deadline.

At nineteen minutes… *Knock. Knock. Knock.*

Chapter Twenty

A part of him expected her to not answer the door. The stubbornness in her that wanted to keep him at arm's length wouldn't let her. But he wasn't about to let her ignore him. He'd brought a few tools just in case.

Quicker than he would have expected, the door opened, and she uttered a resigned sigh. "You again."

"Your obvious delight at my presence warms me."

"You're not going to give up, are you?"

He shook his head. "Nope. My teacher at the academy said I was tenacious." He held up a dark-glassed, corked bottle. "I come bearing a gift. I opted for a red wine since it is, after all, pasta, and…check it out." He waggled a package in his other hand. "I had dessert stashed in my freezer." Dessert being some chocolate snack cakes filled with icing. His weakness because every man had a vice. Calvin now had two, and the second one stood in front of him with pursed lips and crossed arms.

It made a man want to—

"Cal! You're here." Zoe came out of the living room and beamed at him. "You can sit beside me."

"I would be delighted."

The dinner went better than expected, although he didn't say much. Calvin mostly found himself absorbing it all. After weeks of observing and skirting around the edges of their lives, he was now part of the dinnertime ritual.

He felt as if he moved about in a strange country as Zoe showed him how to set the table. From explaining how the little fork with the pink rubber grip was hers—but he could borrow it— to showing him where Mommy stashed the plates in a low cabinet so she could help out. "I'm not tall enough yet for the cabinets up there."

The little girl batted her lashes, and Calvin found himself ready to offer his services to grab things on high places anytime she needed.

Lily brushed past him and whispered, "You are so screwed now."

Screwed? How about blessed? This was how it should be. A man, a woman, and a child sitting down for dinner. Smiling and talking and laughing.

Family.

This was worth fighting for because the payoff could be bigger than anything he'd ever seen. What happened with Lily could make or break his future.

And a lot of that hinged on one little girl's acceptance. Two weeks ago, if asked, he would have said he didn't understand why people had kids. He'd have called them annoying, needy mini-mes, and yet, the more Zoe talked, her very words an exuberant exploration of the world around her, he found himself enthralled.

Especially since she thought he was the cat's ass.

He made sure to rub it in when he did dishes with Lily—yeah, him doing dishes. Mason would have memed it for sure with something emasculating.

"I think your daughter likes me."

"She also likes the weather man on channel five."

"What about the mother?"

"I've never met his mother."

He flicked suds at her. "Don't make me torture it out of you."

"Is that another of your skills?"

"Actually, that's more my buddy's realm. He knows how to make anyone sing." They didn't call him Torment for nothing. If he closeted himself with you in a room, chances were you'd be begging to die before he was done.

"So you don't work alone, Mr. Assassin? Wait, what did that lowlife call you, Sicaro?"

"Sicarius. It means *assassin* in Latin."

"Fancy word. And who else is on your team? Wizard? Archer? Ooh, how about the Warrior?"

"No Wizard, but we do have an archer, Sagittariis." Declan's name and specialty. He was handy with a bow and could hunt anyone on the ground.

"And what about that guy who showed up

at my place?"

"Latet. He finds things that are hidden."

A laugh escaped her. "Do you get together on weekends and plan how you're going to save the city from crime? Maybe roll some dice and do it D&D style while munching on chips and drinking beer?"

"Actually, we usually meet at the office to decide what jobs we'll take."

"Don't you mean what properties you're going to buy or sell?"

"We do some of that, too, mostly for tax purposes, but the real money is in specialty contracts."

She paused washing to look at him. "You know you don't have to keep faking being someone else. I like you just fine as a business guy."

"You like me." He smiled.

"A little."

"She likes me!" He crowed it louder, enough that Zoe wandered in and asked, "Who likes you?"

"Your mommy does."

At that, Lily splashed him, and he laughed. He laughed a lot with Lily and her daughter. Smiled more than he should, too. He felt so at ease around her.

She, on the other hand, acted like a nervous colt once Zoe was put to bed. Calvin was treated to a hug and a sloppy kiss on his cheek. It made him grin stupidly until Lily emerged several minutes later. She seemed surprised to see him in her living room.

"You're not gone."

"Nope." Although the sound of her voice as she read a story to Zoe had almost put him to sleep.

Lily clasped and unclasped her fingers. Uncertainty plagued her again.

He didn't harbor any doubts. He knew what he wanted. Who he wanted.

He patted the spot beside him on the couch. "Come here."

"I should—"

"Come here before I come get you."

"You can't order me around," Lily said, and yet she moved closer, close enough to perch on the very far edge of the sofa.

"Why do you keep fighting it?"

"Fighting what?"

"You and I are attracted to each other." Before she could open her mouth to deny it, he shook his head. "Don't make me prove you wrong. Then again…" He smiled, a slow, stretched, masculine grin. "Go ahead. I think we'd both enjoy me showing you what we both want."

"Wanting isn't enough. I'm not in the right place to get involved with someone."

"Who said we had to do anything serious? We can just have sex." He loved how she couldn't hide the heat. Color rushed to her cheeks.

"We can't just have sex." She said it so primly.

It made him want to kiss her even more than before. "Why not? This isn't the Dark Ages. You're a woman. I'm a man. We both have needs."

"You don't understand. Things are complicated right now."

"Don't care." He didn't. He'd make it work.

Before she could make another silly protest, he moved, sliding across the couch, wrapping an arm around her and pulling her onto his lap.

"We shouldn't." Words softly spoken.

"Shouldn't makes it more fun," was his reply before he slanted his mouth over hers.

She didn't shove him away.

Tugging at her lower lip, he sucked it and could have groaned as her breath hitched. He shifted her on his lap so that she sat squarely across his thighs. Confined in his jeans, his cock pushed and strained, urging him to turn her even more so that she straddled him.

Take it slow. He didn't want to frighten her. Not when he finally had her softly sighing into his mouth. Her hands crept up until they rested on his shoulders, clutching at him, her mouth clinging.

He didn't worry about getting interrupted. Not this time. Since the attack on his neighborhood, he'd taken steps. With the help of his partners, he'd expanded his watching network.

Cameras monitored the entrance to the neighborhood. Alarms would notify him if scanned vehicle plates came up as stolen. Even rentals would cause a ping. And while Lily didn't know it, her house now had a few weapons stashed—just in case.

But, right now, he wasn't thinking about the gun he'd slipped in between the mattresses of her bed or the garrote he'd hung off the curtain pole, hiding it behind the panel. At this moment, all he was thinking of was how good and right she felt in his arms. How perfect she tasted. And how much he needed her.

His hands shoved at her shirt, pushing it up over her silky skin so that his hands might touch without impediment, all the while his lips forged a scorching path down the smooth column of her neck.

"We shouldn't be doing this." The words emerged in between pants. Excitement mixed with nervousness.

"We should have been doing this a long time ago." From the first moment they'd met, his attraction to her had only grown. Now, it raged—a wild and lusty beast that needed satisfaction.

"But—"

He kissed her.

She still mumbled, "Zoe."

That one word reminded him that they weren't exactly alone. The child could wander from her room and find them. They needed to move to a bedroom with a door. A door with no lock, but at least he could close it, and he pulled back the covers on the bed before laying Lily on the clean white sheets.

She stared up at him, her eyelids heavy with passion, her lips plump from the kisses.

He stripped off his shirt and couldn't help but flex at the appreciation in her gaze. He unbuttoned the top of his jeans but left them on. He didn't want to move too fast. Even though she no longer protested, theirs was a fragile beginning that he didn't want to end.

He covered her body with his and found her mouth for another kiss. Her lips parted at his tongue's insistence, and there was nothing tenuous about the way she sucked on it.

Groan. How sweet she tasted. He needed more. His hands once again tugged at the fabric of her shirt. He leaned off her enough to move it up and past her head, leaving her bared to his gaze.

Perfection. A handful of breasts, yet full enough he could cup and squeeze, the tips topped with dark nipples. Fat nipples that begged for him to suck.

How could he refuse the invitation?

At the first touch of his mouth on her berries, she arched and cried out, a soft cry and then a muffled moan as she fought to restrain her fervor.

The nipple between his lips tightened into a hard nub. He sucked at it, pulling on that taut peak. She made such sweet noises. He let the nipple pop long enough to once again plant a kiss on her lips, capturing her soft sighs. But the lure of her body drew him, so he abandoned her mouth to trail soft kisses along her cheek. He traveled down her neck, pausing over the fluttering pulse, a rapid stutter that matched his racing heart. He couldn't help but nip at her skin, a primal urge filling him, one that wanted him to leave a mark. He sucked at the skin before moving down again.

The valley between her breasts beckoned, and he nuzzled his face in that soft space. Her fingers clasped his hair, tugging. He kissed the skin before moving enough to capture the nipple he'd yet to meet, pulling it into his mouth.

The bud tightened as he suckled, and her fingers left his hair to dig into his shoulders. Her body arched against him, pushing more of her breast against his face. Her passion evoked a groan of satisfaction. He was bringing her this pleasure. She responded so sweetly to his touch.

And she made the most delicious noise when he bit down on a nub.

Need engorged him. His cock strained behind the confines of his jeans, and much as he wanted to keep playing with her breasts, he needed more.

I need to sink into her. Claim her as a man claims a woman.

He leaned back as he straddled her thighs, noting how beautiful she looked with passion heating her features.

Her breasts taunted him, the nipples begging for attention. But he was after another treasure.

His fingers tickled down her torso, stroking her skin, watching her shiver as they reached the waistband of her pants. Yoga pants with an elastic top and lots of give. He tugged, pulled them down from her waist over a belly that rounded slightly. She watched as he kept pulling, teasing them over her hips, dragging the cotton panties she wore with them.

When he'd skimmed them off, he tossed them to the side and was treated to a view of her, naked and flushed.

"You are so fucking beautiful."

She licked her lips. "If you say so."

"I do say so. Isn't this proof?" He indicated the bulge and couldn't help but swell as her gaze went to it and stayed.

The damned jeans hurt, so he tugged at his zipper, his briefs not made to contain his erection. It sprang forth, and her eyes widened.

He almost came right then and there. Almost spread her legs to thrust into her.

He held back.

Barely.

Instead, he knelt between her thighs and leaned forward so he could cup her mound. The heat of it scorched, and the proof of her arousal wetted.

Dipping down, he closed his eyes and

inhaled the sweetness of her scent. There was something powerful about knowing how he affected her. A good thing, given how much she affected him. Kneeling between her legs, he maneuvered himself so that they hung over his shoulders and brought his face level with her sex. He nuzzled the moist flesh, and she trembled.

Her hands grasped at his hair as soon as he gave her that first lick.

Mmmm. Honey.

Another lick, then another. He couldn't get enough of her, parting her nether lips with his tongue, probing her for more. The fingers tangled in his hair grasped tighter, pulling him close that he might keep feasting on her flesh. The taste of her made him ache. The need to sink into her and feel her sex clamping around his cock almost made him stop.

But that would mean he wouldn't feel her come on his tongue.

And I want her to come for me.

He licked at her clit, stroking it until she quivered, before latching on to it with his lips.

"Cal!" She said his name on a high-pitched cry, and it spurred him into sucking at her button, teasing it and stimulating her. Her hips rocked and trembled, almost throwing him off. He held fast and kept working her sweet spot with his tongue, circling the clit before sucking it.

Her body tensed, and he knew she was close. So close to coming for him. He wiggled enough to get a hand up close and slid a finger into her moist sex. He groaned at the tightness, the sound of it vibrating against her clit. In response, her sex squeezed his finger, clutched to the point that his cock felt jealousy.

A second finger inserted into her silky sex had her bucking and then thrashing. He finger fucked her, slick digits slipping in and out as he lapped at her clit. Faster and faster until she arched off the bed, body taut and bowed.

She came, the bliss of her climax rolling through her body, causing her channel to clamp down on his fingers.

It was glorious.

But he didn't stop. Even as she still shook from her orgasm, he kept fingering her, thrusting into her and licking, building her back up, loving how she mewled and thrashed. He shoved down his pants to give himself more room.

He had to pause, though, to rip open the condom package. To his shock, and pleasure, her hands helped ease the latex over his shaft, her fingers rolling it and then gripping him.

She held him and stroked, tugging his covered cock toward her.

The tip of him pressed at the opening of her sex, and the thick head rubbed against her clit before sliding in.

He pushed in slowly, holding himself over her on arms that threatened to tremble so great did he have to control himself. He wanted to just plunge to the hilt. Drive his cock deep.

But he went slowly.

Inch by inch. Feeling her squeeze around him.

Oh, dear fucking hell, she squeezed him tight.

She reached for him and drew him down for a kiss. A sweet mesh of lips as he buried himself deep inside her.

He began to move, in and out, short thrusts at first, then longer ones, pulling almost completely out before slamming back in. Each slap of flesh against flesh drawing a soft cry from her and eliciting a squeeze of her channel.

Faster. Thrust. Pump. Retreat. Thrust again.

Their breaths grew ragged and mixed together. Her legs wrapped around his hips, but not so firmly he couldn't move. Under his cock, his balls drew tight, and he had to hold on. He wanted to draw out this intense moment of pleasure.

Fingers dug into his back as she hugged him close, the painful prick of her nails making him rear his head and utter a low, guttural groan. Once more their lips clashed together for a hungry kiss. Her body rocked in time to his thrusts. Her breathing grew short, her body tensed, and she came, came again in squeezing waves that milked his cock.

He could contain himself no longer. With one final thrust, a hard one that took him in to the hilt, he came and collapsed atop her.

They lay like that for several moments,

gathering their breaths, basking in the afterglow.

When she finally stirred under him, he was prepared to counter any argument or regret she had.

To his surprise, she asked, "Please tell me you brought more than one condom."

He had. They put them to good use.

Chapter Twenty-one

I have a lover.

There was no going back once they slept together, and Lily didn't want to. In Calvin, she'd found something she never expected—happiness. Not just the kind that came from good sex, but the kind arising from a man who wanted to be her friend, her helper, someone who knew how to be there and yet give her some space.

A man who made her body sing.

Who knew how to make her smile.

And her child laugh.

It was a glorious week for the newly forming couple, one spent back and forth between their homes. It turned out that Calvin didn't do too badly in the kitchen, and he was excellent with Zoe.

Lily almost forgot the reasons why she had wanted to abstain. Reality slapped her when Friday arrived.

It started at work.

"I arranged a meeting for you," Lisa said after she'd called Lily into her office.

"A meeting?" For a moment, Lily's mind went blank, and then she remembered. "You found someone who can work with my information."

"My friends are very interested in what you have to say. And before you ask"—Lisa held up a hand—"they are one hundred percent discreet. Whatever you tell them will never come back to bite you. Here's the address. Don't be surprised by the location. They might look mundane on the outside, but they're actually something more. Be there on Saturday at eleven o'clock. They're expecting you. And whatever you do, don't tell anyone. I mean it. These guys don't mess around."

"Will I be in danger by seeing them?"

"Only if you screw them over."

Not exactly the most promising reply, but Lily had run out of feasible options.

She slipped the scrap of paper Lisa had handed her, the one with an address that could change everything, into a pocket. It burned there that entire day. Lily felt it, a stinging reminder that she was about to do the unthinkable.

Snitches get stitches. How many times had she heard that?

Maybe I shouldn't tell anyone.

Brock had been behaving. No other incidents had occurred. Perhaps things truly were going to get better.

That stupid bubble of denial popped the moment Brock screeched to a stop in front of her house.

A storm cloud rode his features, he stomped up the steps, and she tried to hide her fear. She couldn't let it show. Calvin probably watched. She'd managed to convince him to stay away while she did the hand-off with Brock. While he might claim he could handle her ex, Lily wasn't about to chance it. No use setting either man off.

"Where's Zoe?" Brock snapped.

"She forgot something in her room. What's wrong?" she asked.

At the dark look he turned on her, her blood ran cold.

Oh, God. He knows about Calvin and me.

"Wrong? Other than the fact my wife won't see reason? Everything is going to shit."

"Problems at work?" Good.

"None of your fucking business, and nothing I can't handle. So keep your nose out of it if you know what's good for you."

She knew what was good for her, and Zoe and silence weren't part of it. Not anymore. "If this is a bad time, I can keep Zoe."

His gaze narrowed, and his lips took on a nasty twist. "You'd like that, wouldn't you? But you can forget it. As a matter of fact, I think it's time I paid the family courts another visit. Arrange for full custody."

"You can't do that. On what grounds?"

"I'm sure I can find something."

Panic fluttered. "You can't do that."

"Daddy!" Zoe emerged with a bright smile, and Lily bit back any other words she might have thrown. "Look what I got." She held up a picture she'd drawn in school. A lovely piece of art made of colors and squiggles signed with a giant, ragged Z.

"That's beautiful, ladybug. What is it?"

"Me and you and mommy and Cal."

Walking hand in hand with his daughter to the car, Lily saw the stutter in Brock's step.

"Who's Cal?"

"The man with the pretty car. He let me ride in it."

Lily bit her lip lest she wince at Zoe's reply.

As for Brock, he shot her a dark look over his shoulder. A shiver went through her, and she hugged herself. She was still hugging herself as Brock drove out of sight. Calvin strode across the strip separating their properties. He wore slacks and a lavender shirt, the color of it emphasizing his dark hair.

Turning away from the road, she managed a wan smile. "TGIF."

"You don't look too thankful. Did he do something?" Calvin glared at the empty street. "You should have let me stay."

"I'm fine. How was work? How come you haven't changed yet?"

"I changed—into a different suit." At her arched brow, he grinned—and just about melted the panties off her. "You need to gussy yourself up, as well. We are going out."

"Why not stay in? Netflix added a few new movies this week." And the couch wasn't far from her bed.

"Because staying in is for during the week when we've got Zoe to watch. It's the weekend." He tossed her a smile. "Time to let your wild side out."

"I don't have a wild side." She immediately wanted to deny it after she'd said it. There was more to Lily than just a mom and a worker. A woman, one with sensuality, who wasn't yet dead or old or boring, lurked inside. That woman said, "Give me twenty minutes." It wouldn't take any longer. She'd had a quick shower after work to refresh herself. Her legs were freshly shaven. All of her was since she'd started sleeping with Calvin.

It didn't take long to throw on a dress, dare to pull the tags off the new underwear she'd bought during her lunch hour that day, and give herself a light coat of makeup—eyeliner, mascara, a hint of blush, and lip gloss.

When she emerged from the bedroom, she found Calvin sitting on the couch. He seemed so serious, but his lips pulled into a smile at the sight of her. He let out a low whistle. "Maybe we should stay in."

"Great idea." She slipped off her shoes.

"Put those back on." He stood with a shake of his head. "You and I are going out. Together."

"In public?" Her nose wrinkled.

"Very much in public. I won't be your dirty secret."

"Speaking of secret, does this mean I get

to meet your buddy soon? The one who's been popping in and out of your place." At very odd hours, too. She feared she knew why—they were still trying to hunt down those drug dealers. Which meant Calvin was in danger.

It made her meeting tomorrow all the more important.

"You want to meet Mason? I wouldn't bother. He's a dork, more into machines and codes than real people."

"That's not very nice. And you shouldn't be mean to him because he's geeky or socially awkward."

"Mean? You should have seen the pranks he used to play on me at the academy. I'm more worried he'll try and talk your panties off. Mason is too smart for his own good. Girls love it. So you need to stay away from him."

She blinked. Then smiled. "You're jealous."

"Insanely so, and if it were anyone else, I'd kill him."

"Because of your mad assassin skills." She chuckled and rolled her eyes. She'd gotten used to his absurd claim. It was just part of his charm. "Where are we going tonight?"

"Charity function."

She looked down at her dress. "Am I dressed up enough? Too much?"

"You are perfect."

With that kind of compliment, they almost didn't make it out the door. As it was, she had to reapply lip gloss to swollen lips. She took a moment to study herself in the mirror—her glittering eyes, flushed cheeks—and couldn't help but realize she looked happy. So happy, and all because of one man.

"I'm ready," she sang, exiting the bathroom.

They took his car, which meant climate-controlled comfort, no fear of sticky spots, and his hand on her leg in between shifting.

Was it any wonder she was addled? So befuddled, she didn't realize where he was taking them. Even when he pulled in front of the swanky hotel, she still had no idea what was going on. But she got a chilling clue when she spotted all the uniforms.

"You're taking me to the mayor's charity ball?" She sat frozen in the car.

"It's for a good cause. It's to benefit the widows and families of those who lost someone working for law enforcement."

She opened her mouth, ready to tell him to take her home. She didn't want to be here. When had the police ever helped her?

But hadn't she vowed to stop hiding from life?

"I didn't realize you were a philanthropist," she noted as they stepped toward the front doors, the glass showing throngs of people dressed to the nines.

"I'm not. But my boss wanted me to check this out."

Of course his boss did. Rich people would be attending this event, and rich people bought foreign property. Calvin was technically working and had chosen to bring her along to make it more fun.

She tried to make light of her fear. "What's our secret mission tonight?"

"Rumor has it there are some people here involved in the drug scheme plaguing our town. I'm here to rattle a few cages and see what pops loose."

"Isn't that dangerous?"

"Actually, by presenting myself to them publicly, that creates a trail. They won't dare to move against me openly."

"They'll just shoot you when no one's looking," she muttered.

"Very astute. Shall we?" He linked her arm through the crook of his and led her in.

It wasn't as awful as expected. People barely spared them a glance, and despite his joking, all Calvin did was circulate around the massive ballroom. The wine he'd snared from a passing tray was weak and tart, but Lily clung to the glass lest anyone see her hands tremble.

When the live band struck up a song, Calvin didn't ask, he simply whirled her out onto the floor.

"You're going to blow our cover if you keep looking so serious," he said, pulling her close as they swayed.

"I'm sorry. I guess I'm more tired than I

thought. Do you mind if we leave early?"

"Leave?" He dipped her and held her a moment longer than necessary. "But we've yet to accomplish our mission." He lifted her upright and spun her away before reeling her close again.

"You can't seriously be thinking of accusing anyone here." Because he was right. She knew for a fact that some of those in attendance knew about and abetted the dirty dealings going on.

"Accuse? No. Hint perhaps, loudly?" He spun her before dragging her close. "Yes."

"You need to stop digging into this drug thing before you get hurt."

"That stopped being an option the moment they threatened you." He ceased dancing for a moment and stared at her. "I won't let anyone hurt you or Zoe."

Staring into his serious gaze, she believed him. But Calvin wasn't aware of everything. He didn't know that—

"What the fuck are you doing here?" Harshly said, and by a familiar voice.

She whirled to see Brock, in full police regalia—her deepest hidden secret—staring at her coldly. The evidence of her lie, a lie of omission, stood squarely in front of her and Calvin.

She wanted to sink through the floor. Calvin would never forgive her for this.

I wanted to tell him. She'd just never found the words.

"*She*"—Calvin reeled her close to his side,

anchoring his arm around her waist—"is dancing with me. The better question is, where is Zoe?"

"None of your fucking business."

"Actually," Lily said, finding some measure of courage in the fact that Calvin didn't immediately stomp off despite her lie. "It is my business since she's supposed to be in your care."

"She's at my mother's, and that still doesn't explain why you're here with him." Brock stabbed a finger.

"She's here because I asked her to." Calvin smiled, a pleasant smile, but looking up at his countenance, she could see the steel in his eyes. "And if you keep pointing that finger, I'm going to break it and make you cry in front of all your friends."

The threat caused Brock's lips to tighten. "See this uniform, asshole? I'm the one with the power here, not you."

"You going to hit me in front of all these nice people?" Calvin leaned closer. "Go right ahead. I dare you."

"You have no idea what you're dealing with."

Casting a glance around, Calvin kept smiling. "I think I do. So stop being a loudmouth pussy." He focused his mocking smile on Brock. "Do something. Right now. Let them all see what a douchebag you are."

"You'll regret this." Brock didn't specify whom as he spun on his heel and stalked off.

This is bad. So very bad. And she didn't

entirely mean Brock's discovery that she dated Calvin.

"I can explain," Lily said to Calvin the moment Brock left. She clutched at Calvin's jacket.

"Explain what? That you forgot to tell me your ex is a cop? I already knew."

"What?" Her turn to blink at him. "But I never told you." She'd done her best not to tell him. How to explain that her psychotic ex was a cop and that was why she couldn't get help?

"It wasn't hard to figure out."

"You knew, and yet you still brought me here?" She poked at his hard chest. "You did it on purpose."

"So what if I did? You obviously felt it would affect what's happening between us. It doesn't, by the way. And while we're on the topic of the truth, I won't keep what we have between us a secret."

"Have? You mean had. I'm going home." When Calvin reached for her, she danced out of reach.

"Don't be mad. Now we have no more secrets."

"No, we don't. Bravo for you. You just ensured that my life would become a living hell." Because Brock would make her pay for this.

"I'll drive you." Again, he made to grab her hand, but she snatched it out of reach.

"No, thank you. I'm leaving." She shot him a look, one awash with anger—and betrayal.

"Alone."

She turned and strutted out the front door, her eyes brimming with unshed tears as she went past all the uniforms and fancy dresses. In truth, not many in the mayor's circle would remember a wife. It wasn't as if she and Brock had gone out often, especially after Zoe's birth. Lily preferred to watch her daughter herself.

For some reason, the fact that Calvin knew her dirty secret and had done this on purpose to force her to admit whom Brock was hurt. It pained her mostly because she should have told him. Should have been honest.

Fear kept her from saying anything. What sane man wanted to get involved with a woman with a cop as her ex? A cop who wasn't afraid to abuse his power.

Except Calvin didn't care. He'd known for a while, or so he claimed. It should have been a relief. Instead, dread gripped her because Brock wouldn't let her have a relationship with another man. The tiny bubble of happy she'd enjoyed popped, just as she'd expected.

She wiped at her eyes as she stood on the curb and held up a hand to flag a cab. A heavy hand fell on her shoulder, and she turned to tell Calvin to go away, only it wasn't Calvin. It was the guy, the one she'd seen at her house.

He smiled and said, "We meet again. Can I offer you a ride?"

Chapter Twenty-two

Calvin watched Lily leave, hypnotized by the angry swish of her hips, and wondered if he should chase after.

He'd seen how the revelation had crushed her, and yet, wasn't he the aggrieved one? She'd never told him that Brock worked in law enforcement. He'd had to find out in the file Mason had compiled for him when Calvin decided he wanted to learn everything he could about Lily. Not a very thick file. High school cheerleader, a solid B and C student. Orphaned while at school. She'd married Brock, a man who'd gotten his badge a year before, soon after college. And then she'd almost disappeared. No social media profiles. Nothing. Not even a speeding ticket. It was as if she didn't exist, a woman shoved into the shadow of her husband. A spouse with anger issues and connections she couldn't fight.

I can fight.

What she obviously didn't yet grasp was that Calvin didn't give a fuck if Brock was a cop. It didn't bother him one bit. A douche nozzle in a uniform with a badge and a gun remained a douche nozzle. No surprise that kind of guy surrounded himself with others of his ilk. It stood to reason, a guy capable of violence against a woman could do just about anything, maybe even illegal things.

Which is why I'm here. Calvin hadn't been kidding when he'd told Lily he came to the ball in order to light a fire under some asses. While he and the boys were making progress clearing the streets of the thugs selling drugs, they'd yet to find out who supplied them. Most seemed to receive their stash via drop, only being notified by text moments before a pickup. The money exchange was done the same way. Except, the payment drops Calvin and the others monitored hadn't borne fruit. Someone must have tipped them off because no one came to collect—and, ironically, those dirty funds were then given to outreach programs.

There were allusions to people in law enforcement being involved. Cops, some lawyers, even a judge, but Harry needed names, not supposition. Most of all, they wanted to know who held the kingpin role at the top of the pyramid. Take that person out, and the whole thing would collapse.

Is that person here tonight?

That possibility was why he let Lily leave, trusting that the protective measures he'd put in place would keep her safe while he completed his mission. Besides, her biggest threat had stayed behind and was here with Calvin.

Calvin mingled, recognizing some of the faces from dossiers, all the while keeping an eye on Brock, who circulated the ballroom on the opposite side. He noted his nemesis—and, no, it wasn't jealousy that made Brock his enemy, the guy was just an all-around dick—seemed to have a few intense conversations with more than a few guys dressed in blue. Did he plan something? Judging by the occasional dark glare Brock shot his way, Calvin hoped so.

According to Mason, douche nozzle had several complaints lodged against him by perps—claims of abuse and more. Rumor had it he also beat his wife, yet nothing appeared on file. Had Lily not had him charged?

Brock's position with the local precinct and ties to other cop shops would certainly explain her trepidation in getting involved with another man. But she couldn't fear her ex forever. Calvin had hoped that by bringing her here to this ball—to confront her past—it would not only get her to admit what Brock was but also make her realize the man couldn't hurt her anymore.

I won't allow it. I'll kill him first. For free. He wondered if his accountant could claim it as a loss of revenue. Snicker.

The note, written on a cocktail napkin in blue ink, arrived slyly, slipped to him by a waiter with a fresh glass of wine. All it said was: *second-floor gallery.*

Someone wanted to meet.

Fantastic.

Calvin wasted no time and headed for the stairs, taking them two at a time until he reached the second floor. Up here, the music could be heard but with an echo as the wide hall ringing the ballroom only had alcoves popping out into balconies overlooking those below.

The area was filled with artwork. Paintings hung at various heights, goose-necked lanterns shining a weak light on them with little cards placed under the canvases displaying titles, artists' names, and prices. Some of them were quite good, and all were local. Calvin tucked his hands behind his back and adopted a casual pose as he browsed.

At the halfway point, farthest from the stairs and at the darkest part of the hallway—drapes pulled over the balcony openings and the lights on the paintings extinguished—Brock pushed away from the wall.

"There's the man fucking my wife."

"If it isn't the a-hole who can't let go." Calvin baited him—and enjoyed it.

"You think you're such hot shit, don't you? Wearing a fancy suit." Brock reached out and flicked Calvin's lapel. "Driving a nice car."

"You forgot to mention the fact that I own my house and have a healthy 401k to retire on."

"How's your health insurance?" snapped Brock.

"Probably better than your life insurance policy. Did we really come here to discuss how much better off I am than you? I'd say it's pretty obvious, given I'm the one sleeping with Lily."

"Motherfucker!"

Calvin caught the punch Brock threw. He held the fist and squeezed. "Too slow." He twisted and sent Brock to his knees. "You just don't get it, do you? I told you before to leave her alone, but, apparently, you're hard of hearing." Calvin leaned down. "I could kill you. Kill you and make sure no one ever found the body."

"So can I," grunted Brock, the pain on his face making him sweat.

And that was when the coward's friends stepped out of hiding. Four of them against one. Shitty odds.

For them.

A policeman's ball meant that Calvin couldn't bring his regular weapons. No gun or knife. He did wear his garrote necktie and cowboy boots, but he wouldn't need those. Not with these thugs. The academy had pitted him against much worse.

A smile pulled at Calvin's lips. It was a smile that his victims would have recognized. It was also the last thing most of them ever saw.

As the guys rushed him, Calvin moved, not waiting for them to attack. He dropped down to avoid flailing fists and swept a leg. Ankles were fragile things, as was balance. Hit that vulnerable joint, and chances were you'd send your opponent down.

He managed to fell two guys. No surprise, one began to moan and cry in a most unmanly fashion.

"My ankle. Fuck. I think he broke it."

Someone needed more calcium if that weak shot had fractured. Calvin didn't bask in his minor victory. He kept moving, diving at the midsection of the big fellow and sending him slamming into a wall. A knee to the gut and a club to the back of his head sent him down to the floor.

He ducked, the fist aimed at his skull cracking off plaster instead, eliciting a sharp yell from his attacker.

Spinning, his right hook took the guy in the face, sending him stumbling into his friend.

A shot from his left hit him in the kidneys. It hurt. Calvin didn't let it slow him, though. He kicked out sideways and pushed that fellow away.

The next few minutes were a flurry of blows and kicks. Grunts and curses. A few punches landed, and Calvin tasted blood at one point. But in the end, only he and Brock remained standing, bruised, and breathing heavily. Ready to keep fighting.

However, Calvin didn't have a gun.

Brock did, and he aimed it.

Calvin arched a brow. "Are you sure you want to do that?"

A sneer pulled the douchebag's lips. "The report will read that we came across you trying to steal the paintings. We got into a scuffle. You pulled a knife." Brock patted his pocket. "We didn't have a choice but to shoot."

"Really? So how are you going to explain

the video?"

"What video? The cameras were disabled, fucktard." Brock sneered, so pleased with himself until Declan—a Bad Boy partner in crime—strode into view holding up his smartphone.

"Smile for the camera, asshat."

The gun veered in Declan's direction. "Give me the phone."

"Won't do you any good. The video was live streamed to my server. We're not amateurs, you know."

Calvin almost laughed at the frustration on Brock's face. It truly was priceless. Even better, the man gave Calvin what he needed to free Lily. "Here's how it's going to go, dickwad. You are going to turn into a model ex-husband. No more threats. No more harassing Lily. I'll allow you to keep seeing your little girl for the moment, but rest assured if you harm one little fucking hair on her head"—Calvin smiled, but it didn't warm his glacial stare— "I will dismember you. Oh, and that goes for your buddies, too. If they so much as drive down her street..." He drew a finger across his throat.

"You won't get away with this. I am a cop. I have—"

"Nothing. So don't cross me. And"—Calvin stepped over a groaning body—"please note, that if you or any of your friends are involved in the drug thing happening around town, this is your one and only warning to shut it down."

"You'll regret this." Brock just couldn't keep his mouth shut.

"The only thing I will probably regret is not killing you now. But...there's always tomorrow. Now, if you'll excuse me, I have a woman to see." And because Calvin also didn't know how to keep his mouth shut, he added, "And touch."

The last smack of his fist against Brock's face felt much too good. The satisfaction of it lasted until he got to Lily's place and saw the car in her driveway.

He entered and aimed his gun. "Move away from her before I shoot!"

Chapter Twenty-three

Lily glared at Calvin. "Put that thing away. You will not shoot Mason. Especially since he was kind enough to drive me home. Or did you forget I didn't have a ride?"

"I offered to drive you. You said no."

"You weren't supposed to listen." Irrational rebuttal, and yet, she was okay with it.

"Well, excuse me for trying to respect you. And excuse me for making sure Mason gave you a ride. Although, when I said ride, that didn't include him sticking around and plying you with his questionable charm." Calvin glared at his friend.

"You mean you had this planned."

"Not the whole you stomping off part, but I did enlist Mason to help me keep an eye on you, given some of our recent troubles."

She ignored the fact that Calvin cared enough to arrange protection and shot a smile at Mason. "Thank you."

"My pleasure," Mason drawled.

"Why does he get the thanks? I'm the one who arranged it."

"Perhaps instead of doing that, you should have been the one to make sure I got home."

"Yeah, what she said," Mason added with

a grin.

The gun that Calvin had lowered rose again. "Don't tempt me to shoot."

"See the thanks I get?" Mason turned puppy-dog eyes on Lily.

"I agree. He is a jerk." She glared at Calvin—it was that or throw herself at him. When she'd left, she'd thought it was over, that he'd finally seen the light and wanted nothing more to do with her. Now that she had evidence to the contrary, her anger threatened to melt.

"I'm the jerk? I'm not the one who was keeping a big secret."

"I would have told you when I was ready." Maybe. She'd enjoyed living in a false reality there for a while. "Let's not forget that you spied on me."

"What else did you expect? Assassin. Remember?"

"Stop it with the stupid assassin thing. This is real life. In the real world, you don't go around stalking women you're interested in."

"I prefer the term ardent pursuit. And why aren't you mad at him? He helped." Pointing a finger, Calvin tossed his friend under the bus.

The whole thing was ridiculous. From the fact that he'd had her checked out, to the fake-spy craziness. But the one thing that wasn't fake? The gun Calvin wielded so casually. "How did you bring a gun to the policeman's ball?"

"I didn't. I keep a few in the car for emergencies."

A few? What kind of nutjob was Calvin? A handsome one who drew her in spite of everything. She stared at him and noticed the state of his clothes and face. "What happened to you?" The concern had her rising from the couch to approach him, her anger melting in the face of his obvious injury.

"Not much. I had a chat with your ex and a few of his friends."

A sharply indrawn breath was all she could manage.

"Don't look scared." A callused thumb stroked her chin. "They look a hell of a lot worse than I do. You also don't have to worry about Brock or his buds bugging you anymore. I took care of it."

"Took care of? What do you—" She tried to protest, but Calvin sealed her mouth with a kiss. A long kiss that she felt down to her toes— and in a certain spot between her legs.

"Ahem. So, I guess I should be going." Calvin didn't reply, but must have made some gesture because Mason grumbled, "Good thing we're friends. I financially ruined the last guy who gave me the bird."

Then the front door slammed shut. It was enough to snap Lily out of the languorous passion threatening to overtake. "I'm still mad at you." She shoved at his immovable chest.

"Okay."

"That's it? Okay?"

"Yes, okay. I freely admit to stalking you

and needing to know everything about you. But in my defense—"

"Is there a defense?" she couldn't help retorting with sarcasm.

"Yes. Because I am falling for you."

Oh. Her mouth opened and shut. A part of her wanted to call him a liar. Another part of her melted into a puddle of warm goo. There was no denying that she wanted this man more than she'd ever wanted anyone or anything. She swayed into him, aching for that feeling she got when in his arms.

"How can you say you're falling for me? My life is a mess."

"So we'll untangle it."

"My ex is crazy."

"I can handle him."

"You could do better."

"In my eyes, you're the best."

"Anyone ever tell you that you're stubborn?"

"All the time. Deal with it."

"Deal with it?" She snorted. "I've never met anyone like you."

"Good. I pride myself on being unique."

"Does anything bother you?" She tilted her head to look at him.

"A few weeks ago, I might have said nothing could rattle me. Then a certain hot mom moved in next door with her kid, and now… The thought of you not being a part of my life isn't something I want to even consider."

For some reason, his words made her lean her head on his chest. His wide chest. Arms wrapped around her, and he nuzzled the top of her head.

"I wish I could believe we could make this work."

"Trust in me."

"I want to." She did. She really did, but—

He wouldn't let her doubt. He also seemed determined to not leave her alone. His arms tightened. "Be with me."

Such a simple request, fraught with possible peril and heartache. Yet, what would pushing him away accomplish?

Why keep fighting it? She sighed, and her whole body relaxed.

He leaned back and tilted her chin. He didn't say anything, but he didn't need to when he showed her how he felt as he crushed his mouth to hers.

Sweet heaven. A tingling awareness swept through her, igniting her senses and firing her need. How she yearned for him. Hungered for his touch. Lily wanted to bask in the sinful pleasure she knew he could give.

Standing on tiptoe, she deepened the kiss as she gripped Calvin's hair. A frantic need overcame her, and she devoured his mouth, sucked on his lower lip, drawing a deep groan from him.

She pressed herself tightly against his body, as if she could merge herself with him.

Maybe then she'd believe him when he said he wanted her. Much as she'd tried to pretend it didn't exist, a bond had formed between them, and she didn't want it to ever break. For this moment, this brief interlude in time, she pretended all was right in the world. He cared for her. She cared for him. For now, it was enough.

The kiss turned gentler, and yet it still fanned her arousal. At her urging, his mouth opened, and she could slide her tongue into the warm recess to touch his. She closed her teeth gently around his tongue, nipping it, and he groaned.

She had the power to make him feel. Need. For a moment, she found herself disoriented as he suddenly swept her off her feet and carried her. Her back hit the mattress of her bed, and she opened heavy eyelids to see him stripping.

No matter how many times she saw him nude, it still made her catch her breath. Chiseled perfection. Muscled all over. Not an ounce of fat. But he did bear scars. She'd traced them one night and giggled at his wild claims. Supposed gun and knife fights. Missions gone wrong. He knew how to make her smile.

And she knew how to make his gaze smolder. As he watched, she removed her own clothing, the little black dress getting flung to the side, leaving her clad in only a lacy brassiere and panties.

"If I'd known this was under that dress,

we never would have left the house," he growled as he knelt on the bed and framed her with his arms.

"I say we never leave this house or bed again."

"That is the best idea I've ever heard." He dipped his head and nipped the lacy cup of her bra, teasing her nipple.

How did he manage to make her feel so sexy all the time? Raising her hands, she placed them flat against the skin of his chest. It never failed to amaze her how soft the hair on his chest was to the touch. A downy fur almost, and, underneath, hardness—a firmness that came from toned muscles. Her hands skimmed his flesh, brushing over his nipples. They protruded in distinct points, and he shuddered as she dragged her nails over them. Her hands kept sliding until they wrapped around him, enough so she could drag him down and have the still-lace-encased nubs of her nipples brush at his chest.

Her turn to shiver.

He dipped his head and resumed their kiss, even as his lower body nestled more firmly between her thighs, the hot hardness of him pressing against her mound, teasing her with what was to come.

He lifted himself from her body, his welcome weight gone, and she made a sound of protest, which turned into a moan as his hands roamed her flesh, teasing the skin, bringing all her nerve endings to life. His lips soon followed the path of his hands, brushing against her, teasing her with soft kisses.

The latch of his mouth on a nipple brought a deep groan to her lips. And when he bit that lace-covered tip? She arched off the bed. He used her movement to slide his arm around her waist, anchoring her in that position, which pushed out her breasts. An offering for him to feast.

He sucked on her hardened nipple, tugged and pulled, each stroke of his mouth sending a jolt to her already wet pussy. He bit her. Nibbled at the tip. Put enough pressure that she couldn't help but cry out and thrash and squirm. Oh, how she squirmed. Her hips bucked as they sought the weight of him. She needed him.

The growing ache between her legs begged for relief. But still, he tortured. Still, he sucked. Teased. Ignored how she moaned and gasped for breath.

When he finally stopped, she let out a mewling sound and then held still, even forgot to breathe as his mouth blazed a trail down over her tummy, right to the edge of her panties.

He grabbed them with his teeth and tugged.

When they didn't cooperate, he tore them.

She managed a feeble, "Those were new."

He growled, "I'll buy you another pair. Make that ten pairs."

His impatience was flattering, the feel of his hot breath against her moist lips shiver-inducing.

Her fingers scrabbled and clutched at the sheets as he went after his prize. His tongue flicked against her clit and sent her spiraling.

He feasted on her and groaned as he lapped. He didn't try to hide his enjoyment.

And enjoy it he did. There was no mistaking the pleasure he took in licking her.

She wondered if he would make her come on his tongue. He did so love to do that. But today he didn't have the patience, or so he claimed as he murmured, "I can't wait. I need you."

Good, because she needed him, too.

It took him but a moment to cover his cock with a condom. Then he positioned himself over her, a big man, a strong man... *My man.*

The tip of him pressed against her sex, stretching it as he sheathed himself. He had the type of endowment she'd only heard of before. Thick. Long. The kind that stretched her and made her feel so freaking full.

A shudder went through her as the walls of her sex gripped his hard length. He moved inside her, thick and pulsing, pushing into her so deeply.

So fucking deep.

He set the rhythm, his thrusts creating the friction that had her gasping for air and trembling. Together, they raced for that pinnacle of bliss, and when she came—with a scream of his name—he came, too.

She wished they could stay intertwined forever.

Wished she could stop time.

She wished for a future without fear of repercussion.

And there was only one way she could really do that.

The next morning, waking up beside Calvin, Lily practiced what she would say to him. He probably expected them to spend the day together. After all, the weekend had arrived, and after the night they'd had, it was a natural assumption. However, if they were to have any kind of future, then Lily had somewhere to be. Something she had to do.

The slip of paper Lisa had given her with the address currently burned a hole in her purse. The thought of going through with the meeting scared the hell out of her. How could she tell her secrets? What if Brock found out she'd snitched?

What if she didn't, and Brock kept terrorizing her? What if, the next time he attacked Calvin, he didn't only use fists?

I have to do something. She couldn't go to the cops. They were a part of it. Forget telling Calvin. Despite his need to act vigilant, he wasn't equipped to deal with this kind of corruption. She wanted to keep him safe.

The meeting today was her only hope. Lisa trusted these people and thought they could do something. That had to be good enough for Lily.

The big male body spooned around her

meant she knew when Calvin woke because a certain rigid part of him nudged her.

"Good morning." She wiggled against him and grinned when he groaned.

"Damn, woman. Can't a man get some rest?"

"I thought assassins went all night."

"Have you forgotten I did? A man needs time to recoup his strength. But—" He rolled atop her and grinned. "If you insist…" He nudged her with his hips, and she couldn't help the world's stupidest, happiest smile. A smile because he just made her so freaking happy.

This is why I have to do this.

"So, listen—"

"By the way—"

They both stopped then laughed. "You first," he said.

"I was just going to say I have to run a few errands this morning."

"Funny coincidence, so do I. Boss texted me about some meeting I have to attend."

Even better than expected. "Shall we meet back here for dinner?"

"Sounds like a plan. I'll grab it," he offered. "I know a place just up the street from my office that does excellent Indian takeout."

"Sounds perfect." She wondered where Calvin worked. They'd never really discussed it. But, if it all went well today, then there'd be plenty of time for her to discover everything about him.

As they showered together—and indulged in some languorous soaping—she hoped he couldn't see how nervous she was. She hated lying to him, but she did this to protect him. Surely, he'd understand.

The meeting today could either be the best or the dumbest thing she'd ever done. No matter what, she couldn't sit back and do nothing. Brock wouldn't stop now that he knew about Calvin. It was either kill her ex or put him in jail.

For some reason, as she waved goodbye to Calvin, a false smile pasted on her face, she couldn't help but wonder if this was how a spy felt as she tried to throw anyone off that might be watching her. Lisa had told her to be careful, and Lily took those words to heart.

When she left her house, she hit several thrift-type stores before the giant flea market on the west side of town. She made sure to mix into the crowd, popping in and out of stalls, constantly moving, especially where it was thickest and busiest. Eventually, she scooted out of there and quickly walked the two blocks to the subway train. She paid cash and hopped onto the first car she saw.

Only once seated on the worn plastic seat did she relax. No one had followed her.

Once at her stop, the directions to the place were fairly easy. The office was in a central part of town and seemed so innocuous on the surface. But, as Lisa explained, things in the open tended to receive less scrutiny.

Since it was a protected office building, Lily had to sign in with a security guard. She flashed a weak smile and, when asked for her business, claimed, "House hunting." That cover got her to the seventh floor. Only when the receptionist—a woman in her forties with teased blonde hair and thickly shadowed eyes—asked her how she could help did Lily get flustered.

"My boss, Lisa Cummings, set up a meeting for me."

"We've been expecting you. First, if you don't mind." The woman came around the desk with a thick baton in hand. "If you'll stand still, this will only take a moment." As the receptionist waved the wand up and down Lily's body, front and back, Lily held still.

"Are you checking me for weapons?" The words emerged on a squeak.

"Weapon. Microphone. You'll have to leave your phone with me, along with your purse."

For a moment, Lily clutched it.

"I promise I won't touch the contents, but we have to be careful."

Of course they did. The people she was meeting couldn't know if Lily told the truth or not. The precautions made sense, but they also frightened her. Just whom had Lisa hooked her up with?

Lily handed over her handbag and the phone tucked in her pocket. She also felt a need to say, "I didn't come here directly. I don't think anyone followed."

"You weren't. Or the operative tailing you from your house would have mentioned it."

"Someone followed me?" And she'd never even suspected.

"If you'll come with me." The woman swept an arm toward a massive set of doors. She slapped a card against it, and the light around the handle went from red to green. The door clicked, and the woman opened it. Lily found herself ushered into a boardroom with several men, including one that she knew.

Her forehead crinkled. Why was Mason here?

He stared at her, his mouth opening, then pulling and stretching into a wide grin. He started to laugh, and before she could ask why, the door behind her was flung open and Calvin boomed, "What the hell is my girlfriend doing here?"

Chapter Twenty-four

Despite knowing he looked like an ass, Calvin couldn't help but glare.

How had he not known Lily was the missing link in their case? Why had no one told him? Declan must have known when he trailed her that morning. Hell, Declan had to have seen him leaving the fucking house.

Damned conspiracy by his teammates to shock him. They'd thought it funny. Calvin? Not so much.

Lily was in more trouble than he'd expected. Her ex-husband was but the tip of a deadly iceberg. Lily had names of those involved. Even addresses. Apparently, Brock was heavily involved in the cover-up and drug operation. He was the one, along with his buddies, siphoning goods from out of the lockup.

Harry asked questions while the others took notes.

Calvin just stared.

Stared and feared because he knew, by Lily giving them this information, she'd just made herself a target.

Lucky for her, he was a man who knew how to minimize that risk.

If she ever talked to him again, which at

the moment seemed unlikely.

When he'd first walked in, she'd shot him a startled glance, and then her gaze had narrowed. "What are you doing here? Did you follow me?"

"I work here."

"As a realtor?"

"On the surface. As you might have guessed Bad Boy Inc. is just a cover. In actuality, we are problem-solving specialists."

Her lips flattened. "So you're part of some kind of underground vigilante group."

"Underground, yes, vigilante, no," Harry explained. He spread his hands. "We are a group with special skills. Graduates of an academy that is very picky about its candidates."

"There's a school for what you do?"

"More than a few around the world founded decades ago when it became clear that sometimes local laws and government weren't enough. We are the ones called in when regular channels don't work."

Her lips flattened. "You're mercenaries for hire."

"In a sense."

"Which means you're really a killer." At that statement, Lily finally looked at Calvin, and what he saw on her face didn't encourage. Especially when he nodded, and her shoulders slumped. "I knew there had to be something wrong with you." And that was the last thing she said to him.

Things turned back to business at that

point. Words spilled out of her as Lily told them everything she knew. Gave them a list of names, many of them part of her ex-husband's posse. She gave them an address, a swanky place in a gated community that Brock had once driven them to before taking them on a family trip to the beach. Business, he claimed.

She told them of the suitcases full of cash. The duffel bags full of drugs.

He watched as her fingers twisted and turned in her lap as she related to them all the things she'd observed.

At one point, Mason, that fucking idiot, asked her, "Why didn't you rat him out before?"

Calvin answered for her. "Because that douche wad beat the shit out of her."

Lily ducked her head and nodded. "He's been threatening me for years. Not only is he a cop, he's also Zoe's father." Her shoulders lifted and dropped. "I didn't know who to tell."

So why her sudden change of heart? Did he dare even imagine it was because of him?

When the meeting adjourned, Calvin left his buds talking over a plan and instead chose to follow Lily. She ignored him as she stabbed the elevator button. He wouldn't let her walk away this time. As soon as the elevator door closed, he confronted her.

"Why didn't you tell me about all this before? You knew I wanted to do something about the drug problem in this town."

"I didn't tell you because I thought you

were a realtor playing a game. But all along, you weren't what I thought. You really are a killer, aren't you?"

Did the gun and the fact that he took care of himself not make that clear before? "I never lied about that."

"No, you didn't, but I thought you were joking. I mean, seriously, who the hell kills people for a living?"

"I do."

At that stark announcement, her face turned ashen. "I'm sleeping with a killer."

"You're sleeping with a man who sometimes gets rid of bad people."

"And who decides if they're bad? You? Them?" She spat the words at him and slashed out her arm. She closed her eyes and leaned against the cab. "I can't believe this is happening."

"Who I am hasn't changed."

"Perhaps not, but it means that, once again, my radar is off." She opened her eyes. "I left Brock to start a new life with Zoe. One free of violence. And instead, I'm right back in it."

"I told you I wouldn't let anyone hurt you. I even offered to take care of your ex."

"By killing him? Are you going to murder anyone that gets in your way or pisses you off? Are you going to kill me if I don't do what I'm told? Hit me." She got right in his face as she yelled. Her cheeks held a flush, and her eyes flashed with anger—and hurt. "I just want a safe and normal life."

Before he could say anything, the elevator doors opened, and she walked out.

The words he wanted to speak hung on the tip of his tongue. *All I want is you.*

But how to make her understand that?

He needed to vent his frustration. Lucky for him, he had a list of places and people he could take it out on.

A few hours later, he stared down at the body slumped on the ground with a hole in his head. He didn't feel sorry for the lowlife. The fucker was peddling underage girls and drugs. With him gone, there was one less danger to Lily and Zoe.

Killing the lowlife didn't make Calvin feel any better. He kept seeing the hurt and fear in Lily's eyes. The truth had made her scared of him.

How can she be frightened of me? Doesn't she know how much I care?

He cared so much that he'd assigned Jerome guard duty over his woman. He kept an eye on her in between Calvin's hunt for asshats. He noted her bedroom door closed on the video feed. Did she cry behind it?

Argh.

The pain gripping him, an emotional pain he'd not experienced since his youth, meant he spent that night cleaning up the streets. Those that didn't die got one chance to leave. The ones that refused? No one would ever see them again.

Calvin didn't hunt alone. Declan provided

backup while Mason did what he did best—siphoned the dirty money. Took all the profit out of it.

Meanwhile, Benedict and Harry put their heads together and sifted through the clues, looking for the link they were missing because, while what Lily had given them uncovered some secrets, they were still missing one thing. The person in charge of it all.

Maybe if Calvin got rid of that threat, then perhaps Lily would look past his job and see the man who just wanted to protect her.

A man who had everything but felt as if he'd just lost it all. An assassin in love.

Chapter Twenty-five

In her room, knees tucked to her chest, Lily couldn't stop thinking about Calvin. Ruminating on the fact that he was a killer.

Yet treated her so gently.

She thought about how he felt no remorse about what he did.

But looked so chagrinned when he'd broken one of her kitchen chairs; he'd taken it upon himself to fix it and the other three.

Violence was a daily part of his life.

And yet he'd promised to keep her safe.

Now that he was gone, because she'd chosen to walk away from him and everything being with him entailed, she found herself scared again. She spent that Saturday night huddled in her bed for a while, sobbing before emerging to perch on the couch, wrapped in a blanket, fearing every car that drove by. Flinching at every creak.

She stayed that way until the wee hours of the morning, tense and jerking when a flash of lights briefly lit her window. She knew what that meant, but she popped from the couch to peek and saw Calvin's car pull into his driveway. Hidden behind her curtain, she spied and thus saw him get out of his car. He didn't immediately go inside. He paused and stared at her house. For a moment, she wondered—hoped—he'd cross that slim expanse and force her to face him.

Disappointment brought tears to her eyes as he, instead, pivoted and entered his home. Still, knowing he was close eased some of her tension. Only then did she relax enough to fall asleep. A restless slumber that saw her running through dark alleys, looking for her baby, hearing Brock's taunting laughter as he chased her.

Breath whooshed from her in hard pants. The alley seemed never-ending, shrouded in fog and shadow. She couldn't see far and ran into something hard. Something that didn't move. Bouncing back, she raised her head and saw Calvin's face.

Relief made her blurt, "Help me."

His lips moved. "You told me to stay out of your life."

"I didn't really mean it," she sobbed. "Please. Please don't leave me." But he turned his back on her. Left her to face her demons alone, and that demon, wearing Brock's face, laughed and laughed as he—

Lily jolted awake violently enough that she rolled off the couch onto the floor.

Damned floor proved hard and unsympathetic. Her body protested the abuse. It wasn't the only part of her that didn't welcome the harsh wakeup. Her eyes felt gritty, her mouth pasty and dry as if she'd not drunk in days. A glance at her phone on the coffee table—a basic wooden table that Calvin had built using recycled palettes he'd grabbed from the side of the road, then sanded and stained into something beautiful—showed it was late afternoon. She'd slept longer than expected. If only she felt rested.

She doubted she'd sleep well ever again. She'd finally done the unthinkable. She'd snitched.

And snitches get stitches.

She shook her head and regretted it. How sluggish she felt. She needed a caffeine jolt in the form of a cup of coffee, more coffee than water. It served to wake her up a bit. She had to wake up, given Brock would bring Zoe home in less than an hour.

I can't let him or Zoe see me like this. Broken. Hurting. And all because of the truth, not fists.

Who knew the truth could hurt so badly?

She forced herself to move, showering, dressing, and managing a light snack.

Five o'clock came.

No sign of Brock. The minute hand kept ticking. Minute after minute passed. At quarter after, with anxiety making a pit in her stomach, she texted.

No reply.

At five-thirty, hands clammy, she called his cell phone.

No answer.

Panic threatened, and she fought to control her breath as she called and texted, again and again, until, finally, Brock did reply with a text. One word.

Gone.

No. No, he couldn't do this. No. No!

She screamed the word as she threw her phone. How dare he. He had no right. She wouldn't let Brock keep Zoe.

I will get my daughter. But how? How to get her baby from a bastard who didn't fight fair, who had the law on his side?

Only one person could help her. She only trusted one man.

She banged on Calvin's door. Banged so damned hard. When he answered, he caught her in his arms, and she couldn't breathe. Her chest was too tight.

"What's wrong?"

"He's got her. He's not bringing her back. Oh God, he's keeping my baby." Calvin caught her when she would have fallen.

"No, he's not. That little girl belongs with you."

"But he has her." She raised a tear-streaked face. "He says she's gone. What if— What if—" The thought was too terrifying to say out loud.

"Zoe is fine. I promise." Calvin gripped her tight by the forearms. "I will get her back for you, Lily. Do you trust me to do what has to be done?"

She looked into his face. A face she'd grown to care so damned much about. A man who'd shown her such kindness, such consideration such…love.

She thought of Brock. Thought of the hell he'd put her through and still kept putting her through. The danger he put their daughter in with his sick games. No more.

"Do it. Don't let him take my baby from me, Cal. Please. I'll do anything."

"I don't want you to do anything. I'll bring her back to you. I promise." He lifted her chin. "I will fix this."

She hugged him, and he crushed her back, his solid presence just the thing she needed, his words the balm to her fear and rage.

He set her from him. "I've got to get ready." By get ready, he meant go into the attic, a space that looked benign from below, but once her head popped above the ceiling height, the illusion disappeared, and her mouth rounded in surprise.

"This is your lair," she exclaimed.

"Lair?" He chuckled as he tossed her a look over his shoulder. "I guess you could say that, except I don't have a bat suit or a cape."

"But you do have lots of guns." She couldn't help but notice them on the wall, held in racks, gleaming metal, hard-looking plastic, the smell of oil heavy in the air.

"Guns. Knives. A man in my line of work never knows what he'll need." He knelt down to throw open a chest. A gleaming array shone from its depths.

"Does it bother you?" she asked. "The killing?"

"If you're waiting to hear me say I break down and cry, then you'll be disappointed." His gaze remained steady. "I kill people, Lily. Mostly bad people, which helps justify it to some, but sometimes, it's just a job."

"Have you ever killed a child?"

At that, his face tightened. "No. Never. There are some lines even I won't cross. Just like I don't kill women."

She couldn't help but ask, "What if they try to kill you first?"

"Then I'd probably do what had to be done. But if you're wondering if I'd ever hurt you, then the answer is no. You could take this knife and plunge it into me." He turned it so that the blade rested over his heart. "I would let you. If I ever did anything that made you so desperate, then I probably deserve to die because the last thing I want to do is hurt you."

The rawness of his words, the blazing sincerity in his gaze wrapped tightly around her. It was almost too much.

Tears blurring her vision, she turned from him and glanced around the rest of the attic space, a cowardly way of not answering. She couldn't respond, not while Zoe was missing. "What's this for?" She swept a hand to encompass all the monitors, most of them flipping to show various camera views. Some she recognized, like her street. And… "Is that my living room?"

"I told you I was keeping an eye on you."

She wanted to feel angrier, and yet, oddly enough, the fact that he did watch over her strangely comforted. "What will you do when you find them?"

"What's necessary." He didn't elaborate.

"I don't want Zoe to see any violence."

"She won't."

Lily bit her tongue lest she ask what he planned to do to Brock. She didn't care. The man had brought this on himself.

She watched as Calvin armed himself. Ankle holster with a gun. A matching one on the other side with a knife. She noted a rack of ties, only they weren't ties, she realized as he pulled one off the rack and snapped it. Even his sense of fashion was practical.

Last of all, the cowboy boots, and she wondered if they hid any surprises. She followed him downstairs as he gave her final instructions. "Don't leave the house. I've got it armed to keep people out."

As Calvin put his hand on the doorknob and prepared to leave, a sudden fear that he wouldn't come back had her throwing herself at him. "Be careful."

"Never. Careful won't get the job done. But I will promise one thing," he said as he hugged her. "I'll bring her home to you."

At that, it occurred to her that, "Maybe I should go with you. Zoe might need me."

"This will be easier if I'm not worrying about you. If Brock has gone off the deep end, then there's no telling how he'll react if he sees you."

Good point, but it didn't ease her anxiety. "Call me the instant you find her."

"I will. Remember. Stay inside."

"Am I in danger?"

"Just call it a gut instinct. I don't know what I would do if someone hurt you."

Implying he'd go on a murderous rampage of vengeance should have made her recoil. Instead, she threw herself at him once more and plastered her mouth to his. The kiss was a short, fervent thing that left them both flushed.

"I'll be back."

When Arnold said it in *Terminator*, people giggled. When Calvin said it, she shivered.

The door shut, and the light on the alarm pad turned from red to green. She peeked out the window and saw his car pull out. She had to have faith that Calvin would find Zoe and bring her back safely.

He'd said he would call—

Call me how? I left my phone in the house.

Dammit. Dammit. Dammit.

She could kick herself now. Especially since the alarm was set.

No matter. She could wait. How long would it take for him to drive to Brock's and find Zoe and then make it back? She knew the route.

But what if something happened? What if Zoe needed her or got hurt? *What if she's already hurt?*

Being a mom meant thinking of the million things that could go wrong. Add to that Calvin had said to stay inside. But she wasn't the one in danger.

No one had bothered them in weeks. Surely, she could take a minute to pop out and grab her phone.

What of the alarm system?

Once she had her phone, she could call Calvin and let him know it was a false alarm. He had an app for it. He'd probably give her hell, but she could handle that. It was better than the not knowing.

Still, she hesitated. Paced.

Waiting was awful. Especially since she wondered if a message waited. What if Calvin had tried to call and she didn't answer? He'd worry.

So many reasons for her to pop out. Screw it. She was going. She couldn't stand the not knowing.

Exiting the house, she kept the door propped open so it wouldn't lock behind her and ran over to her place. She'd left in such a rush, she'd forgotten to lock the door. The phone remained where she'd tossed it in the kitchen. She stooped to grab it and noticed not a single missed call or text.

A sigh of disappointment left her. She straightened and caught a flash of motion from the corner of her eye. A blow to the back of her head sent her into darkness.

Chapter Twenty-six

As Calvin sped towards Brock's place—the address already accessible to him through his research—he contacted Mason to let him know what he was doing.

"Douchebag took Lily's daughter. I'm going to get her back. But that means no one is watching my place." And he couldn't get a hold of Declan, who was probably sleeping or hunting. "Can you swing over?" Ever since the attack on Lily, Calvin had made sure someone kept an eye when he couldn't. He wouldn't allow anyone to terrorize Lily again. But with her so frantic and worried about Zoe, Calvin couldn't wait for a replacement.

"Sure, I'll head over, but it will take me a good thirty minutes or so."

Better than nothing. Calvin didn't figure he would be more than an hour or so, but he didn't like leaving Lily unguarded, especially given how many people in the drug trade they'd taken out in the last week or so.

Bad Boy Inc. was cleaning up their town, and those who didn't cooperate paid the price and became an example for others. Unfortunately, more than a few were thick-headed and didn't get the message. They thought they could strike back. A cop and ex-lover tried hitting Benedict. It didn't end well. For them.

Things were at the boiling point, ready to explode, which meant Brock was unstable, and Calvin needed to tread carefully lest the bastard do the unthinkable.

Calvin hung up with Mason, satisfied Lily was taken care of, and kept his speed within limits. People watched movies and had this misconception that assassins lived by no rules. In books and on screen, they owned fast cars, drove like maniacs, and did all kinds of stupid shit to draw attention.

Wrong.

Assassins only lived to retirement if they were smart and remained hidden. Being discreet meant not getting pulled over for speeding or shooting the neighbor's dog because it liked to bark its head off at the crack of dawn.

Calvin took his time and planned what he'd do when he got to his target location. He had dropped into work mode, the only way to deal with the anxiety that threatened over the thought of the sweet little girl he'd grown fond of in possible danger.

Here was what he knew. Lily's ex lived in their old house, a single-floor bungalow. The basement windows were below grade and set within wells, making access through them impossible for a man his size.

According to Calvin's file, Brock didn't have an alarm system, though, which meant entry through a window on the main level, if done quietly, wouldn't raise any alerts. But before taping any glass and smashing it, Calvin did something very simple first. He infiltrated the property via the yard.

After ascertaining that there was no one in the kitchen, he tried the back door. The door opened with hardly any sound. Not that anyone would have heard over the blaring of the television in the other room.

Creeping across the tile floor doing his best to make sure his boots didn't make a scuff, Calvin held his gun in his left hand, which tended to screw with most people who expected a righty. The academy had taught him to be ambidextrous. He slid past the wooden table and the matching chairs, sporting flowered cushions that he suspected was a remnant of Lily's touch, as were the ceramic canisters and other kitchen decorations bearing spotted cows. Real men went stainless all the way.

The canned soundtrack of audience laughter came from the front of the house, through the kitchen, and past the dining room with its dark mahogany surfaces. Calvin made it to the living room without the man in the fat, upholstered, reclining chair being any wiser.

Easing forward, Calvin had the gun pressed against the back of Brock's head before the guy said in a slurred voice, "Go ahead. Shoot me. I deserve it."

Given Calvin had expected him to beg for

his life, maybe throw out a few profane *motherfuckers*, the pity party request took him by surprise.

"Where's Zoe?" First things first. He needed to locate Lily's daughter.

"Gone."

"What do you mean gone, asshole? If you harm a single hair on that little girl's head…" Hell couldn't devise a punishment for Brock that would hurt as much as Calvin would. *I'll torture him slowly, and make him scream.*

"I would never hurt her!" Brock squirmed in his chair, turning around enough so that the barrel of the gun resided between his eyes. He glared at Calvin. "I love Zoe. She is my kid."

"Then where is she?"

The bravado faded. "They took her. Took my ladybug."

"Who did?"

At this, some of the anger returned to Brock's face. "They did. The fuckers you wouldn't leave alone. They told me to do something about you and your fucking poking. And so I did. That night of the ball, I told you to stop meddling, but you just couldn't walk away. You just kept pushing and interfering in things you shouldn't."

"So your partners took Zoe? That makes no sense."

"They took her because I told them I was done. I wanted out." The resignation once again hit Brock, and he slumped back in his seat. It didn't mean Calvin eased the pressure on the trigger of his gun.

"They won't allow you to quit."

"Nope. And not only that, now I have to prove myself to get her back." Brock took a swig from the brown bottle clenched in his fist.

"Prove yourself how?"

"They want me to kill Lily for starters because, apparently, my lovely ex-wife couldn't keep her fat fucking mouth shut."

"Only because she was attacked in her own house."

"What?" Brock didn't feign surprise. "I didn't know that."

"Even if she hadn't talked, we were coming after you."

"Who is this we? The boss keeps saying there's a gang coming after them. Some bullshit about some classmates wanting to wipe him out because he knows too much."

At those words, Calvin couldn't help but ask, "Your boss? Who is it? Is he the one who has Zoe?" And which of his classmates had gone off the rails? They hadn't all kept in touch after graduation, so he wasn't sure how to figure out whom they needed to target—and eliminate.

"If you want a name or face, you can forget it. He's too smart for that. We only ever saw him wearing a black hood. I can't even tell you what color his eyes are. Hell, for all I know, it's a girl under there with a deep voice."

A shrouded leader. The circle got even

more convoluted. And fascinating. Who was this foe with a grudge?

"I need an address."

"It won't do you any good. The place is well guarded."

"I don't give a shit." He poked the gun at Brock. "Get up."

"Why? Won't shoot a man sitting down?"

"I'm not shooting you, but you are coming with me on a car ride."

"Need a place to dump the body? I can show you the spot we usually use." Said with a sarcastic laugh as Brock rose from his seat with a stagger.

"I'm not killing you. Not yet, but we are going to get Zoe, and then I'm going after your boss."

"You won't be able to save her by yourself. The warehouse is fortified. One man can't penetrate it."

"I'm not just any man. And who says we're going alone?" Calvin had friends, lots of them, and they loved to bring toys—and mayhem.

They wouldn't blow anything up until a certain little girl was safe. But then...

His phone buzzed in his pocket, the silent vibration sending a forbidding feeling through him. Holding the gun on Brock—because he didn't trust the fucker at all—he pulled it out and frowned.

The alarm text noted the front door on his

house had opened and stayed open. Lily had gone out. But why?

He fired a text off to her, one-handed; the other still aimed the gun. An assassin knew how to multi-task.

"Move outside," Calvin ordered as soon as he hit send.

Brock did as told, if in a lurching, drunken fashion. The idiot protested when a click on the key fob opened the trunk and Calvin ordered him to, "Get in."

"Fuck y—"

Whack. The clubbing of his gun on the back of Brock's head silenced his feeble protest. The man only lived because Calvin still needed him. Calvin dumped the body in the trunk and shut it. Leaning against it, he texted Lily again, and then immediately called her phone. It went right to voicemail.

He dialed Mason. Forget a hello. "Are you at my house yet?"

"Just pulling onto your street."

"The alarm's going off." And more worrisome, he couldn't get a hold of Lily.

Was that why she'd left his place? To grab her phone? It occurred to him that her track pants and T-shirt didn't have a spot to stash her phone.

"Your front door is wide open. And so is hers." Mason's grim announcement made Calvin's blood run cold.

"Check her place first."

Having trained at the academy, Calvin had had panic drilled out of him a long time ago. He was the man with ice in his veins. Who never rushed.

That all changed the moment Mason announced, "She's gone. And they left you a note."

We have the woman and the girl. We want you. Come alone, or they die.

They'd also kindly provided an address.

It turned out Calvin didn't need Brock after all, which was why he left him in the trunk. But being a man who lived by the rules of darkness, he didn't obey the part of the note that said to come alone.

And let his friends miss out on the fun? Like fuck.

Screw with one Bad Boy, and you screwed with them all.

Screw with Lily and Zoe, and you wouldn't live to see the dawn.

Chapter Twenty-seven

The throbbing in her head didn't come from a hangover. Stupidity, though, that was another thing.

I should have never left Calvin's house. But no, Lily had been the proverbial stupid girl—the one who took a shower in a haunted house, the one who went into the basement, the one who got killed—and now, she paid the price. The only shining light was the fact that she didn't wake alone.

"Mommy!" Her little girl sobbed her name a second before she threw herself at Lily. Zoe clung to her as she cried.

"Oh, baby." Moisture pricked her eyes. Tears of relief at finding her daughter and fear because, what did Brock intend to do with them? Why imprison them both?

It took only a few babbling words from Zoe for Lily to realize, though, that things were more dire than she'd thought.

"The bad man took me from Daddy and said I couldn't go home until Daddy did something."

"What bad man, ladybug?" Who was this stranger who dared to harm them?

"The man with the white hair."

Want to wager it was the same one who'd attacked Lily in her house? She now understood why Calvin joked it was better to kill an enemy than leave them alive. Alive they could come back to steal your daughter.

Give Lily a gun, any weapon really, and in that moment, she would have gladly taken care of that error.

"It's all right, ladybug. Mommy's here. I'll fix this." Though how she would get them out of this mess remained a mystery.

"I want to go home."

"So do I." Lily looked around, noting they appeared confined in some kind of storage room. Overhead, an empty socket mocked, the dangling string not even long enough to hang a mouse. The only light came from a dirty window set a few feet high in the wall. Around them, their cage was formed of solid walls, the plaster covered by peeling, green paint, the floor stained with mildew and riddled with scuff marks and holes. Other than the useless window, there was a door, the surface dented and more than likely locked. She doubted anyone who went through this kind of trouble to get them would just let them walk out. On the off chance she might be wrong, she tried the doorknob. It didn't budge no matter how hard she twisted.

The flats of her palms slapped the slab in frustration.

Given it seemed too solid for her to kick open, not to mention she didn't think making noise was a bright idea—a racket might bring someone—she whirled around, looking for any other option. No air vents, or at least not the kind big enough to crawl in. The only other true opening in the room remained the window.

Craning on tiptoe—cursing her shortness—Lily grabbed the sill and peeked through the crusted pane, noting they were on the ground floor. The source of their feeble illumination didn't appear, but given they seemed to be in some sort of warehouse, she imagined it was a security light of some kind.

It didn't matter which direction she looked; Lily didn't spot a single person outside. No one she could cry to for help. She shoved at the window, surprised when it opened, the pane lifting up until it reached the end of its folding brackets, leaving only a narrow slot.

The opening was much too small for Lily to climb out—her handful of boobs would work against her—but someone slimmer and smaller could fit. A little girl could be dropped out of the aperture and sent running for help—or at least out of harm's way.

Before Lily could talk herself out of the danger of sending her child out into the night alone, she'd picked up her daughter and slung her onto a hip.

"Listen, ladybug. Remember how the princess in your favorite story has to be brave?"

A chin dipped in a nod.

"You're going to have to be just as

courageous. I'm going to help you get out of this room, and you need to go find some help. So Mommy's going to lift you out that window, and you're going to have to jump. Remember how you bend your knees at gymnastics?"

Zoe nodded.

"Same thing. Once you hit the ground, I need you to pop up like a bunny and run fast. Fast like the wind."

"I'll run faster than you," Zoe stated with a tremulous smile.

"Mommy can't come with you, baby. The window is too small."

"By myself? I'm not allowed." The soft lisp almost broke Lily's heart.

"This time is an exception. You have to be the princess that saves me."

At this, her daughter clung, tight. "B-but I don't wanna go alone. I want to stay with you." The sobs shook Zoe's tiny frame.

Lily wanted to join her. How to explain that she feared them both dying if she stayed? Lily could endure a lot, but she wouldn't survive knowing she could have saved her daughter.

"I'm too big to come with you, which is why you have to be brave. Find someone with a phone and tell them to call…" Who should Zoe call? The cops? What if the dispatch went to one of the corrupt ones? It was a chance she'd have to take. All that mattered was getting Zoe out of here. "Call 911."

"I don't wanna go," Zoe sobbed as she

held tightly to Lily.

Lily pried Zoe's hands from her neck, feeling her own eyes welling with tears and her throat tightening. "We have to do this, ladybug."

Before she could change her mind, she raised her daughter high. She slid Zoe's legs through the window first and, standing on tiptoe, lowered her by the arms until her daughter dangled as far as she could reach.

"Remember what I told you." Lily's voice cracked as she let go. A second later, she heard a thump. She peered through the opening and saw her daughter standing there, cheeks wet with tears. "Run, ladybug. Run!"

With a sob, Zoe turned and ran, little feet pounding pavement. She quickly disappeared from sight, the light from the building not extending far. When Lily couldn't hear the steps anymore, she slumped and leaned her forehead against the wall, praying even though she didn't believe.

She heard the door open and whirled to find a familiar smirking face topped with shocking white-blond hair.

"You," she snarled.

He peeked around the room. "Is it me or did your brat disappear? I hope you didn't send her wandering outside. I guess it's too late to mention the boss has snipers on the roof with orders to shoot anything that moves."

A cold fist clutched her heart. "She's just a little girl."

"No, she's what we call a liability."

A man from outside shouted, "I see something moving."

At those words, Lily whirled and gripped the window ledge, straining to see, opening her mouth to cry out for her daughter.

Crack. The gunshot rang out, loud and clear, but it was the shriek, Zoe's scream, that sent Lily reeling from the window.

Dear God. They'd killed her child.

"No. No. No." Lily sank to the floor and sobbed, great shuddering heaves of agony.

"Must you make that noise?"

At the words, Lily uttered a cry of pure rage and launched herself at the man.

"Bastard!" Lily pummeled at her captor, and he laughed. Laughed as he grabbed her hair and yanked. But that pain couldn't compare to the agony in her heart.

Let him kill her. She didn't want to live in a world without her Zoe.

Chapter Twenty-eight

Staking out the warehouse, Calvin noted the guards on the roof. A pair to be exact; one on the east side, one on the west. A high, chain-link fence surrounded the property, leaving an open space of at least forty yards, a wide swath with no cover. The front bay doors were wide open but guarded. A guy stood just outside, rifle slung over his shoulder. Sloppy. Their old sergeant would have had him running the quad until he puked then would have made him clean it up before running again. Within the building, crisscrossing in plain sight, he saw more men wandering. Laughing and talking.

They wouldn't be laughing for long.

I will kill you all. That was his plan. But did they seriously expect him to use the front door?

He was tempted. Just stroll right in and pick them off, one by one. By the time they realized he was coming, most would be dead.

However, given this was a rescue mission, he had to exercise caution. Also, he'd promised Harry that he would wait for backup, something about not keeping all the fun for himself.

He appeared to be the first one to arrive for the party. While he waited for the other boys to get their asses into position, he wasn't completely idle. He located some sentries outside the fence line. Snuck up behind them both actually—they never heard death coming—and ended their miserable lives with a twist of hands and a sharp crack of their necks.

With them unable to raise an alarm, Calvin paced around the outside of the building. The warehouse was like many in this quarter, built of stone block for the first ten feet or so and then metal siding for the rest. A door at the back allowed entry and had a pair of guards. *Had* being the keyword. The silencer on his gun meant he barely made a sound when he dropped them. Perfect headshots, just like the academy had taught him—because anything else saw the students punished.

Four down, a mini army to go. Calvin looked for more points of entry. Windows were spaced along the side of the warehouse, too small for him or anyone other than maybe Kacy to squeeze through. On the second floor, the apertures were wider, but inaccessible.

Returning to the front, Calvin froze as he noted motion at one of the small windows on the west side. A set of legs dangled then a body. A little girl was dropped to the ground.

Zoe! His first impulse was to vault over the fence so he could run and grab her. Mason emerged suddenly from the shadows and held him back.

"You'll get shot," his friend hissed. "You need to take out the guys on the roof. Give me a second. I've got a rifle in my bag." Good idea, given a pistol at this angle and distance would be iffy at best.

As Mason rummaged through his bag of goodies, Calvin knew he couldn't remain idle. As the little girl ran across the space, he dropped to his knees and pulled the wire cutters from his pocket—no assassin ever left home without a few tools of the trade.

As he snipped, Calvin didn't know if Zoe could see him, but it wouldn't matter once she got close enough. He trimmed a hole in the fence as fast as he could and was pulling the loose wires out of the way when he noticed Zoe's gaze alight on him. Despite the shadows, she recognized him.

Her mouth opened, and she took in a breath. He quickly put a finger on his lips and shook his head.

Smart girl, she clamped her mouth shut, but someone still noticed her.

"I see something moving," shouted the fucktard on top of the building. Took him long enough.

Calvin reached out and pulled Zoe through the hole, immediately tucking her behind his body as the roof sniper took aim. The gun atop the roof cracked loudly as the man fired, poorly, he might add. Little Zoe let out a shriek of fright.

He had no time to comfort as Mason slapped a rifle in his hand, once again equipped with a silencer—a must in his profession. Calvin didn't miss—because he was a pro, unlike these wanna-bes. Their very existence offended him. The fact that they'd shot at Zoe pissed him off.

Who the fuck shoots at a kid? Not these assholes. Not anymore.

Zoe hiccupped and sobbed behind him, still not saying a word but unable to hide her fright.

He turned and pulled her against him, stroking her hair, soothing her even though he'd have told anyone who asked he didn't know how. But it came instinctually. "Shhh, princess. I'm here. You're okay."

"Momm—mmy," she stuttered. "Mommy's inside."

Calvin shot a look at the window Zoe had escaped from. He still wouldn't fit, but that wouldn't stop him from going in.

He stood, Zoe in his arms. "Mason, take Zoe to safety." He handed the little girl to his friend.

"Calvin, what are you doing? You can't go in alone. Wait. The boys are coming."

Except Calvin couldn't wait. He didn't dare wait. People willing to shoot a child wouldn't hesitate to kill a woman. It wouldn't happen, not tonight, not fucking ever.

Calvin shed his coat before palming a gun in each hand. Only then did he reply. "Those b—" The word he wanted to say burned at the tip of his tongue, but he remained all too aware that little ears listened, so he changed it to, "Bullies took something they shouldn't have. I'm going to get her back."

And he wasn't going to hide while doing it. Someone had given him an invitation to a party, and Calvin was going to make them fucking dance.

He took long strides toward the opening in the gate that led to the front of the warehouse. He began shooting even before the guard noticed his approach.

There was a time and place for subterfuge. This wasn't that time. He also didn't plan to show any mercy.

You dared to touch people I cared about.
For that, they would all die.
Bang.

Chapter Twenty-nine

When the screaming started, Blondie already had Lily halfway up a set of stairs. The grip on her hair didn't ease, which meant she couldn't turn around and look. Not being able to peek didn't make her deaf.

Lots of shouts erupted along with pops and cracks of gunfire.

At the top of the stars, Blondie kept dragging her along, but she now had a side view of the action. A one-man show currently played out. When her abductor abruptly let Lily go with a shove, she broke her fall with her hands and crouched. From the catwalk ringing the first floor, Lily watched, and despite the leaden lump in her chest, she couldn't help but admire.

It was insane and yet also beautifully elegant the way Calvin delivered death. He moved so fluidly, shifted in ways no man should be able to. His body ducked and flowed, almost as if he wasn't entirely solid as he evaded bullets. Either the aim of those below sucked or he was just really freaking lucky because, despite the pops and cracks, he kept moving farther inside, his own aim steady as he took out those standing in his way. Headshots for the most part, which meant once they went down, they stayed down.

She felt no sympathy for those who died. Those men had allowed a little girl to be kidnapped and taken hostage. One of those men might be the one who'd killed her daughter. Scum like them didn't deserve to live.

So she might have grimly smiled and cheered with dark glee as Calvin swept in and meted out a well-deserved justice.

Those he targeted didn't die quietly. Nor did they run. They thought numbers would prevail…

"Shoot him!"

"Jesus, someone kill him."

"How did you miss?"

"Holy fuck, he just shot—" Followed by abrupt silence.

Someone whimpered.

A low pop, and it stopped.

Everyone in the room below died.

It wasn't enough to save her, though. To one side of her was a man wearing some kind of hood over his face. On the other side of Lily stood Blondie with a gun trained on her. She didn't doubt he planned to use it.

Once the shooting stopped, the hooded one—who'd interestingly done nothing to stop the carnage—spoke, his voice oddly lacking inflection, the monotone almost machine like. "I see you got my invitation, Sicarius."

At the words, Calvin finally looked up. "Who are you? How do you know my name?"

"I know all the boys at Bad Boy Inc. But

you're the one I was interested in. You've been poking around in things that don't concern you."

"It became my business when you dragged Lily into it. You should have left her and this town alone."

"Why do you care what I do in this town?" Gloved hands waved, and she noted the man wore a long leather duster, the front of it closed. It hung down to the ankles, allowing the black combat boots to peek. The pure villainous look and lack of identifying characteristics spooked. As did his method of speech. "The academy teaches its students to not grow attached."

"The academy taught us many things, but that doesn't mean they're all right."

A short bark that was meant to be laughter emerged from the hooded man. "Don't let them hear you. The academy doesn't like those who speak against it. In many ways, you're a rebel, like me, which is why you should join me instead of fighting."

"Like hell." Calvin snorted. "What makes you think I'd join a drug-dealing lowlife who threatens women and children? How about, instead, I do the world a favor and put a hole between your eyes?"

"Shoot, and your girlfriend dies." The man in the hood tilted his head. "Then again, if you don't shoot, she will still die. My compatriot has been itching to pull the trigger. Seems you embarrassed him. I warned him he was no match for someone academy trained. But…" The man in the hood shrugged.

"Who are you?" She could hear the curiosity in Calvin's query. "Why do all this? And don't say you're doing it for money. We both know if you went through the academy that you have the skills to make it without resorting to drugs and other petty crimes."

"But everyone loves drugs. Especially the rich."

"Yet you're killing your buyers."

"Killing is such a harsh word. No one is forcing the little shits to snort and get high. They don't even care that they might die. If you ask me, they rather enjoy the Russian roulette they're playing because guess what? Business is as brisk as usual. You should thank me, not hunt me. I'm ridding the world of unfit future leaders. A Darwinism of sorts."

"Why put the academy logo on the drugs?" Calvin kept talking, and Lily had to wonder why. It didn't seem like him. He had yet to move from his spot. Was he waiting for something?

The hooded guy must have wondered, too. "Do you expect me to break down and give you some grand speech about how the academy screwed me and owes me? They don't. The academy saved my life. It brought me out of the shit pile that used to be my existence. It gave me purpose and skills. It seems only right I give something in return. Enough chitchat, though. I know you're stalling, waiting for your friends. However, they won't arrive in time. I'm afraid they've been detained."

"I don't need help."

"You don't, but your girlfriend does. Any last words before she dies?"

Blondie grinned as he steadied the gun aimed in her direction. Even if Calvin got off a shot, chances were he'd be too late. Her captor was too close to miss. She looked death in the eye, and it sneered as he pulled the trigger.

She closed her eyes so she wouldn't see it coming.

Bang.

Thud.

A body hit the ground, and it wasn't hers. Lily opened her eyes as she heard a second gunshot and only briefly noted the blond-haired fellow sporting a third eye in his forehead. His mouth gaped as he sank to his knees, a dead man.

Good riddance. But then, who was the body on the floor in front of her?

A glance had her gasping. "Brock?"

Her ex-husband lay on the metal catwalk, a hole in his chest pumping blood, some of it frothing at his lips. She scooted to his side, horrified because that should have been her. Shock gripped her as she realized Brock had stepped in front of a bullet for her. She stared at him, knowing he wouldn't survive, and she could see by the resignation in his eyes that he knew it, too.

"Take care of Zoe." He gasped. "Tell her—" A bloody cough. "Tell her I love her. Don't let her know her daddy was a crook."

She didn't have the heart to tell him it was too late. Zoe was dead.

With one final gasp of air, he died. To her surprise, she cried. Hot, fat tears rolled down her cheeks, and it took a moment for her to remember that, even with Blondie dead, she wasn't safe. Where was the masked man? She whirled behind her to look, but he was gone. Calvin, however, had arrived, and he pounded across the metal catwalk. She half rose before she was gripped tightly in his arms.

He buried his face in her hair. "I thought I'd lost you."

She couldn't help but sob. "Zoe."

"Is fine. Mason has her."

At those words, she froze and raised a tear-streaked face. "She's alive?"

"And well. Probably twisting Mason around her little finger as we speak." He brushed the hair out of her face. "Come on. I'll take you to her."

"But…" She couldn't speak, just stared around at the carnage.

"Don't worry. I know people who will clean this up."

"Clean?" For some reason, she couldn't help a hysterical giggle as she imagined a tiny army arriving with mops and spray bottles. She felt so out of her depth.

"Let's get you out of here and back with Zoe."

Yes. Zoe. The most wonderful thing she'd ever heard.

As they headed for the stairs, someone came jogging into the warehouse. Calvin briefly raised his gun and lowered it.

Lily recognized Benedict, and he seemed a little agitated. "Get your ass moving. This place is about to blow."

At those words, Calvin grabbed Lily and tossed her over his shoulder. He took the stairs two and three at a time, leaping down them, jostling her hard, but she didn't care. She held on. He sprinted across the warehouse floor toward the open door, and as he ran, she managed to look back, saw past the bodies and violence to the red lights gleaming in the shadows at the back. A clock counting down.

Eleven.

Ten.

Nine.

Eight.

She kept a silent count as they hit the outside.

Four.

Three.

Two.

Calvin dropped and covered her with his body.

Boom. The explosion was louder than she would have imagined, and though they'd escaped the heart of it, the blast still hit them in a wave of pressure and heat.

Debris rained down, chunks of the building and even a body part or two.

So gross. But who cared if she had to wash guts out of her hair? She was freaking alive, and so was her little girl.

Calvin didn't stick around to watch the blazing inferno left behind. Once again, he scooped her up, this time into his arms, and followed Benedict, who'd appeared out of the smoke and shadows to beckon.

In moments, they had piled into a large SUV and sped out of the way, to who knew where. But Lily didn't care because from the moment she heard, "Mommy!" she couldn't see through the tears.

Chapter Thirty

The night ended with a bang, literally, but everyone who mattered had escaped more or less unscathed. Even Calvin's car, which Declan had borrowed for the night and returned the next day smelling of perfume.

But Calvin didn't care. The things he truly cared about had survived.

After a parade of showers to rinse the strife of the night from their skin, they'd dressed in clean clothes and partaken in the biggest pizza they could order. Not long after the meal, Zoe's eyes drooped from her spot on her mother's lap. She held out her arms to Calvin, though, when Lily declared it was time for bed. She tucked her head against him, and a speck of dust irritated his eyes.

Fuck, but he loved this child. He couldn't have said how or why it happened; it just had.

A sloppy kiss later for him and Lily, and Zoe slept in the spare room of his house. The trauma she'd suffered would take time to heal, especially the loss of her father. But she was young, and Calvin planned to be part of that healing.

Harry was dealing with the aftermath of the explosion. Hard to hide what had happened when cops and fire trucks were on the scene, scooping up body parts and putting out flames. On a positive note, it did erase the evidence of Zoe's and Lily's presence. The word already circulating was that rival drugs gangs had battled it out.

He wondered how they would spin it once it was discovered via DNA match that Brock and some of his police cronies had been present. Probably be painted as hero cops who tried to save the day and got killed while on duty.

It made him want to gag to think that people might believe Brock was a hero instead of a crook. But he'd allow it for Zoe's sake.

All that mattered tonight was sticking close to Lily. He'd come so close to losing her.

It made the relief in him almost euphoric that they'd both survived. It also made him fucking horny.

We've alive. And together.

He couldn't stop touching her.

She, on the other hand, shook. The events of the evening, along with Brock's death, had hit her hard. It made Calvin want to kill the man again for putting Lily through this shit, but at the same time, he wanted to thank the bastard—who'd managed to pop the trunk and insert himself into the unfolding drama—as he had proven himself to not be a complete douchebag when he'd taken the bullet meant for Lily.

In time, she'd get over it, especially once she remembered why Zoe had gotten taken in the first place. It was why he didn't expect anything when he told her she was sleeping at his house that night—and every night thereafter. No way was he leaving her out of his sight. "It will be safer. The guy in the hood is still out there."

She didn't argue. Just collected some clothes and other items with him standing guard. She'd not said much at all to him. She'd saved most of her soft words for Zoe as she tucked her in.

Only once the door closed behind Mason, who'd watched over Zoe while Calvin helped Lily gather her stuff, did her shoulders droop.

"Is it over?" she asked.

Should he lie? "Possibly not."

"Do you think we're still in danger?"

"Probably." He wanted to shoot himself for the honesty, but Lily deserved it.

She raised her gaze to meet his. "Being with you means sleepless nights and watching my step."

"Yes."

"You'll protect us."

"With my life."

At that, her lips curved into a smile. "Let's hope it doesn't come to that."

"Does this mean—"

"That I want to be with you?" She cocked her head and paused, making him wait. "Yes. Which is probably crazy, and yet, you came for me. You went after Zoe."

"I will always come for you both. You are

my world now. My reason for everything."

The most beautiful smile lit her expression. "I love you, too."

"You do?" For some reason, the hope in him refused to flutter free. For so long, he'd been unloved, unwanted. How could this woman, this wonderful fucking woman, love him?

"I most definitely do. I might not agree with your job"—her nose wrinkled—"but then again, the world isn't always as black and white as I'd like. Look at Brock. He was supposed to be one of the good guys." She shook her head. "In the end, good really is in the eye of the beholder, and in my eyes, you're a good man, Calvin Jones. My man." She wrapped her arms around his waist. "Just do me a favor and try not to bring your work home."

He laughed. "I'll do my best." Everyone at Bad Boy Inc. would do their best to ensure this town, this place they'd staked and claimed as theirs, was safe.

This is our home. And they'd defend it with their lives.

"I say we seal the deal."

He expected a kiss. Instead, she caught his hand and tugged at him. He followed her up the stairs to the second floor, tiptoeing past the guest bedroom—Zoe's room—to the master suite.

She shut the door and leaned on it. Her eyes hooded, her lips parted.

"Strip for me."

A man didn't argue with an order like that.

Calvin grabbed the hem of his T-shirt and couldn't get it off fast enough.

Lily matched him, tugging off her own shirt, revealing her bra. The *mom bra* as she called it. Beige and covering her breasts entirely; yet, in his eyes, so fucking sexy. He stared, and her nipples puckered through the fabric.

She always reacted to his stare, but then again, so did he, his cock swelling and aching.

"Pants now."

In moments, they'd both shed their pants, but she kept on her underwear. White cotton had never looked so tempting.

Her hips swayed as she took the few steps needed to bridge the gap between them. His entire being prickled with awareness when she placed her hands flat against the tense muscles of his abdomen.

"Lie down."

"Yes, ma'am." This assertive side of her was proving very arousing. Somehow, by finally declaring their feelings for each other, the last hint of resistance, the part of her she held back, was unleashed.

And he got to benefit from it.

He lay on the bed, hands laced behind his head, a willing slave to whatever she had planned.

"You are a big man, Calvin Jones." She crawled onto the bed and straddled his waist. Her head cocked to the side. "A really big man." Her gaze dropped to his cock, which jerked in reply. "But I think I can handle you."

"Show me," he teased, his voice husky and low. Her breasts proved too much of a temptation. He reached to cradle them, his thumbs stroking over the fabric hiding the tips.

Her head tilted back, and she sighed as he touched her. He pinched the tips, and she squirmed, the crotch of her panties wet and teasing.

Tugging at the cups of her bra, he freed her breasts, the peaks jutting proudly, begging for his mouth.

"Bring them to me."

She leaned down, enough that he could latch on to a pert tip and suck. He hummed as he lavished her breasts with attention. She kept squirming, making happy sighs and moans that drove him fucking wild.

All too soon, she pulled her nipple free, but he couldn't complain, not when she went on her knees and kissed a trail down his body, her teeth nipping at his nipples.

Inch by inch, she worked her way down, brushing her mouth over his tense stomach muscles and lower still. She shifted down his body so that she straddled his thighs and could stare down at his cock.

It rose to attention.

She wrapped her hand around his shaft, the fingers not quite able to meet. She squeezed, and he groaned. She slid her hand up to the ridge and smeared the pearl at the tip with her thumb. When she reached down to lick, his hips jerked off the mattress.

She licked him again, and again, laving him, showering him with attention, leaving no part of his cock untouched by her tongue and mouth. Aroused beyond belief, his fingers dug into the sheets as she worked him, taking the head of his shaft into her mouth, sucking it, the suctioning pressure so damned good. His hips bucked, and his whole frame trembled as she slid her lips up and down the length of him.

It felt so fucking good. Calvin fought for control, tried to hold on, especially since he had other plans. Finishing in her mouth, while awesome, wasn't one of them.

With a growl of, "My turn," he rolled and repositioned them until she lay under him and he was nestled between her thighs. He left her panties on, choosing to suck at her through the fabric, adding a layer of temptation.

She moaned and thrashed on the bed, her hips undulating, her honey soaking through the thin material.

He tore the cotton from her, eagerly latching on to her sex, feasting on her glorious flesh. But he wouldn't let her come.

Like hell.

Once again, he rolled them and told her to, "Sit on me."

She needed no other urging. She positioned herself above his shaft, the moistness of her sex teasing the tip of his cock. His hands grabbed hold of her hips and pulled her down, filling her with his cock.

Her head reared back, and she let out a cry. "Cal!" Nails dug into his chest as she rode him, her entire body undulating and gyrating, drawing him deeper into her trembling flesh.

He couldn't help but watch, reveling in the intimate connection of their bodies, noting the pink blush suffusing her skin. Her lips were open on a sigh, her eyes closed as she basked in the pleasure.

When she came, he came, too, their climax a thing of absolute bliss, a joining of bodies and soul.

This was what he'd been looking for all his life. This woman. This moment. This love.

He even loved the morning after when a little body crawled atop the sheets and announced, "I'm hungry. Calvin, can you help me get a bowl?"

Fucking right he would. He'd do anything for his family—as soon as he found some pants.

Epilogue

A week or so later…

Lily watched Zoe merging with the other kids wearing the uniforms and couldn't help but hug herself. Leaving Zoe anywhere still brought a feeling of trepidation.

An arm slipped around her waist. "She'll be fine here."

"I know she will." Unlike other schools, this academy—not the one Calvin had studied at but a private prep school for rich kids and famous parents—boasted the finest security. Zoe was safe here.

But Lily was a mom. She worried.

The one thing she didn't worry about was her choice to be with Calvin. Any second thoughts she might have had about getting involved with Calvin didn't survive amidst the knowledge of the depths he was willing to go to make this family work. And they were a family.

Calvin saw Zoe as his daughter. He gave her the affection and attention she needed. And Zoe needed it with Brock out of the picture. Who wouldn't love a man who took steps to make sure their home was a secure fortress?

Sure, he might not have a conventional job, and she dreaded his first out-of-town trip next week, but then again, that was what she got for falling in love with the assassin next door.

Life was finally turning out to be the happily-ever-after she'd always wanted. And the sex was freaking fantastic—and, yes, she did brag to Jenny every chance she got. But she'd drawn the line at taking pictures to prove his size.

And as for the drug ring? Gone. The hooded man had vanished into thin air, leaving behind a vacuum that proved easy to disperse.

Bad Boy Inc., though, was watching. Waiting. And ready to kill—for a price.

*

I don't know if this job is worth the price.

Kacy felt like an imposter sitting in the fancy restaurant. White linen on the tables. Candles. Snooty waiters. Even snobbier clientele. Harry had explained during his debriefing that the joint had some kind of Michelin star. She wasn't sure what tires had to do with food, but her boss sounded impressed. Kacy, on the other hand, kept wanting to fidget.

When it came to places like this, girls like her usually worked in the kitchen or as waitstaff. They certainly didn't sit in the dining room as patrons. She may be a fake diner, but still. The things she did for work. Like wearing a damned bra. Horribly confining thing.

She tried not to scowl too much. Harry would ream her out if she busted her cover before she'd even begun. *Stupid sexist mission.* Posing as some rich dude's girlfriend because he was scared of getting his pansy-ass shot off.

Harry refused to tell her much about the guy, claiming their meeting and getting to know each other had to look authentic to anyone watching. Hence the blind date setup.

And the bra that dug into her skin. She'd also had to wax her legs, but she drew the line at a Brazilian. There wasn't no man, client or not, who was getting a peek at those goods.

A deep voice rumbled at her back. "You must be Kacy."

Standing, she turned and beheld a chest. A really wide chest covered in a snowy white shirt. She had to look up, even in her heels, and she noted a craggy face, piercing eyes, and lips pulled tautly in displeasure.

"Yeah, I'm Kacy. You must be Marcus."

"You're awfully small," was the first mistake he made. The second was to loom even closer, crowding Kacy.

A man who liked to intimidate? She'd met her fair share and knew how to handle them, too.

She pressed into him and smiled—as her hand tucked between their bodies and squeezed his balls in a vise. "Call me small again, and I'll make sure you sing soprano for life."

Because this pint-sized killer didn't take shit from nobody.

The end, but stay tuned for the next Bad Boy Inc. story:

Pint-Sized Protector.

More info at: EveLanglais.com

CPSIA information can be obtained
at www.ICGtesting.com
Printed in the USA
BVOW03s2155110717
489116BV00001B/41/P